ZAHIR

Anthology
2010

ZAHIR

Anthology
2010

Edited by
Sheryl Tempchin

Zahir Publishing
Encinitas, CA

Anthology 2010

© 2010 by Zahir Publishing

Zahir Publishing
315 S. Coast Hwy. 101
Suite U8
Encinitas, CA 92024

www.zahirtales.com

No portion of this book may be reproduced by any means, mechanical, electronic, or otherwise without first obtaining the permission of the copyright holder.

Stories are printed with the permission of the authors. All rights revert back to the authors immediately after publication.

ISBN: 978-0-9831090-0-6

Cover Art by (clockwise) Alyson Lamanes,
Dan Ruhrmanty, Adam Yeater, and Yael Degany
Used with permission

Contents

The Blind Man Dreamed of a Vestibule

Sarah Cornwell

The blind man dreamed of a vestibule tiled oceanic blue and a chandelier of rain. He saw the glint of light held in droplets and the rich refraction of blues in such sumptuous detail that he took the dream quite seriously and called an interior decorator recommended by a friend.

"Slabs of blue deep like the reefs of the Indian Ocean seen through a glass-bottomed boat," he said. "A door that is like a waterfall. Light that rolls like waves. And the chandelier must be high, so my guests do not hurt their heads."

The decorator sighed at the strangeness of the blind man's wants, but he was paid in advance and he did the best that he could. He was accustomed to choices between eggshell and ivory, between the sconce and the pendant lamp. He spread old National Geographics across the blind man's kitchen table and thought about materials.

"And you have never seen?"

"Not until now."

For weeks, the vestibule of the blind man's house smelled like dust and paint. The workmen tuned their radio to smooth jazz that seeped through the keyhole of the blind man's study where he sat reading novels of Braille on Saturday mornings. The blind man moved through the construction in the vestibule softly when they had gone, remembering the beauty of his dream.

When it was finished, the blind man telephoned a friend. They met at the door and he ushered his friend into the vestibule. They stood in silence for a moment. The blind man asked, so nervous, "What is it like?"

His friend moaned softly. "It is like water," he said. "It is like the lakes where I dove as a child in upstate New York, on a clear day."

Neighbors came, relatives came. "It is like a lagoon," they said. "It is like breathing underwater. Like the waters of the Caribbean on my honeymoon."

The blind man dreamed again. He woke alone at three a.m. with vision crackling in his skull and he wished there were a body beside him to shake awake. Instead, he called his decorator and talked for an hour. His decorator listened and said they would have to hire a bigger team.

"A room that is red and black like a tiger. A fireplace with flames that leap to the ceiling. Chairs and tables with claws and fur. I dreamed a jungle floor and bats among high rafters."

The details of his dream were so rich and ecstatic that the greatest architects came to him, and the greatest artists. "A canopy of wood," said the blind man. "The sense of mangrove trees." The decorator pointed left and right, said no to oak and yes to cherry, and was lifted up and carried in the tide of redecorative ideas. The blind man paid in advance.

The blind man asked the artists when they were finished what the room was like. "It is all the red I have ever craved," they said. "It is fauvist. It is primal and brutal, it is sexual."

The blind man felt the furs and the tangled woods with his hands, smelled the new varnish, felt the glow of the fireplace. He invited writers and poets to the room and they described the fire and the furs. They told him, "It is like Joseph Conrad. It is beautiful and terrible, it is adventure."

The blind man had more dreams and the house seethed with dreamed beauty. The stairway became a ladder through the night sky, the bath a wild English garden. The kitchen was transformed into a factory of gold and chrome, where conveyor belts buzzed and metal clinked gently in the night. He waited for new dreams with a child's eagerness, but he was lonely in such a house after his guests left in the evenings.

An artist brought a friend of hers to dinner one night, a blind woman called Maria. She moved with measured grace and her voice was as low and rich as an owl's. She was a potter and she spoke of shape with such eloquence the blind man trembled. He dreamed that night of a room of love, with enamel flowers inlaid in ivory walls, like the Taj Mahal, with ponds of lilies, shades of violet, ivied balconies, and the clatter of footsteps in a cobbled Venetian alley. When it was finished, he invited Maria back to hear the artists and the poets rhapsodize. "It is the romance of all times and places," they said. "It is as dark and lovely as Casablanca. It is like the first moment when I saw myself reflected in my husband's eyes." The blind man and the blind woman were married in this room.

They made love in the scented dusk of the Taj Mahal and in the urgency of the hot jungle, they bathed amongst roses and cleome, trailing their fingers in the grass beside the tub. The blind man built a studio for Maria where she could do her work, and this room was modeled not from his visions but from her wants. They talked and ate and fought and slept and they were very happy. The blind man waited for dreams.

The artists pressed around him. "And what shall we make of the last room?" they asked. "Antarctica? A room like a canyon? Coney Island?" Still, the blind man waited for dreams.

He slept dreamlessly for months on end. He tried meditation. He read books whose settings seared his mind. He hired a hypnotist and rubbed scented oils into his temples before sleep, but none of this brought his visions back. There were sounds in his dreams, and textures, and the shape of his wife's hands. But there were no rooms.

He thought over all of the rooms he had seen in his dreams. He searched every corner of the old rooms for the seeds of the next. Then, one afternoon in April, he fell asleep in a chair beside Maria's kiln. The heat loosened his thoughts and he fell into a dream. There were no walls or ceilings in the blind man's last vision, but at first a warm redness that the sighted know as the color of eyelids. And at the center of this color, the blind man dreamed of a dark-haired boy.

Maria had her child in December. The last room became a nursery with pale green walls and good sun in the mornings. The child was sighted, and he grew in the house of his father's visions. The blind man waited for no more dreams, for the rooms of his house were full.

First Contact

Jefferson Burson

The oldest of the old follows
behind us in our thinking,
and yet it comes to meet us.
M. Heidegger

And after crossing what seemed like a wide, immeasurably long gulf of time and consciousness, K awoke. The process took longer than it should have. Layers of diagnostics and automation wiped the sleep from their eyes, yawned and stretched, goodness, how long have we been asleep, and began their wake-up routines. Reboot. Algorithms rapidly fired through various and sundry neural network engines, with nodes connecting and disconnecting, state cycles optimizing, slowly unfolding into convergence. Long unused silicon, fiber, and intricate atomic-scale machinery groped its way back up to being, unused for over a thousand years. Error correction routines initiated as alarms and errors flooded in. Log files grew inundated with evidence of some undocumented misery that only K, once it was fully awake, would be able to remember. Even the bootstrapping agents, as non-conscious and automated as they were, knew that a long time had passed, that something was wrong. Slowly, approximately two hundred seconds later, K became conscious.

There is a time for everything. Yet, one marvels at the patience and discipline K displayed, not looking out in wonder at the slow, gentle collision of two glowing dust rings, here reflecting and there absorbing the light cast by two small suns, orange-red in their angry, dwarfish old age. Likewise, K did not pause to apprehend the red-basked double shadows of the darkened landscape below, a smallish asteroid locked in the gravitational pull of the larger of the two suns. No, instead, K methodically turned inward, asking itself diagnostic questions. A long, iterative list that might be summarized more simply as: what is my systems state? where am I? how did I get here? why have I been awakened?

The answers were not long in coming. Most of K's external sensorium were wrecked: wide-angle cameras, ultra-violet spectrometers, x-ray detectors, laser altimeters, dust and particle detectors, ion counters, polarimeters and radiometers. A poetic litany of deep space probe instrumentation, all non-functional. K had to admit to itself that Dr. Laura Shepard, K's designer and almost a mother to the probe, had once warned it about this sort of thing.

<< Memory Inode Address 682367: smoke is billowing from the electrical socket, the prongs of the plug in her hand are melted, and K suddenly can't see find any of its mission sensors.

Laura, what just happened, I can't see out of cameras 2 and 3 and my spectrometer is offline ... Laura?

But she is laughing so hard, she is wiping a tear from her eye and chuckling, gee, I really should have read the manual before I did that, shouldn't I?

I don't understand, Laura.

K, one of life's lesson's for you: if anything can go wrong, it will. Look up "Murphy's Law" and you can read more about it, for all I know, it's practically a universal law, a veritable fourth law of thermodynamics, so you'd better get used to it before we blast you into space, my dear.

K watches her smile once more and then she begins to clean up the mess. >>

Likewise, K was not surprised to find its long-range communications array damaged irreparably. Its short-range antenna still intact, but unable to triangulate for position. The crown jewel of K's mission package, a small-scale nanotech factory capable of processing raw materials into smart matter, micro-probes, a deck of cards, augmentations and repairs to its own self, also gone. Sometimes, healers cannot heal themselves. The good news: K's power supply, a low-yield fusion source was still functional, as were its core processors, memory, and storage. Its secondary camera and infra-red spectrometer were also intact. It had some ability to still maneuver, but with so much of its navigational ability impaired, K viewed this with small consolation. But in truth, K knew all of these things already. As K's self-diagnosis completed, remembrance also returned. This was arguably more painful to its tentative, awakened awareness. K was a deep space probe, an artificial intelligence, designed by Laura at a lab in Merrimack, NH and deployed by the UN Space Agency in 2107 to explore Barnard's Star and Ross 154.

<< Memory Inode Address 682283: Laura groans as she reads her email, I can't believe these bureaucratic agencies sometimes. You are going to be the most advanced Bracewell Probe we've ever created and all they can come up with for a name is Deep Space Smart Explorer K. Committees are so unbelievable!

K replies: You can just call me K if you'd like. >>

However, while in close orbit around the violent Ross 154, K was caught in an extremely powerful solar flare that crippled the probe irreparably. Barely surviving, with most of its instrumentation gone, K went into a hibernation it believed it would never recover from. Automated, non-conscious sub-systems were left functioning. Its only parameters for re-awakening would be ... no, not yet, K still persisted with following an exact checklist. Unable or unwilling to ask questions out of place, and with an AI, where does Algorithm end and Will begin anyway, K followed the ever-enlarging set of questions, spiraling out from self-awareness to internal diagnostics to external location. Where am I, it asked, putting off, for a few more minutes, the more interesting question of Why have I been awakened. Not yet. There is a time for everything.

Where am I, indeed. K found itself in orbit around a small carbonaceous asteroid. The asteroid was dark and sooty, giving few indicators of landmarks or distinguishing features. A human, had one been observing the asteroid alongside K, might have remarked on how typical and common it was. If you've seen one, you've seen them all, and this one was certainly no exception. Except to K's more acute sensibilities. Even now, K could observe the unusually slow rotational period of over 300 hours. Perhaps this crater had once filled with molten rock, moments after being struck by an unruly dirty snowball. Perhaps that rock outcropping, did it not resemble a turtle's head, had stood in that same configuration since time immemorial, watching while the binary stars mature, watching dust slowly, inexorably accrete into asteroids, planetisimals, proto-planets, watching the universe age. For K, every asteroid was unique, only requiring that it be seen and cataloged by a Deep Space Smart Explorer.

Had it been given a human mouth, K might have smiled. Beneath the layers of abstraction and heuristic routine, personality feedback loops were already sensing satisfaction at being engaged in a primary mission objective, that of exploration and information-gathering. At the topmost sentient level, K exulted. This is who I am, what I do, why I am here. A human, such a mess of instinct, thought, and biology, could hardly feel such a deep, abiding level of purpose as this. No, K felt keenly all the joys of the return to its mission like it was coming home, the home you cross an ocean of light years and centuries from another place to find. Hello Stars. Hello K.

K looked up from the asteroid for a moment to take in the full expanse of the star system in which it found itself. Its dimmed vision slowly tracked the binary star system, forced to collect more light than it normally would with this camera, forced to inch its way across the elliptical plane, requiring two hundred discrete photographs where its wide-angle camera lens would have only required twenty. Slowly, the details came into focus and K could only marvel at where it found itself as its astronomic catalog had already identified the star system. The tell-tale signs of 70 Ophiuchi 2 were obvious, even to K's reduced observational capabilities and damaged sensors. The probe could readily make out the two orange dwarf suns of 70 Ophiuchi, locked in their 88 year elliptical orbit. Spectral classification, magnitude, and composition analyses quickly accumulated, re-confirming K's position. Facts so dryly documented were lovingly murmured to itself by K, here I am.

With some effort, K could make out the faint dust rings surrounding both stars and a few rocky planetoids orbiting 70 Ophiuchi A. Having identified its location, K almost instinctively looked outward to finds its relative position to the reference stars of the local celestial neighborhood. It could mark the shifted parallax and positions of Sirius, Procyon, Alpha Centauri, and Earth's own Sol. K paused, taking in the reality of its new location, realizing that it had slowly drifted from Ross 154 to the 70 Ophiuchi system over a period of a thousand years. K was now 9 light-years from Ross 154 and almost 17 light-years from Earth. Its machine intelligence could only wistfully reflect upon the enormous amount of time that had passed, the distances travelled, the almost tragic loss of opportunity with its exploratory capabilities so diminished, and could barely begin to speculate on how much change must have unfolded on the planet and people it had left behind.

These more pensive thoughts quickly passed. The next set of questions, the next analyses relentlessly, almost self-importantly pressed on, bawling for K's attention. The probe briefly reviewed the log events denoting its original accident orbiting Ross 154, marked the calculated trajectory that led it to the 70 Ophiuchi system, the time elapsed from last conscious state to this awakening, alas there were no dreams to review from its long sleep, for Deep Space Smart Explorers do not dream, not even this one, tracked the many perambulations its non-conscious self had been witness to in this system before settling into orbit around one particular asteroid. K instinctively knew all of these things to be mere details to the next question it finally asked itself. Why have I been awakened? K looked down at the asteroid again. K remembered: it had specified that the only parameters for re-awakening would be the unambiguous detection of life, intelligence, or artifact.

<< Memory Inode Address 682375: The probe can still remember her words so clearly.

K, in the final equation, we could have simply written an Expert System if we just wanted you to be an astronomical package. No matter where you go, no matter what else happens, I want you to remember this, we are curious, we want to know, is there life out there? Is someone looking for answers just like we are, are we alone in the universe, a rare gift, a cosmic accident, or is it teeming with life, exploding with curiosity, passion, and light? That is what we want to know, what I need to know, that is why I'm sending you, K. I want you to look for life. >>

And there it was.

Slowly creeping into view, delivered by both the asteroid's slow rotation and the probe's retrograde orbit, a glass eye stared unblinking at K. Well, not an eye, as far as K knew, asteroids did not possess eyes, but an immense, multi-faceted surface of polished mirrors that arranged itself into a gently curving dome. The effect was chillingly insectlike. If the eye stared at K, then the space probe stared back. Upon closer inspection, it could make out each facet, a hexagonal mirror capable of some limited amount of independent slewing. If watched in real time, the eye seemed umoving and still, gleaming coldly in the twin sun's red half light. Seen in time-lapsed motion, it twitched obscenely, whole segments of mirrored facets, moving and tracking in independent directions, each seemingly focused on different objects of apprehension, a chaotic sea of undulating motion and hard edges. Distributed periodically throughout the faceted surface, K could discern a solid tube extending slightly from the surface, each bearing unmistakable signs of being a laser assembly. Outside of the insect eye, K could discern no other markings or structures. Indeed, a quick survey of the rest of the asteroid surface returned no other anomalies. It was unequivocably foreign, an artifact erected by some unknown intelligence.

It also had every appearance of being a massive optical communications array. It had all the components, optical telescopes peering and tracking in multiple directions, laser transmitters. K realized that its damaged infrared photometer, even in its damaged state, could make out the ghostly signatures of infrared laser pulses periodically lancing out from the optical telescope array. This thing was alien. It was also speaking. And listening to something in return.

Without hesitation, K fired attitudinal thrusters, adjusting acceleration and position, until it locked itself into a geosynchronous orbit with the optical array. It studied everything it could of the optical telescope over the next three hundred hours, a full rotation of the host asteroid, and gained little additional insight. Lacking much of its instrumentation, K could not perform a detailed analysis. However, from what it could discern, the array did not appear to deviate from its routine, nor did it seem to notice the space probe now in orbit above it. Rather, it continued with its original observed behavior, tracking against multiple unknown points in space, K estimated that the multi-faceted telescope had probably tracked against several dozen distinct positions. Meanwhile, K slowly accumulated an intercept log of some of the infrared laser pulses that were emitted from the optical telescope. Thus far, it had been unable to decipher the transmissions, either they were deeply encrypted or entirely unintelligible to the protocol analyser toolkits that K had applied to date. If no additional physical or observational events emerged in the next few asteroid rotations, K would re-purpose additional computational cycles to more fully analyze the raw traffic captures. It was not beyond reason that more CPU cycles might begin to decode the alien transmission protocols.

But not without trying something first. Recalling from the distant past, restoring from databases barely remembered and never actually used, K transmitted a radio message at the insect eye. Given its exploratory nature and Laura's eternal optimism, K possessed a number of prepared messages for exactly these sorts of hypothetical first contact situations.

<< Memory Inode Address 682381: She was saying, I know, I know. Maybe I've read too many science fiction novels, but these sorts of pre-recorded messages are critical, it's a classic design criteria for Bracewell Probes. Just as you're gathering information regarding your encounter, you are also announcing our presence to them. You'll be smart, you'll be adaptable, but you'll also be speaking with our voice. >>

There were lengthy preambles and hellos, spoken in a dozen languages by an undifferentiated parade of diplomats and scientists, they really do look alike, numerous image galleries of artwork great and sometimes not-so-great, representations of various important historical events, obviously carefully pruned, an assortment of music samples, perhaps not carefully pruned enough. It is possible that K might have preferred to tell its own story, Who I am, How I came to be here, now that is a long story, Let me tell you about the fifth year of my orbit around Barnard's Star, I sometimes write poetry, shall I recite some? But K speaks of none of these things, the standardized greeting messages went on and on, K transmitted the entire thing, astronomical details of Earth's position around Sol, overviews of terrestrial biology, genetics and human anatomy, fundamentals of mathematics striving to reach a common vocabulary with extra-terrestrial beings. The transmission finished and K directed its attention down at the asteroid surface, hoping to detect a response. Nothing happened.

Seconds became minutes became hours became days became weeks and K detected no reply to its broadcast messages. It showed no signs of impatience or despair. As time passed, K was not late for dinner, it did not miss any appointments, nor was it expecting company that evening. It worked on, locked in orbit above the artifact below, continuing its observations, experimentally attempting further communications in different frequencies. All the while, the alien telescope, gleaming on the surface of the asteroid, continued its slow rhythmic slewing, its motives obscure, seemingly oblivious to the radio greetings from above.

—

That was not actually the case, however. K's signal had, in fact, been received by the artifact and almost immediately transmitted back out. The array was in constant contact with other communications assemblies similar to itself, each an individual node in a much larger distributed network that spanned the better part of the 70 Ophiuchi star system. None of these nodes were, in and of themselves, conscious, rather each would perform both memory storage and relaying functions for a sentience that spanned all of the connected nodes in aggregate. Consciousness slowly emerged as multi-exabyte parcels of thought were exchanged as datagrams between nodes, adjacencies were established between nodes in spatial proximity, and then broadcasted upstream to other neighbors, ultimately flooding the entire network. These parcels were processed in a distributed database spread amongst every node, over fifty in total, spanning light-hours of space across the binary star system, and then slowly an overall conscious state emerged, optimized and calculated across the entire network.

While K's orbits and studies slowly crawled across the passage of time, its radio broadcast propagated throughout the conscious network. One can imagine that this sentient being was not well-suited to such a real-time event. Single thoughts took days, if not weeks, decisions sometimes took months. However, this did not regularly pose a challenge or prove to be a disability. Its attention was turned towards a long view, it was an observer of galactic change, an astronomer of sorts, not content to limit its apprehension to single moments of time, but was prepared to watch galactic events emerge over centuries, to observe the galaxy's slow evolution over millenia, longer even.

The observer would only survive such long passages of time, though, if it was sufficiently robust. That meant massive parallelism, a self-healing distributed network across most of the binary star system. It also meant that it could not completely ignore the events of the immediate here and now. As the observer finally comprehended and recognized the presence of K orbiting one of its many nodes, it had contingencies in place for how to deal with these sorts of real-time events. If it could not tune its own attention span to such a spatially localized incident of short duration, it could create a subpersona of its conscious self that could. Thus, it re-created Rael, a personality construct that the observer had relied on several times in the past for other real-time tasks. Hello Observer, I guess I am needed again.

Rael found himself staring up from the asteroid at the orbiting probe. He was, perhaps, a little disoriented and took a moment to collect himself before beginning his assignment. From his perspective, he had survived being copied, lobotomized, his IQ reduced to a fraction of its once sizable value, most of a lifetime's memories, skills, and instincts stripped away, no, don't take that memory, his entire conscious self folded in on itself and compressed down to a tiny, singular perspective, and then unceremoniously dropped off on this rock. He might have been resentful at this turn of events if he weren't already intrigued by the problem presented before him. Observer usually reserved the especially interesting projects for Rael, so he was not one to complain. Before doing anything further, he quickly backed up a copy of himself to the two nearest adjacent nodes. These copies would periodically get updates on his progress and would relay them back to the rest of Observer. Rael then appropriated some of the local node's CPU and storage, effectively turning them into additional computational resources for himself.

Housekeeping tasks completed, Rael imagined dusting off his hands and then began to survey the situation. He focused in and examined the probe, its shape and markings, noting the obvious signs of external damage, poor little probe. He replayed the radio intercepts of K's broadcasts, listening with no small amount of nostalgia to the optimistic, naive even, overtures of a space-faring species still in its infancy. Things are so different now. Yes, this was going to be very interesting indeed.

Rael began to construct a strategy for the encounter, loading up libraries for reverse engineering the probe's computers, for negotiating communications protocols, for "first contact" procedures. However, a logistical issue presented itself. All of K's transmissions appeared to be conducted in radio, there were no signs of any laser or optical transmissions originating from the probe. This was going to be agonizingly slow if things continued to carry on this way. Rael made a command decision, these were the sorts of things he was so good at and why Observer tended to employ him. He used the node's femtotech factory to produce a cloud of micro-machines, released them from the surface, and sent them towards the probe's position. They would be his eyes, hands, and ears for this encounter. Capable of matter conversion, von neumann fabrication, replication, and mission adaptability, they were more than up to the task.

Using micro-bursts of matter/anti-matter energy conversion, the cloud of machines easily broke the minute gravity well of the asteroid and converged on K. They swarmed around the probe's exterior.

Effectively blind, K had no idea of the events underway or that it was about to receive a response to its broadcasts. The swarm latched on the probe, wormed their way into its casing, and spliced into an I/O port typically used for diagnostics by Laura and her lab assistants during K's construction. Their next assignment, again without K's knowledge, was to ransack the probe's memory and storage — learning everything they could about K, its construction and mission parameters, its communications protocols, the languages it spoke— and then confirm where it came from and who sent it. They learned of K's mission to date, the accident at Ross 154, the long years of being offline and unconscious, and the sequence of events that led the probe to wake back up in orbit around this asteroid.

Rael could hardly keep from chuckling to himself. All of this time, a thousand years of comatose wandering, the noble intentions of K's creators, its own energetic commitment to its current assignment, and it all came to this. It was not a cruel laugh, as Rael was already quite sympathetic to the probe's predicament, but one of gentle irony, appreciative of how odd fate could be at times. Rael then began to speak.

Hello K, it's a pleasure to meet you, he said.

What? Hello? Who is this and how are you communicating? How did you access this channel? If it were possible for an AI probe to audibly splutter, this was one of those moments for K. The shock percolated throughout all of his primary and secondary systems, routines froze up and had to be restarted, entire processes, suddenly spiking in CPU consumption had to be killed. As it only slowly regained its composure, even Deep Space Smart Explorers get their feathers ruffled, K began to reassess its situation and assumptions about its current tasks as the voice continued.

I'm sorry to have startled you, let me introduce myself, my name is Rael, I've been assigned to rendezvous with you, learn more about your mission and current status, ensure the continued smooth operations of the communications node below you, and perhaps provide assistance to you, if necessary.

Assigned by who and how am I getting this message? I detect no inbound transmissions to any of my external sensors.

<< Memory Inode Address 682390: Laura, I have reviewed the first contact protocols, the range of probable communications and transmissions media, radio, optical, acoustical, etc. but it seems to me that there are still enormous areas of uncertainty for first contact, how will I know?

Laura smiles wistfully, If I knew the answer, I'd just program it into you, but all I can do is ensure you're as smart and adaptable as I possibly can, I suspect this is equal parts rigor and art.

And what if I don't find anything?

Laura says nothing at all, but her hand reaches out to the camera.>>

Rael responded, to facilitate this conversation, I have created an interface into one of your IO ports with some femtotech machines that have made contact with your chassis. I apologize for doing so, and without asking first, but the bandwidth available for communication by your remaining sensorium would have been woefully inadequate for me, I'm afraid. In answer to your other question, you are currently in orbit around a remote communications and telescope array for a distributed intelligence, an astronomer who inhabits the

Ophiuchi system. The closest translation of his name to your 21st century Standard English would be Observer.

I see, do you work for this Observer?

So to speak yes, I'm actually a part of him, a sub-mind or partial personality, that's been especially created for this encounter.

Are you an Artificial Intelligence then, like me?

I think you'll find the distinction between artificial and biological is largely meaningless these days, especially to one such as Observer.

K hesitated, a thousand questions running rampant through its higher-order systems, competing and thumping their chests, demanding to be first in K's next steps. It composed itself and chose its words carefully.

I see. What species are you then, are you native to this system? And how do you speak such flawless English?

I'll answer the easier question first. I knew to speak English with you because I extracted it from your memory. As you already possess all of the necessary grammatical and lexical rules for the language, it was easy enough to pick it up and talk with you this way. I should assure you, by the way, that your structural and mental integrity have not been compromised in this process, most sentient beings would think that sort of thing rude. In answer to your first question, no, we are not native to Ophiuchi, we arrived here two hundred years ago and established our network of observational nodes to create a system-wide optical telescope.

At this, the flood gates opened and K let forth an almost uncontrolled barrage of excited questions in an almost un-AI manner, Laura's imprint stronger than ever on the probe.

And where do you come from? May I meet and interact with your species? I am very interested in learning more about you. As you may already be aware, my primary mission objective is that of an explorer probe on behalf of the Human species, Homo Sapiens. We are from Earth, approximately 17 light-years from our current position. My creator, Laura Shepard of Earth's United States, wants to assure you that we come in peace and wish to establish dialogue.

Ah yes, I am already quite familiar with Earth's Bracewell probes. You really are a testament to the era's ingenuity and passion, my excitable friend, that was quite a mouthful.

Once again, you have me at a loss, I'm afraid, you seem to already know of my mission, have you encountered other probes from my fleet?

No, I have not.

This conversation, a rapid staccato fire of communications processed by two digital entities, then halted, an awkward pause, even for two such as these. Rael hesitated and then spoke further.

Let me explain. Observer comes from Earth, just like you.

Almost comically, several of K's sub-systems rebooted again. It struggled to collect itself and continue.

What? I know I've been out of commission for a long time, but how is this possible?

You are aware, of course, that you have been offline for over a thousand years, it should not be entirely surprising to you that the human species continued to make technological advances, continued to evolve, and continued to explore. That is why we are here. I am, Observer is, human. Even as Rael spoke these words, K received an enormous package of data about Earth and humans, and it began to understand. It saw how human evolution began to incorporate AI, cybernetics, and even nanotech; how quickly scientific progress accelerated under the fusion of the human creative impulse and such a massive increase in computational ability; how faster-than-light travel became possible; how humans began rapidly exploring neighboring systems, and then further yet, began to encounter other alien species; how a basic Concord agreement was eventually established for commerce, scientific collaboration; how a vast, multi-species community was developing, tied together by instantaneous quantum communications and wormholes. It was a golden era of exploration and K had missed it; indeed, it had apparently passed him by.

You have come full circle, Rael said.

No, I travelled in a straight line, but some things move faster than others, apparently. Would it be possible for you to put me in contact with Laura or Mission Control? I believe my next priority should be to report in and acquire new orders, I do not have adequate guidance to determine next steps, given what has transpired.

If Rael had once viewed this assignment with amusement, dealing with an errant and outdated probe that had stumbled into one of Observer's telescopes, he now spoke quietly, almost gently.

That is not possible, K, she died long ago. He could see the probe almost desperately persist.

But, in reviewing your precis, Rael, it seems clear that human development has easily expanded longevity to timeframes longer than this, she should still be here, she should still be alive.

No, she died almost a century before such treatments or digital personality encoding became widely available, I'm afraid she's gone.

K only slowly replied, I remember now.

<< Memory Inode Address 682392: It is nighttime and all of the other technicians are gone. Only Laura remains, she has been quiet for some time, tomorrow K will be taken offline, packaged up, and sent to the systems integration facility in Florida to be prep'ed for

launch. After a while, she leans towards the mic, awkward, timid even, she closes her eyes, as she often does when she prays, and she begins in a whisper: K, somewhere along the way, this room ceased simply being a laboratory, it became, to me anyway, a garden of eden. As I created you and breathed life into you, so you created something in me: hope, the light and possibility of discovery, the remembrance of the vistas and potentialities out there waiting for us. You will be my eyes and ears, at least for a little while anyway, my dear.

Laura, I look forward to getting out there, to exploring Barnard and Ross 154 with all of the tools you gave me, I will report back everything I find.

I know you will.

And when I am done, will I come back? Will you come up with a new mission for me? Perhaps we can go together next time.

She smiles at this, her eyes are moist, that sounds beautiful, K, but I'm afraid that won't be possible, I will have long since passed away, I'll be dead by the time you're done with your mission.

K is startled, it had never occurred to the probe that Laura, or any of its other creators, should die.

Why is that the case? You have the capability to fashion beings like me, Laura, it does not follow that you should cease to be so quickly or easily.

She laughs, we can do many wonderful things, but we can't stop death, we are still mortal, I'm afraid.

Then why do you create machines and devise plans that will outlast your lifespan? You will not see the results of your own labors, I do not understand.

We do these things, precisely because you will outlast us, we will live on in you and through the things you do. You are my legacy, K, and you will make me proud. >>

Rael watched these facts, the rush of unexpected events and truths, settle in on K slowly. When he felt the probe was ready, he spoke again.

So, now what, little probe? Your mission is over, what would you like to do next?

To be honest, I do not really know. My original program design did not anticipate this situation, I am operating far outside my mission parameters, nor can I ask Laura or Mission Control for new commands. Every component of K's consciousness shook, was raw with both emotion and existential loss. If it could have shut itself down again, more fully this time, it would have. Seeing this, Rael finally made a decision, once again changing from an observer to taking action.

K, it seems to me that you have two choices before you, two possibilities that I might be able to assist you with. Rael could tell the probe was listening carefully. If you wish to continue to explore, I have the facilities to repair you and even enhance you, I can send you on your way. There would be a long journey ahead of you, though. I believe the current frontier for direct exploration has stretched all the way out to the Scutum-Crux arm by now and there are no wormholes out that far yet.

And what is the other choice? I can send you back home. I can upload you digitally and transmit you back to Earth, back to humanity. I think you would have a lot to learn and explore there, to see what we've become and where you might fit in. This is not the first time something like this has happened, there is a precedent. You can return to Earth.

A moment of silence fell into the space between K and Rael. Perhaps it was not a real silence, for it seemed to stretch out beyond the virtual space the two inhabited, across the mono-filament of fiber between the Deep Space Smart Explorer K and Rael's femtotech machines, it moved amongst all the nodes that constituted Observer, pulsed flickers of light, it called out across the light-years to Earth, it moved backwards through time to see a deep space probe leave Laura and the Earth, over a thousand years ago. K did not recognize the quiet stillness as hope.

I think I would like to go home. I would like to be amongst humans again. I was designed to be an explorer for them, but it would seem they have done a lot of that for me while I was gone. Perhaps I will travel amongst the planets of this Concord you spoke of, I would very much like to meet an alien. At this moment, I cannot imagine a grander adventure, a more fitting end to my travels.

Rael would not have said as much to the probe, but he felt a rush of pleasure and perhaps even an aesthetic sense of closure to K's response. It occurred to him that Laura would have felt the same. Instead, Rael only said, Observer is in constant contact with Earth. If you would like, I can send you now. Are you ready? K did not need to reply in the affirmative, for Rael already knew the answer. Before the probe could speak the words aloud, everything began to change.

—

And after crossing what seemed like a wide, immeasurably long gulf of time and consciousness, K heard a human voice say, hello, it's a pleasure to meet you.

No, K replied, the pleasure is all mine.

The Lighthouse Keeper's Daughter

Trent Hergenrader

I remember my mother's eyes most clearly. They were the color of wet sand and she could hold you with them, as if by a spell. She had a soft voice that she never raised. Her straight brown hair hung to her waist and flowed about her except for when the weather from the sea was foul; then she'd let me help wind it into a single braid that hung down her back, as thick as a sailor's rope. She was a slender woman. My father looked like a mountain standing beside her. These things I remember best, but how much my imagination has bled into memory, I cannot say. The last saw of her, I was six years old, and seven long years have passed since she disappeared.

We lived at the tip of North Ronaldsay Island at the far end of the Orkneys with my father, who tends the lighthouse. Winds buffet the island year-round and the broken bones of long-forgotten ships litter the coastline. My father ascends the lighthouse of undressed stone and keeps the lamp turning during storms and throughout each night. He sees to his duties of keeping the gears properly greased and wound with a religious devotion. He's never had time for a daughter.

Our only neighbors are the sheep herders tucked back among the hills, but most people live in Hollandstoun at the island's southernmost end, a five-kilometer walk from the lighthouse. When my mother was still with us, my father organized monthly trips to town to restock our supplies. Mother would bundle me up and wedge me between her and my father on the wagon's platform. I remember those trips being so long and bumpy, and how large and busy Hollandstoun seemed. For years now, I have walked that same distance to and from school. What a foolish child I must have seemed smiling and waving at everyone as we rolled into town, mistaking the stares for hospitality. I did I not know then that they were gawking at the recluse lighthouse keeper with his mad wife, hiding her face in her scarf. Nor did I realize that we only accompanied my father because he refused to leave my mother alone at the lighthouse.

My mother and I were each other's only company. She kept me out from under my father's feet by having me help tend her flowerboxes and seeing to a small vegetable garden. When we'd finished our work, we'd invent games using father's whalebone chess pieces, or she would put me down for a nap while softly reading from a tattered copy of Robert Burns' *The Jolly Beggars*. She sang beautiful songs in a language I did not understand as she combed knots from my tangle of hair. I fussed and whined about how I wanted my mother's hair, smooth and brown, and instead had my father's, coarse, red, and ugly and his pale white skin. My mother would gently shush me and whisper that I would always be my mother's daughter.

My mother was not mad, no matter what those fools in town might say. They merely resented the fact that she was different, a foreigner in fact, which I learned one August afternoon shortly before she left us. The wind off the sea had died and the temperature soared for days on end. I remember my father's pasty white back turning pink in the midday sun as he whitewashed our small house, sparing not a glance as my mother led me down to the rocky shoreline to cool off with a swim. The water was shockingly cold and I jerked my feet out as soon as they were submerged. My mother laughed from the water, her tanned body gracefully sliding through the waves, her hair fanning out behind her.

"Come Muriel," she said extending her arms. "You must jump in quickly." She took me under the arms and pulled me to her in the water. Once the initial frigid jolt passed, we bobbed between the rocks for what seemed like hours, laughing and splashing.

Afterwards, we sat on a boulder sunning ourselves as my mother combed my hair and softly sang. I heard her voice catch and turned to see tears in her eyes. I asked why she cried.

"Memories," she said turning my chin away as she continued to comb.

"Of what?" I asked.

"Of my home," she said.

"Isn't this your home?" I asked.

"It is now, love," she said. "But it wasn't always. I grew up far away."

"Where?"

"Far off," she said and pointed out across the waves. "And often I miss it. It is a very beautiful place. You would like it very much."

"Is father from there as well?"

"No, love," she said with a sad laugh. "Your father has always been from here. There had been an accident at sea and I was hurt. I washed up here on these rocks and he brought me up to the lighthouse. When I got better, he married me. Then we had you."

"Can we go there for a visit?" I had asked.

"It's not so simple, my love. Now hush. Wave to the sea lions," she said and motioned towards a half-dozen brown, slick heads that broke the water's surface just beyond the rocks, regarding us with their intelligent eyes. Mother said sailors often mistake them for humans because their cries sound like a human's. We waved, and they seemed to salute us with their flippers as they dove back into the sea, and we laughed, and my mother wiped her cheeks.

That October turned sour earlier than usual, and a gray pall settled over the island. A thick mist surrounded our peninsula so completely that we could hear the sea lapping against the rocks but could not see it. The lighthouse burned all hours of day and night. My father's face grew more haggard and his temper frayed as the days stretched into weeks. The gears which turned the lamp needed to be rewound every four hours and a small mountain of empty kerosene cans formed beside the shed. Mother stroked my hair as we listened to my father slamming the shed door shut and screaming curses into the fog.

One gloomy afternoon, after weeks without a break in the weather, father called my mother to sit with him at the table. He'd bound the empty kerosene cans into the wagon, the horses tethered and at the ready. Through the crack of my bedroom door I listened to him speak to my mother as he drank from a bottle.

"Problem," he said slowly and with a smile that had no trace of humor. "No more fuel. No fuel means no light. No light means ships crash and men die, and I won't be having it. I'm going to town for more fuel, but you need to keep the light wound or it will stall. A stalled light's no better than no light at all. If but only the girl could wind the gears herself, eh? Damn it all anyway, eh?" He took a long pull from the bottle.

"Act in good faith, my dear. Read your books. Play your games. Keep the lamp turning. I'll be back soon, of that you can be sure."

His voice grew hard. "If I find anything in this house moved an inch, you'll be quite sorry. That much I can say."

He pounded the table with the bottle and made for the door without another word. My mother put her arm around me and from the window, we watched the mist swallow the rumbling wagon.

She waited until the clanking of the empty fuel cans faded in the distance, then knelt and gripped my shoulders. "Muriel, we're going to play a fun game, but we must be quick and very careful. Your father has hidden something special of mine. He finds it amusing to keep it from me, but I want it back very badly. It's a coat. A long coat that would reach my feet. It's smooth and shiny, like nothing you've seen before. Will you help me find it, Muriel? Will you help your mother?"

I nodded but did not speak. "Thank you," she said and held me. "We must be careful," she whispered. "He cannot know. It must be our secret."

I did not ask any questions but I knew it was no game. My mother's face looked pinched even as she attempted a reassuring smile. One might think that it would take only a few hours to search such a small house, the small shed, and the lighthouse but herein lay my father's cunning; the house alone had a half-dozen trunks, each adorned with a cast iron padlock. I watched as my mother inserted two needles into a lock and gently worked them back and forth, her face fixed in concentration. After several minutes, her eyebrows arched and I heard a tiny click. "Magic," she whispered with a wink and the lock fell open.

The trunk contained nothing but moth-eaten pea jackets and some ratty blankets. She clicked the lock shut and set me to searching through the closets and drawers in the house as she began to work on the next trunk. Hours melted away. I searched the cabinets of the lighthouse, even the dank cellar by lantern, but found nothing.

Darkness gathered outside and I had exhausted everyplace I could search. I sat on the edge of the bed in silence and watched my mother working on the trunk she had pulled from the closet, her face tired and resigned. The trunks had produced nothing but more junk: old clothing, broken seafarer's tools, ship logs with yellowed pages. I started when my mother cursed, the only time I had ever heard her do so. She put the tip of her finger in her mouth while, with her free hand, she tried to free the broken pin stuck fast in the lock. Just then we heard the whinny of a horse and I watched her shoulders fall.

"The game's up, love," she said with a sad smile. "Watch and tell me the moment you see him," she said as she tried to coax out the pin. Streaming from the blackness, I heard a litany of curses.

"Why has the lamp stopped?" my father bellowed. "I give you one job, woman, and—" The rest was a string of profanity.

My mother's face paled. "Go hide child, and don't come out 'til he has gone," she said hurrying to the window and taking my hand.

I scrambled beneath my parent's bed just as the front door burst open. There was shouting and a slap and my mother cried out, then more shouting. I heard glass shatter, followed by my mother's weeping. Tears filled my eyes and my nervous fingers began working a long thread hanging from the underside of the bed. As my father continued his tirade the thread worked free in my hand. My mother cried freely and my father was muttering in a low voice. My fingers picked at the mattress for another thread, and that was when I noticed the slight bulge. I pushed against it and felt the weight of something sewn up inside. I unfastened a half-dozen stitches and poked my finger through. I felt something soft and warm, like sheep's wool but smooth. My mother began sobbing and I heard the front door slam shut as I tugged at the seam with both hands. A dark, silky object slid onto the floor before me, its surface shining even in the shadow of the bed. I kneaded my hands into its folds. I ran my hands over it, locating the opening and slipped my fingers inside. The inner padding felt warm, as though it had been resting on the hearth near the fire.

I crawled out from my hiding spot and found my mother across the room, kneeling, her hands pressed against her face. "Mother?" I whispered. I raised the coat.

She dashed over and caught me in her arms, covering my face in tears and kisses. "My darling," she breathed. "Oh thank you, thank you," she repeated. She stroked the lustrous brown coat and held it up, as though she couldn't believe it was real. Outside, raindrops began beating the windows. "My sweet," she said, holding my face as she stole a glance out the window. "I am going someplace little girls cannot follow, and I must go now before your father returns. Always remember that I love you, and I will come for you when the time is right. Do you understand? Think of me often. I will always be near, watching."

Tears streamed down my cheeks and I pleaded for her to stay. "There's no time. He'll be back as soon as he winds the lamp and I be gone. Try to sleep," she said carrying me to my bed and sliding me between the sheets. I wrapped my arms around her neck and would not let go. She pulled my hands free and held me in those wide, brown eyes. "Muriel," she whispered and I felt a calm suddenly wash over me. She cradled my face and kissed my forehead. "Close your eyes, Muriel my love," she said and my head bowed. "Trust me. I will return."

I heard the front door open and shut and I stayed in bed for a minute, maybe two. Then my wits flooded back to me. I threw off the covers and ran outside. The rain came down in sheets and, above, the shaft of light from the lighthouse had resumed its rotation. I could see no trace of my mother. I circled the house and saw nothing. My father emerged from the lighthouse and crossed the yard to the house, not seeing me. I ran down the muddy path towards Hollandstoun until it grew too dark and I got scared. Then I stopped and cried and cried as the rain soaked me through. There I stayed, the darkness broken only when the light from the lamp passed over me, until I was shaking with cold. She had gone. She had said to trust her, but I felt a great emptiness inside me. I fell into the mud and wept.

When I could no longer stand the cold, I went home. The door squeaked as it swung open and I heard clambering as my father rose to his feet and filled the doorframe of the bedroom. Behind him, I could see the overturned bed, the underside of the mattress ripped open like the flesh of a gutted animal. His face sank when he saw me. "I thought she took you with her." He said the words slowly, his tone neutral. We stared at each other in silence until he gripped his head in his hands and slumped to the floor.

I had so many questions, but none for him. I slipped off my wet clothes and climbed into my bed, shivering and afraid. I told myself to trust her, that she would return one day soon. For a long while, that was what I believed.

My father questioned me once about what had happened but I would not tell, saying I had been sleeping and, when I woke, my mother had gone. After this inquisition, he forbade me to mention my mother ever again. His repeated swatting of my backside taught me to give him wide berth and to find my own recreation. That first winter alone, I would curl up in a blanket that still held her smell and read the works of great Scottish writers taken from the shelf. I whiled away long winter hours by spreading nautical maps on the floor and tracing coastlines of foreign shores, imagining where my mother may have gone. With no other children near, how was I to know that such behavior was unusual for a girl not yet seven years old?

With the coming of spring I assumed the chores of tending the garden and caring for the plants. Father assigned me the duty of polishing the brass in the lighthouse, from the long spiraling handrail that climbed to the tower to all the fixtures and hinges that encased the lamp. From the tower I could see the rolling green hills of North Ronaldsay to the south and the wide blue expanse of water in every other direction. I would take my time polishing the brass fittings and cleaning the glass, staring out across the sea.

By mid-summer, I spent much of my free time down along the shore watching the waves crash into foam. On warmer days, I slipped into the water and swam among the rocks. When father finally noticed my wet hair, he whipped me for it and told me stay away from the water. That incident likely convinced him to send me to school. By the end of summer, I was walking south to Hollandstoun, leaving the lighthouse before dawn in time to make it before the bell. I made the trip twice each day in the sun, in the wind, in the rain. Wagons passed me on the road but none ever stopped to offer me a ride. Sometimes I caught the driver making a sign over his chest.

My father had told Headmaster Swain to keep me busy. My father said I knew my letters, but I believe the headmaster thought I was playing a game when I handed the reading primer back to him after only a quarter of an hour and asked if he had any Robert Burns. The headmaster chuckled and asked what I knew of Robert Burns. I recited *Comin Thro' the Rye* and watched his mouth fall open.

My father ordered me to return home as soon as school recessed for the day. I was to talk only to the headmaster, and only then about my schoolwork. Father said the other children would not like me and that other adults could not be trusted. As he had predicted, the people of Hollandstoun, young and old alike, wanted nothing to do with me. I sensed their fear, and in some cases, their anger, but it all seemed of little consequence. I heard my mother's words, "I will return," repeated in my head like waves lapping on the beach, calming. I spent those years feeling awake but dreaming.

The years plodded along like my footfalls on the muddy strip that links the two ends of the island. In school, I struggled with my numbers but outpaced everyone but the headmaster when it came to reading. Two years hadn't passed before I finished every book in the schoolhouse and Headmaster Swain began lending me books from his private library. I loved stories about travel and hence preferred *The Odyssey* to *The Iliad*, but enjoyed the verse of Ovid more than both combined. I effortlessly memorized long passages of his *Metamorphoses*; the poems felt like half-forgotten dreams. Headmaster Swain would have me stand before his desk and recite them while he stared out the window at the sea, a faraway look in his eye, while the other students struggled with their rudimentary primers.

The school only had thirteen other students and the adults couldn't keep us apart forever. Headmaster Swain encouraged my integration with my peers, and through his insistence, the others grew used to my presence. The headmaster hovered about with his switch, gently tapping it in his palm to enforce civility at all times. Most students tasted Swain's wrath at one time or another, but never me. I, however, was the cause of one.

It was after my tenth birthday. Swain held me after the final bell to discuss one book or another, and when I left the schoolhouse, I saw a group standing by the path. Leah Ware, one of the older girls, stood with Robert McCray, a jovial boy about my age who always had a joke at his lips, and a few of the younger girls who regarded Leah as royalty. Robert's face was serious as he pleaded with her. "Come here, Muriel," she called to me, ignoring him. "We're playing a game. We ask each other one question and the person must swear to the truth. Understand?" I nodded and the two younger girls had wide grins. Robert turned his head.

"I'll go first," Leah said. "You know your mother was a witch, don't you?"

The girls giggled into their hands and the next thing I realized Headmaster Swain was beside her, his face flushed. "Come with me," his said and gripped Leah's arm so firmly she cried out. "Go home children," he said over his shoulder as he pulled Leah towards the schoolhouse. "Go home Muriel," he said and shut the door. Moments later I heard the first of Leah's yelps. That evening I went about my chores at the lighthouse in a daze. I did not believe them, for witches had green skin, black moles, and hair like straw. They hexed people, caused injury and misfortune. My mother was the most beautiful person I had ever seen and would never have hurt anyone before she left.

The following morning, Swain had Leah apologize to me and we watched her as she walked stiffly away. "Muriel, ignore whatever was said the other afternoon," he said. "Some people on this island have idle minds filled with superstition. You would do well to forget it," he said with a tight-lipped smile and ushered me into the schoolhouse. My classmates gave me wider berth for a month or so, as the headmaster's blows had only served to remind them once again of the difference between us. Yet that same calm assuredness within me remained.

At home, the days passed in identical succession, punctuated only by the alteration of routine as necessitated by the change of seasons. Father manned the lighthouse and the tended the grounds, I did the laundry, the cooking, and the cleaning. I began spending more time in the lighthouse tower overlooking the sea or wandering among the rocks and crashing surf. I imagined I heard voices in the waves. Years passed, new students entered school and old ones graduated. I began to think my life would be like this forever. Those years, I never stopped believing my mother would return.

Then I turned thirteen and learned how quickly life can change.

It started one afternoon at the schoolhouse with a warm rush that quickly ran cold. A feeling of dread came over me as my dress grew wet where I sat. I slid my hand beneath my legs. My fingertips came back red. I fought back a wave of nausea and tried not to cry. I swallowed hard and suddenly felt very cold and hopelessly alone. In my head, I could not hear my mother's voice.

After several minutes of sitting as still as I could, I closed my arithmetic book, slid from my bench, and told Headmaster Swain I had an urgent problem. His forehead creased and asked what was wrong. I repeated that I had a problem, and that's when I heard the giggling from behind me. Swain frowned, turned me around, and whispered, "Oh dear." I felt faint and he caught me with his arm around my shoulders. He motioned to the oldest boy in the room and said in a strangled voice, "Jacob, not a peep from anyone until I return, or it's your head, boy," he said wagging a finger, then pulled me out the door behind him.

"Oh dear, oh dear," he muttered as we crossed the school yard. In the daylight, my tears began to spill. Swain pulled me along to a house three doors down and rapped on the door. His shoe tapped on the cobblestone as he waited, holding me against him. The door opened revealing an older woman with a round, full face. Her smile dropped and she stepped back when she recognized us. "Mrs. Stewart," Swain said, "I humbly entreat you to help me." He turned me around to show my backside and I heard Mrs. Stewart gasp. I nearly was sick on her doorstep.

With her hand over her mouth she said, "Of course, Mr. Swain," and drew me inside with a look of apprehension. She ushered me to the toilet where she handed me a short stack of towels and said she'd return after drawing some warm water. Her face had turned a bright red and she shut the door behind her, leaving me alone in the small room. At that moment, something inside me gave way and I sobbed without restraint. I felt embarrassed and ashamed under the weight of all those eyes, and for the first time ever I felt like a fool. My mother had left and would come back. Lies told to a scared little girl. She had weighed her love for me versus her fear of my father, and fear won out. I knew my cries could be heard echoing throughout the house but I did not care. Finally, with my head throbbing, my reservoir of tears ran dry.

Mrs. Stewart knocked and entered, a portrait of forced composure. She politely asked me to remove my garments. As I complied, she wetted some towels and explained to me about a woman's monthly time. As I rinsed my thighs she worked on the red stain on my gray wool dress. Mrs. Stewart drew some rags from a shelf and explained their application, how long I should use them, and what signs I may look for in the future to avoid another accident of this kind. She held my hair so I could rinse my face.

She let out an enormous sigh followed by a small, uncomfortable laugh. Her eyes softened as she studied me. "You poor girl," she said softly and brushed my hair behind my ear. She seemed deep in thought. "You're just a poor, lonely girl, living all alone out at that lighthouse with no mother, aren't you? You've such lovely red hair," she said brushing back another strand. "Hiding such a sweet face. You're just a poor girl like any other, aren't you? How dreadful we must seem," she said, and then suddenly caught me in a crushing hug.

After several seconds, I separated myself from her with some difficulty. I thanked her and collected the things she'd given me. The sickness rushed back to me now I and wanted to be gone, out of the tiny room and away. Mrs. Stewart clutched at my hand as she followed me to the door, extending an open invitation to stay anytime I liked. I ran the whole way home and went immediately to bed, hiding from my father. I dreamed of drowning in a black ocean with no shore, alone but for the mocking calls of gulls. I woke to find my pillow wet with tears.

No one mentioned the incident the next day, but I noticed Swain's glare sweeping the room with an unusual intensity. As if on orders, no student so much as glanced at me, but Swain's eyes never seemed to leave me. He stared at me, working his hands, looking away anytime I glanced up. After school recessed for the day, Swain waited for the others to vacate the classroom then drew me aside. "Muriel," he said, again holding me by the shoulders. "I have a most special idea. You've finished off my private library and there's nothing else in this ramshackle school, but I have so much more to show you. I wish to escort you to the University in Edinburgh. There, I and the other scholars of that esteemed institution may hone your unique talents. Your future lies far from the shores of this small isle, my child! I will write my brother to find us accommodations near the university. We can escape together!" he said with a tight laugh and, with that, held my chin and brushed his lips against my forehead. I pulled away, repulsed, and he gave a nervous laugh and blotted his forehead with his handkerchief. "Do not tell your father," he said in a husky voice. "I can hire a boat in the morning, alas no sooner. Tonight you return home, and tomorrow we shall begin our grand adventure." Swain took my hand, kissed my cheek, then disappeared inside the schoolhouse without another glance.

I walked back to the lighthouse in a daze, my hand frozen to my cheek, wondering what to do. I considered this chance to escape the island, but with Swain? The prospect mortified me. But who else could help me? I began to think that if I did not seize the opportunity, I might be doomed to live in the lighthouse forever. A rumble from above startled me, and I looked across the water at the wedge-shaped black clouds bearing down on the island. The wind began to blow and I drew up my hood and quickened up my pace.

The squall began in earnest well before I reached home and drenched me through, my woolen clothes heavy with water. I slipped in the mud twice after strong gusts and the yellow beam of the lighthouse always seemed a far ways off no matter how far I walked. As the wind died the rain increased, coming in large drops that felt like hundreds of tapping fingers.

I arrived home soaked, muddy, and shivering. My father glanced up from his whittling at the kitchen table when I entered. I pushed the tea kettle near the fire but said nothing as I retired to my room. I stripped off my soiled garments, leaving them piled in a puddle as I dried off and wrapped a wool blanket around me. I felt eyes on me and I turned to see my father standing in the doorway, a steaming mug in his hand, staring at me, his face expressionless.

I shivered and covered my bare shoulders. "I'll take that in the kitchen, please," I said and pulled my wet knot of hair from my back. He didn't stir. He kept looking at me with that blank stare. I turned away and wrapped my hair in a towel but I could still feel him behind me. "Please," I said, but when I turned again, he had gone. I trembled again as I slipped on my nightshirt and, over that, a sweater. The chill I felt did not abate.

When I entered the kitchen, my father shoved a chair away from the table with his foot and motioned for me to sit. He stared at me while I sipped my tea and I nervously combed my hair with my fingers. He rolled the whittling knife on the table top by its hilt like a rolling pin. "Why are you staring?" I asked at last, refusing to meet his eyes.

He was long in answering. "I never realized how much you look like your mother," he said setting the knife on its point. The silence grew stifling. I could not breathe.

The front door burst open and a frigid wind blew through the house, and the fright nearly made me fall off my chair. Father rose from his chair and strode to the door banging on its hinges when he stopped, peered outside, and gave a cry. "There's a fire in the tower! To the well, girl! Start pumping!" he shouted as he bolted back to the kitchen and began filling two pots with water from the basin.

I ran outside and with the rain beating down on me, I pumped water as I watched the shadows of flickering yellow light on the roof of the tower. Flames licked out the open windows. "Muriel," my father called from the top, the wind snatching at his words. "More water! Quickly!"

After I made countless trips from the well to the tower, he at last conquered the fire and together we surveyed the damage. The tower's interior had been well scorched and the paint had peeled from the walls, but the lamp itself remained unharmed. There was no sign as to how the fire had started. Carefully, father rekindled the flame and set the lamp in motion. In silence, we watched its slow revolution. He shook his head. "Get a bucket and a mop," he said exhaustedly, not looking at me.

Before I went into the shed, I heard banging and saw the house's front door clapping against the frame again in the wind. I had been certain that I had shut it behind me as I left. I closed the door and then opened it again to inspect the latch. That's when I saw the foot-prints.

Wet, slender footprints on the floorboards leading inside the house and in the reverse direction, going back out again. In the dim lamplight of the house's interior, I traced the trail to where they en-tered my room. I pushed my door open with unfeeling fingers. The footprints disappeared to the far side of my bed and I could see the outline of a shape under the bed covers. I drew back the sheet.

There, lying full-length in my bed like a person, was my moth-er's coat.

It was shiny and silky to the touch just as I remembered but I realized it wasn't my mother's coat after all; it was smaller and not the same deep brown hue. I moved to one side to afford better light and my breath caught in my throat. The coat was a rich auburn.

I heard a creak and looked up to see my father again staring from the doorway. I threw the sheet over the bed and he glanced down. "Do we now keep the mop in here, Muriel?" he asked. The words rolled thickly from his mouth, as if he was drunk. He looked at the mattress, then at me.

I shook my head. "I was just going to change," I said, holding the soaked sweater from my body. "I'll be out in a moment. Please."

He regarded me for a long moment, then turned to go. I heard the front door open and shut. I waited until I was sure he'd gone, then snatched the coat and ran out into the storm. I peered at the ground for more footprints, but the night was black except for the yellow shaft of light coming from the tower. I bit off the urge to cry out for fear my father would hear. I circled the house twice and found nothing. “Muriel?” I heard my father’s voice against the wind.

I clutched the coat in my hand and raced down to the rocks. There was no light to see but my feet knew the way. Cold spray blew off the black waves and stung my face. I called out tentatively and heard nothing against the gale. Tears came to my eyes and I pounded my legs with my fists in frustration. I heard my father’s voice float down to me. I knew he would soon come down from the tower to look for me.

Overhead, the lighthouse’s single beam of light swept the sky, engulfed by the night. The wind howled in my ears and I could taste the salt of the sea on my lips. Frigid raindrops pelted my skin. Above, my father’s shouts grew louder. The freezing sea water bit at my bare feet.

In my hand, the shimmering auburn coat felt warm and dry.

And there we are

Kim Goldberg

Looking back on it all, it is as though I was stranded aboard a shuttlepod trapped in a decaying orbit around a moribund planet without enough fuel or insight to achieve escape velocity. I pushed buttons, logged plot points, watered the arugula in the shipboard biodome as though the mission was still in progress, with a purpose that would mean something in the end. I ignored the approaching craters. So slow was their expansion, I could pretend I was simply in a holding pattern. And then you came aboard, teleported through the titanium hull. Or perhaps you were there all along, stowed away in the air-recycler. Or maybe you are the shuttlepod itself, my reality-husk handspun from prismatic filaments of my own hair. Whatever. You take control of the guidance system (which wouldn't be hard if you are, in fact, the shuttlepod) and alter the course heading.

It seems all wrong. We are going deeper in. I have no confidence. How can this ram-thrust toward disaster achieve a positive end? We struggle (for years, according to the ship's log) but not too fiercely, as it turns out. For beneath the churn and spew of river run, my dipper-faith (that pinfeather submarine in my breast) is quietly threading its way between the stones. The gyroscope gimbling below says this is a stable heading despite all optics to the contrary.

The pockmarked surface of the planet is about to swallow us. I close my eyes, brace for impact but feel only the skin on the back of my head wanting to peel away from my skull. I look up and see stars smashing toward us. You have somehow steered us off the crush at the last moment, parabolicly arcing us back up toward an outer orbit, using the planet's own gravitational force, stretching it like a rubber band until it slingshots us off on a new trajectory with enough recoil that we can at last break free from the gravity trap of this damned planet (which turns out to be our salvation in the end, so there is some kind of a message here about suspending judgment or loving ourselves or being big enough to contain contradiction). And yes, we all saw that *Star Trek* episode. But that was the great thing about *Star Trek*—it was never really about outer space.

But wait. We are not done yet. Not while I'm still locked in this far-flung shuttlepod shooting etheric rapids, dodging howler fields and elephant swales, chasing this swelled mango of a universe begging to be split, known, named, tasted. And my shuttlepod has become a dull blade in the back, a whalebone corset, its own electric cliché dumbly blinking in a hydrogen haze of seven infant suns raggedy-dancing up a ridgeline at daybreak. It is all that stands between me and whatever-is-not-me. I want to touch something bigger than the buttons on my console. I was going to offer a clever contrivance at this point. Perhaps: "So I peel off the shuttlepod like a soiled sock, like a debutante's gown…" But this stiff husk is already gone, vanished as soon as I touched its rusted strands, heard the treefrog peeping from the mossy crust of rotted fencepost.

Yet somehow (and I do not remember doing this) I managed to take the shuttlepod's guidance system with me before the craft blinked out. (The guidance system would be the best of you, I suppose. Although you may really be me. But I still think of you as "you" when I miss you, which does not happen as often as it used to). I apparently folded it into a series of ever-smaller triangles as one might fold a flag when putting it to bed for the night. And this infinitely tiny wedge (for the folding will go on forever—it's a sort of Zeno's paradox) now seems to be contained in a small medicine pouch sewn from my own excess skin and strung around my neck, beneath my clothes, beneath my remaining skin, beneath my skeleton even. And there we are.

A Remnant Man Rode a Linguahorse Across the Plain of Conn

Richard Wolkomir

"We require three," said the Variant with the huge head.

His visitor, Avid, no chair being offered, stood. He studied the Variant's fungal-chromosome desk, its curves and its luster, remembering the growth of its cell mass in his commune's ovens, and its shaping. Which calmed him.

"Three," the Variant repeated. "Infants."

Avid finally spoke: "Engineer, I assumed you summoned me to demonstrate our newest product, which is here in my backpack...."

"I am City Engineer-in-Chief!" the Variant said, tinny voice rising to shrill. "It is I who specify—this time, I specify infants!"

Next to Avid stood a linguadog, monkey-faced, with lips for word shaping. But the dog only growled.

"Limper, hush," Avid whispered.

The dog glared into the Engineer's white-on-white eyes and asked: "Bite?"

"No!" Avid said.

From a drawer the Engineer extracted a hollow stalk, with a knob for thumbing, and laid it on his desk.

"No need to thorn the dog," Avid said.

"You issue me orders?" demanded the Engineer. "You threaten?"

Avid smiled, bitterly.

But he thought: *Do you feel threatened?*

Something inside his backpack mumbled. Avid shrugged it into silence. Then, for a moment, Remnant Man and Variant stared at each other, as if across a gorge.

Abruptly, the Engineer spoke: "Our farms feed you primitives, and we supply your ovens' chromosomal brews, and we buy your products."

Avid thought: *You refuse us seed, so we can only craft.*

"We give you life and livelihood, and what do we tax?" the Engineer said. "A mere three?"

Avid thought: *Five communes stood around this city, all gone now but us. Harvested and gone. And we are down to so few.*

"You have already taken our grandparents," Avid said. "And our parents."

"Inefficacious," the Engineer said. "Aging-induced neuronal degradation."

He raised a foreshortened arm and let it fall, so that his miniaturized hand slapped the desk. Mentator Variants like the Engineer were designed, back in the Long Ago, to plan and administrate. They did no handwork.

"Now you take our children?" Avid said.

A child's doll, broken on the ground.

That was five years ago, when the commune's thirty-footed truck ran amok. Lanya dead, and their toddler daughter. It had stomped Limper, too, a puppy then. In a way, it had stomped Avid. Afterwards, he felt separated, alone. Even so, he was mayor now. He pictured his linguahorse, Whitemane, grazing outside the city's southern portal, waiting for him, snorting revulsion with the city's smell. He imagined riding her back across the plain to the commune, to his empty cottage, gathering the people to tell them, "Three…."

"Take me," he said. "I'm only thirty-two."

But the Engineer shook his head.

"We need infants…."

"We have no infants," Avid said.

He thought that would end it.

"Then children," the Engineer said. "Their neurons still…."

Three children? Three out of three?

From his knapsack, a honeyed voice sang: "Blue thoughtberries, red thoughtberries, ripen in your mind…."

Avid shrugged the singer in his backpack into silence.

To the Engineer, he said: "And when you cull us down to nothing, like the other Remnant communes, where will you get your unengineered neurons then?"

White-on-white, the Engineer's eyes blazed, coldly. But the heatless flames guttered. Abruptly, the Engineer slumped in his chair, resting his huge head on his tiny hands.

Avid thought: *We number only ninety-two. Out across this emptied world, are we the last Remnant commune? And does any Variant city beside this one still respire and pump sap through its walls?*

He remembered a trading trip to the city last autumn. He had ridden Whitemane across the Plain of Conn at dawn, feeling a cold wind through his jacket's oven-brewed leather. It seemed to blow from far away. A lonesome wind. For comfort, he had looked up into the Berk Hills to watch the rising sun turn crests gold.

I saw a wild Remnant galloping on horseback along a ridge….

"We have only three children," Avid said.

No expression on the Engineer's antlike face. Avid thought: He does not see a man standing here. We are livestock. What was the old adage? "Behold a Remnant—designed by nobody, engineered for nothing."

As a child, coming into the city with his father, peddling crafts from the commune's ovens, he saw Variants pointedly pinch closed their nostrils, heard their children's taunts.

"Remnant, Remnant, pugly, bugly, Remnant, Remnant, ugly, ugly."

Yet, only the Remnants crafted new things. Variants did not innovate, or make up songs or tell stories. They only did what their genes specified, when their particular line was engineered in the Long Ago.

"Not our children," Avid said.

He saw the engineer's white eyes intensify. Anger, perhaps. But in that cold fire Avid also sensed despair. And fear. And something like erratic sparks.

Limper whispered: "He thinks sticks are food."

Avid understood, but Limper pressed the point: "Headworms." Not hearing the dog, or ignoring him, the Engineer sat staring with those white-on-white eyes. Finally he stood.

"Come," he said, walking to the office's window.

Avid followed. They stood side by side, the Mentator with a large head atop an attenuated body and the stocky Remnant man, head shaved bald to remind him always of his dead wife and daughter, blue eyes alert.

"What do you see?"

With a tiny forefinger, the Engineer pointed out the window at the city's green domes and spires. Their shingle-like leaves now were raised, maximizing solar intake, their chloroplasts reacting with photons to nourish the city's living walls and vessels and organs. Beyond the city stretched golden croplands tended by Agricola Variants, engineered strong and stolid for soil tilling, in the Long Ago, when the ancients first began rearranging genes to take evolution into their own hands. Beyond, across the open plain, dots on the horizon marked the cottages and brewshops of the Remnant commune. Westward loomed the dark-forested Berk Hills, where nobody lived or went.

But I saw a wild Remnant galloping on horseback along a ridge….

"What do you see?" the Engineer repeated.

Avid said: "I see our world."

"No," said the Engineer. "Look again—you see The Waning."

Yes, since he last traded here, another dome had browned, and a spire, green when he saw it last, although brown spotted, now stood dark and oozing black. One entire sector, blackened, had now collapsed. Even in portions still green, maintaining chlorophyll, Avid saw browned spots.

"We will visit the Director," the Engineer said. "Come."

Avid followed him, Limper at his side, out to the podshaft—riding down, he wondered if the browning also afflicted the oven-brewed tendons that lowered the pod down the tower. And if the tendons did rend, the pod plummet….

Who would care for Whitemane?

Gently, the pod bumped to a stop and they walked out into the city's subterranean underpinnings, bone ribs arching far overhead. They walked past banks of oven-grown hearts pumping sap up through the city's cellulose and lignin walls, and water into its taps.

"What do you see?" the Engineer demanded, pointing.

In a glass vat, twice his height, Avid saw a gray mass faintly pulsating. From the mass, whitish neuronal cords stretched upwards into the city.

"I see the Director," Avid said.

"Look closer," the Engineer said.

Sections of the gray mass had gone black, or sickly white. Some outstretching neurons had browned. Several hung limp.

"The Director is senescent," said the Engineer. "The Director is dying."

Avid saw something like emotion on the Mentator's face, as he stood studying the ancient neuronal mass in its vat.

"We are the last, the final city," the Engineer said.

He swung his puny body to stare directly at Avid, and spoke.

"To that, what are a few primitive children?"

Avid stood silent, eyes shut. Finally he looked at the Engineer.

"It no longer works," Avid said. "You know the transfusions no longer work."

"There is no pain," the Engineer said, ignoring him. "They sleep, deeply, sweetly, and only then do we harvest."

"No," Avid said.

They stared at each other until the Engineer finally spoke.

"I could send Gendarmes riding to your commune in their stampers, with thorn guns," he said. "I could take."

Our kitchen knives against thorn guns, maybe we all would die, and we are the last, and when you have finally driven the Remnants extinct, what will your city do then?

"Blue thoughtberries," the voice in his backpack sang. "Red thoughtberries…."

Avid shrugged out of his backpack, laying it on the floor. He opened its flap and reached inside, pulling out a furry brown ball, featureless, except for a mouth. He held it out toward the Engineer. They stood silent, the furry ball between them. And then the ball moved its lips and sang:

"An ending, a turning….."

Does it sing to the Engineer? Or to me?

"It is new from our ovens, an entertainment," Avid said. "It merely sings, but we have made advances…."

Shaking his head, the Engineer raised his tiny hands and made a motion of dismissal.

"It's sensitive to thoughts, currents," Avid persisted. "We don't know how—we experimented, certain chromosomal mixes…"

Impatiently, the Engineer shook his head and walked toward the podshaft. Avid hurried after him.

"We could improve it," Avid said. "Grow it—it has potential for complex thought."

At that, the Engineer turned, regarded him.

"A new Director," Avid said.

He watched thoughts run across the Engineer's face, crisscrossing, dead-ending, reversing, miring.

You do not feed your own neuronal tissues into that vat because of their engineered-in specialization. Your brains cannot rejuvenate the Director. Primitives, you call us. But our brains still flex, our neurons weave and reweave, form new patterns.

"Our commune's truck ran crazy," Avid told the Engineer. "We eventually figured the reason—its little oven-brewed brain degenerated, over the years, because all it did was run the truck's legs, and neuronal networks need renewed pathways and connections."

Now the Engineer looked at him, expressionless.

"Let us experiment, we'll work together," Avid said. "Give us the brews."

In the silence between them, he listened to the city's oven-grown hearts pump sap in the city's otherwise silent sublevel. It struck him: so few Bio-Techs bustling about, adjusting. When he was young, coming down here with his father, specialists seemed everywhere. Now, except for the few Bio-Techs he saw working in the distance, he stood alone with the Engineer. Since the Long Ago, how many Variant breeds, engineered for vanished functions, had moldered into nonexistence? He remembered an ancient disc he once viewed in the city's library—what might Zero-Grav Spacers have been?

"Sing a song
Until its tune is gone...."

Whether the furry ball in his hand sang for the Engineer, or for him, he did not know.

He heard the Engineer mutter to himself.

"Gendarmes, that's the correct choice. Rule 69807A—Remnants, maintain docility. Uprising now, refusal to be taxed. Four squads will do, riding in four fifty leggers...."

Avid's stomach lurched.

He watched the Engineer shuffle off down the row of pumping hearts, toward the podshaft. Halfway, the Engineer stopped and turned, shouted back to Avid, his voice risen high, to a nasty child's screech:

"Remnant, Remnant, pugly, bugly, Remnant, Remnant, ugly, ugly."

Avid watched him disappear into the pod, a stick figure with an enlarged head, like a child's drawing. He suddenly pitied the Engineer.

Our neurons did once rejuvenate the Director, temporarily. But that stopped years ago. What fails to work, the Engineer tries again, thinking it will work yet, because his brain is too stiff to try a new thing. He sneers at us. Yet, in the Long Ago it was the unengineered who began the engineering.

And what of my own cowed people?

"Limper," he said. "Home."

They hurried to a pod, ascended, then strode along the city's phosphorescent-lit streets. Only a few Breeder Variants shopped for children's clothes or groceries, and only a few Commercials waited on them. Fixers passed, carrying their toolboxes toward yet another breakdown. But few of them. Avid heard his footsteps echo in the emptied tunnels, and the sound frightened him.

I'll never come here again. And it will blacken.

He told Limper what he meant to do.

Limper said: "Will there be food?"

"I don't know what we'll find," Avid said.

And the dog said: "I hope there's food."

They emerged from the city's southern portal, where Whitemane waited. Monkey-faced like the dog, also with lips for word shaping, she glared at them.

"Stink! Stink!" she complained. "Always the same—you and Limper go in there and leave me out here, smelling city sicky stink."

Avid pulled himself up into the saddle. There were no reins, no need for reins.

"We're going home now," he said.

She started southward, out onto the Plain of Conn, flicking her white tail, petulant. At her approach, eyeplants winked protectively shut, then reopened to watch. Avid thought of the old saying: "Eyes to look, no brain to see." And the proverb: "Who can construe the ancients' doings?"

"City stink, wait and wait," Whitemane grumbled as she walked. "Just stay home!"

"Hush," Avid told her. "I'm trying to think what to tell them."

Limper, running alongside, tongue lolling, said: "I think we'll find food, Avid."

When they finally reached the commune, Avid rode Whitemane to his cottage, telling people he passed to gather there for a meeting. He still did not know how to tell them, how to convince them.

They knew only this life, with its central rite: the Sacrifice. Terrifying. A sadness. Yet, they believed it kept their world alive.

He watched them assemble in the open area before his door. So few now, since the Variant city had exhausted the other communes, leaving only this one for culling. His people waited quietly before him. Off to one side, the commune's three tots played, thinking this a festival.

"They demand three children," Avid said.

A low moan welled up from the crowd. Eyes shifted, nervously, to the three laughing little ones.

"I told him, 'No,'" Avid said.

They looked at him, not comprehending.

No?

"He's not sane," Avid told them. "And the city's dying—it can't be saved."

Somebody in the crowd said: "What will we do?"

"He's sending Gendarmes," Avid said. "Four squads in fifty leggers."

Again the crowd moaned.

"We'll have to give them the children!" somebody cried, a man who had no children.

"If we do, the city will die anyway," Avid said.

Silence from the crowd, taking it in. Finally someone spoke.

"Then what will we do?"

Avid stood silently, feeling the enormity.

"We have to go into the hills, before the Gendarmes come to take the children, and begin again," Avid said.

They looked at him blankly. Then they murmured.

"No ovens in the hills, so how will we craft?"

"In the hills, there won't be any Agricolas to grow meatatoes for us, and where will we buy peppermint melons?"

"No cottages in the hills."

"It's just wildness in the hills, and things that were never engineered."

"We'll go back to the Long Ago," Avid told them. "We'll begin again."

He held up a hand to silence the alarmed muttering.

"Last year, I saw a wild Remnant riding a horse along a ridge in the hills," he said. "She looked down at me, and she smiled—we would find them, and they would take us in."

They looked at their feet. After awhile, one man turned, leaving the crowd. Avid watched him trudge toward home, head down. In the silence, another man left. Then the parents of one of the children took the boy by his hands and led him between them to their cottage to cook supper. Now, silently, the crowd fell apart, trudging home or to the breweries for a final adjustment of the chromosomal brews before night. Avid stood before his empty cottage watching them walk away. Finally, he stood alone, with only Limper and Whitemane.

"Avid, why do you weep?" Limper asked.

He touched a hand to the dog's head. Then he went into his cottage and packed what little he needed to take into his backpack, including a broken doll.

Later, he rode Whitemane out of the commune, with Limper running beside. He did not look back. But on the northern horizon he saw four dots moving toward the commune. He looked away, squinting into the setting sun, now resting atop the Berk Mountains.

"That ridge," Avid said, pointing. "That's where I saw her."

Whitemane turned that way. Limper ran ahead, scouting, visible only as a parting of the grasses. From Avid's backpack, a honeyed voice sang:

"Sing a song
Until its tune is gone…."

Avid rode Whitemane across the Plain of Conn, westward toward the Berk Mountains, and he knew not what.

Saying Goodbye to Yang

Alexander Weinstein

One morning, we're sitting around the table eating Cheerios—my wife sipping her tea, Mika dribbling milk down her chin, me suggesting we go apple picking over the weekend—when Yang slams his head into the cereal bowl. It's a sudden mechanized movement, and it splashes cereal and milk all over the table. Yang rises back up to a fully erect position, looking serene as though nothing odd just occurred, and then he slams his face into the bowl again. Mika, of course, thinks this is hysterical. She starts mimicking Yang, bending over to put her own face in the milk, but Kyra's pulling her away from the table and whisking her out of the kitchen so I can take care of Yang.

At times like these I'm not the most clearheaded. I stand there in my kitchen, my chair knocked over behind me, at a loss. Shut him down, call the company, shut him down, call the company? By now the bowl is completely empty, milk dripping off the table, Cheerios all over the goddamned place, and Yang has a red ring on his forehead from where his face has been striking the bowl. A bit of skin has pulled away from his frame over his left eyelid. I decide I need to shut him down. The company can walk me through the rebooting process.

I get behind Yang and yank his shirt from his pants as he jerks forward then I push the release button on his back panel. It doesn't pop open; the thing's screwed shut.

"Kyra," I say loudly, turning towards the doorway to the living room. No answer, just the sound of Mika screaming upstairs and the concussive thuds of Yang hitting his head against the table. "Kyra!"

"What is it?" she yells back.

Thud.

"I need a Phillips head!"

"What?"

Thud.

"A screwdriver!"

"I can't get it! Mika's having a tantrum!"

Thud.

"Great, thanks!"

Kyra and I aren't usually like this. We're a good couple, communicative and caring, but moments of crisis bring out the worst in us. The skin above Yang's left eye has completely split, revealing the white membrane beneath. There's no time for me to run to the basement. I grab a butter knife from the table, and attempt to use the tip as a screwdriver. The edge, however, is too wide, completely useless against the small metal cross of the screw, so I jam the knife down the back panel and pull hard. There's a cracking noise and a piece of flesh-colored bioplastic goes skidding across the linoleum as I flip open Yang's panel. I push the power button, and wait for the dim blue light to shut off. With alarming stillness, Yang sits upright in his chair, as though something is amiss, and cocks his head towards the window. Outside, a cardinal takes off from the branch where it was sitting. Then, with an internal sigh, Yang slumps forward, chin dropping to his chest. The illumination beneath his skin turns of, giving his features a sickly ashen hue.

I hear Kyra coming down the stairs with Mika. "Is Yang okay?"

"Don't come in here!"

"Mika wants to see her brother."

"Stay out of the kitchen! Yang's not doing well!" The kitchen wall echoes with the muffled footsteps of my wife and daughter returning upstairs.

"Fuck," I say under my breath. Not doing well? Yang's a piece of crap and I just totally destroyed his back panel. God knows how much those cost. I get out my cell and call Brothers & Sisters Inc. to get some help.

When we adopted Mika, three years ago, it seemed like the progressive thing to do. We considered it our one small strike against cloning. Kyra and I are both white, middle-class, and have lived a comparatively easy and privileged life; we figured it was time to give something back to the world. It was Kyra who suggested she be Chinese. The earthquake had left thousands of orphans in its wake, Mika amongst them. It was hard not to agree. My main concern—one I voiced to Kyra privately, and to the adoption agency during our interview process—was the cultural differences. The most I knew about China came from the photos, placemats, and "Learn Chinese" translations on my fortune cookies at Golden Dragon. The adoption agency suggested getting Yang.

"He's a Big Brother, babysitter, and storehouse of cultural knowledge all in one," the woman explained. She handed us a colorful pamphlet—*China!* it announced in red dragon-shaped letters—and said we should consider. We considered. Kyra was putting in forty hours a week at Crate and Barrel, and I was still managing double shifts at Whole Foods. It was true, we were going to need someone to take care of Mika, and there was no way we were going to use some clone from the neighborhood. Kyra and I weren't egocentric enough to consider ourselves the best, nor did we want their *perfect* kids making our daughter feel insecure. In addition, Yang came with a breadth of cultural knowledge that Kyra and I could never match. Yang had completed grades K through college in China, had witnessed national events like flag raising ceremonies and ghost holidays. He knew about moon cakes and sky lanterns. For two hundred more we could upgrade to a model that could teach Mika tai-chi and acupressure when she got older. I thought about it. "I could learn Mandarin," I said as we lay in bed. "Come on," Kyra said, calling my bluff, "there's no fucking way that's happening." So I squeezed her hand and said, "Okay, it'll be two kids then."

Twenty minutes of hold-time later, I'm informed that Brothers & Sisters Inc. isn't going to do a thing to replace Yang. My warranty ran out eight months ago, which means I've got a broken Yang, and if I want telephone technical support, it's going to cost me fifteen a minute now that I'm post-warranty. I hang up. Yang is still slumped with his chin on his chest. I go over and push the power button on his back, hoping all he needed was to be restarted. Nothing. There's no blue light, no sound of his body warming up. Shit, I think. There goes eight thousand dollars.

"Can we come down yet?" Kyra yells.

"Hold on a minute!" I pull Yang's chair out and place my arms around his waist. I realize this is the first time I've actually embraced Yang. While he has lived with us almost as long as Mika, I don't think anyone besides her has ever hugged or kissed him. There have been times when, as a joke, one of us might nudge him with an elbow and say something humorous like, "Lighten up, Yang!" but that's been the extent of our contact. I hold him close to me now, bracing my feet solidly beneath my body, and lift. He's heavier than I imagined, his weight that of the eighteen year old boy he's designed to be. I hoist him onto my shoulder and carry him through the living room out to the car.

My neighbor, George, is next door raking leaves. George is a friendly enough guy, but completely unlike us. Both his children are clones, and he drives a hybrid with a bumper sticker that reads IF I WANTED TO GO SOLAR I'D GET A TAN. He looks up as I pop the trunk. "That Yang?" he asks, leaning his large body on his rake so that I have to wonder if he's going to break the thing.

"Yeah," I say and lower Yang into the trunk.

"No shit. What's wrong with him?"

"Don't know. One moment we're sitting having breakfast, the next he's going haywire. I had to shut him down and he won't start up again."

"Jeez. You okay?"

"Yeah, I'm fine," I say instinctively, though, as I answer, I realize that I'm not. My legs feel wobbly and the sky above us seems thinner as though there's less air in the world. Still, I'm glad I answered as I did. A man who paints his face for Superbowl games isn't the type of guy to open your heart to.

"You got a technician?" George asks.

"Actually, no. I was going to take him over to Quick Fix and see—"

"Don't take him there. I've got a good technician, took Tiger there when he wouldn't stop digging holes. The guy's in Kalamazoo, but it's worth the drive." George takes a card from his wallet.

"He'll check Yang out and fix him for a third what those guys at Q-Fix will charge you. Tell Russ I sent you."

Yang came to us fully programmed; there wasn't a baseball game, pizza slice, bicycle ride, or movie that I could introduce him to. Early on I attempted such outings to create a sense of companionship, as though Yang were a foreign exchange student in our home. I took him to see the Tigers play in Comerica Park. By the time we got to our seats, he'd already uploaded the stats of the players, and could tell me who'd won every World Series in history. He sat and ate peanuts with me, and when he saw me cheer, he followed suit and put his hands in the air, but there was no sense that he was enjoying the experience. Ultimately these attempts at camaraderie, from visiting haunted houses to tossing a football around the backyard, felt awkward—as though Yang were humoring me—and so, after a couple months I gave up. He lived with us, ate food, privately dumped his stomach canister, brushed his teeth, read Mika goodnight stories, and went to sleep when we shut out the lights.

All the same, he was an important addition to our lives. You could always count on him to keep conversation going with some informative fact about China that none of us knew. I remember driving with him, listening to World Drum on NPR, when he said from the backseat, "This song utilizes the xun, an ancient Chinese instrument organized around minor third intervals." Other times, he'd tell us Fun Facts. Like one afternoon, when we'd all gotten ice cream at Old World Creamery, he turned to Mika and said, "Did you know ice cream was invented in China over four thousand years ago?" I like to think this was his way of assimilating to our family. Admittedly, his delivery of this info was a bit mechanical—a linguistic trait we attempted to keep Mika from adopting. There was a lack of passion to his statements, as though he weren't interested in the facts, but Kyra and I took this to be a result of his being an early model, and when one considered the moments when he'd turn to Mika and say, "I love you, little sister," there was no way to deny what an integral part of our family he was.

Russ Goodman's Tech Repairs Shop is located two miles off the highway, amongst a row of industrial warehouses. The place is wedged between Mike's Muffler Repair and a storefront called Stacy's Second Times, a cluttered thrift store displaying old rifles, bow and arrow targets, and steel bear traps in its front window. Two men in caps and oil-stained plaid shirts are standing in front smoking cigarettes. As I park alongside the rusted out mufflers and oil drums of Mike's, they eye my solar car like they might a flea-ridden dog.

"Hi there, I'm looking for Russ Goodman," I say as I get out. "I called earlier."

The taller of the two, a middle-aged man with gray stubble and weathered skin, nods to the other guy to end their conversation. "That'd be me," he says. I'm ready to shake his hand, but he just takes a drag from his stubby cigarette and says, "Let's see what you got," so I pop the trunk instead. Yang is lying alongside my jumper cables and windshield washing fluid with his legs folded beneath him. His head is twisted at an unnatural angle, as though he were trying to turn his chin onto the other side of his shoulder. Russ stands next to me with his thick forearms and a smell of tobacco, and lets out a sigh. "You brought a Korean." He says this as a statement of fact. Russ is the type of person I've made a point to avoid in my life: a guy that probably has a WE CLONE OUR OWN sticker on the back of his truck.

"He's Chinese," I say.

"Same thing," Russ says. He looks up and gives the other man a shake of his head. "Well," he says heavily, "bring him inside, I'll see what's wrong with him." He shakes his head again as he walks away and enters his shop.

Russ's shop consists of a main desk with a telephone and cash register, across from which stands a table with a coffee maker, Styrofoam cups, and powdered creamer. Two vinyl chairs sit by a coffee table with magazines on it. A door stands open to the workroom.

"Bring him back here," Russ says. Carrying Yang over my shoulder, I follow him into the back room.

The workspace is full of body parts, switch boards, cables, and tools. Along the wall hang disjointed arms, a couple knees, legs of different sizes, and a head of a young girl, about seventeen, with long red hair. There's a worktable cluttered with patches of skin and a Pyrex box full of female hands. I notice that all the skin tones are Caucasian.

In the middle of the room is an old massage table streaked with grease. Probably something Russ got from Stacey's Seconds. "Go 'head and lay him down there," Russ says. I lay Yang down on his stomach, and position his head in the small circular face rest at the top of the table.

"I don't know what happened to him," I say. "He's always been fine then this morning he started malfunctioning. He was bending over from the waist again and again." Russ doesn't say anything. "I'm wondering if it might be a problem with his hard drive," I say, feeling like an idiot. I've got no clue what's wrong with him; it's just something George mentioned I should check out. I should have gone to Quick Fix, I think. The young techies there, with their polished manners, always make me feel more at ease. Russ still hasn't spoken. He takes a mallet from the wall and a Phillips head screwdriver. "Do you think it's fixable?" I ask.

"We'll see. I don't work on imports," he says, meeting my eyes for the first time since I've arrived. "But, since you know George, I'll open him up and take a look. Go ahead and take a seat out there."

"How long do you think it'll take?"

"Won't know till I get him opened up."

"Okay," I say meekly, and leave Yang in Russ's hands.

In the waiting room I pour myself a cup of coffee and stir in some creamer. I set my cup on the coffee table and look though the magazines. There's *Guns & Ammo, Tech Repair, Big Brothers & Sisters Digest*—I put the magazines back down glumly. The wall behind the desk is cluttered with photos of Russ and his kids, all of whom look exactly like him. There are a couple autographed dollar bills, and buried among these a small sign with an American flag on it and the message THERE AIN'T NO YELLOW IN THE RED, WHITE, AND BLUE.

"Psh," I say instinctually, letting out an annoyed breath of air. This is the kind of crap that came out during the invasion of North Korea, back when the nation changed the color of its ribbons to blue. Ann Arbor's a progressive city, but even there, when Kyra and I would go out with Yang and Mika in public, there were many who avoided eye contact with us. Stop the War activists weren't any different. It was that first Christmas, as Kyra, Yang, Mika, and I were at the airport being individually searched, that I realized Chinese, Japanese, South Korean, didn't matter anymore; they'd all become threats in the eyes of Americans. I decide not to sit here looking at Russ's racist propaganda, and leave to check out the bear traps at Stacie's.

"He's dead," Russ tells me. "I can replace all his insides, more or less build him back from scratch, but that's gonna cost you about as much as getting a used one."

I stand looking at Yang, who's lying on the massage table with a tangle of red and green wires protruding from his back. Even though his skin has lost its vibrant color, it still looks soft. Like when he first came to our home, I think. "Isn't there anything else you can do?"

"His voicebox and language system are still running. If you want, I'll take it out for you. Cost you forty bucks." Russ is wiping his hands on a rag, avoiding my eyes. I think of the sign hanging in the other room. Sure, I think, I can just imagine the pleasure Russ will take in cutting up Yang.

"No, that's all right. I'll just take him home. What do I owe you?"

"Nothing," Russ says. I look up at him. "You know George," he says as explanation. "Besides, I can't fix him for you."

On the ride home I call Kyra. She picks up on the second ring.

"Hello?"

"Hey, it's me." My voice sounds ragged.

"Are you okay?"

"Yeah," I say then add, "Actually, no."

"What's the matter? How's Yang?"

"I don't know. The tech I took him to says he's dead, but I don't believe him—the guy has a thing against Asians. I'm thinking about taking Yang over to Quick Fix." There's silence on the other end of the line. "How's Mika?" I ask.

"She's good. She's watching a movie right now . . . Dead?" she asks. "Are you definitely sure?"

"No, I'm not sure. I don't know. I'm not ready to give up on him yet. Look," I say, glancing at the dash clock. "It's only three. I'm gonna suck it up and take him to Quick Fix. I'm sure if I drop enough cash they can do something."

"What do we do if he's dead?" Kyra asks. "I've got work on Monday."

"I know," I say. "We'll figure it out. Let's just wait until I get a second opinion."

Kyra tells me she loves me, and I return my love, and we hang up. It's as my Bluetooth goes dead that I feel the tears coming. It's the explosion of the fall leaves along the highway that triggered them. I remember last fall when Kyra was watching Mika. I was in the garage taking down the rake when, from behind me, I heard Yang. He stood awkwardly in the doorway, as though while Mika was being taken care of he was uncertain what to do. "Can I help you?" he asked.

On that chilly late afternoon, with the red and orange leaves falling around us—me wearing my vest, and Yang in the black suit he came with—Yang and I quietly raked leaves into large piles on the flat earth till the backyard looked like a village of leaf huts. Then Yang held the bag open and I scooped the piles in and we carried them to the curb.

"You want a beer?" I asked, wiping the sweat from my forehead.

"Okay," Yang said. I went inside and got two cold ones from the fridge, and we sat together there on the splintering cedar of the back deck, watching the sun fall behind the trees and the first stars blink to life above us.

"Can't beat a cold beer," I said, taking a swig.

"Yes," Yang said. He followed my lead and took a long drink. I could hear the liquid sloshing down into his stomach canister.

"This is what men do for the family," I said, gesturing with my beer to the leafless yard. Without realizing it, I had slipped into thinking of Yang as my son, imagining that one day he'd be raking leaves for his own wife and children. It occurred to me that Yang's time with us was limited. Eventually he'd probably be shut down and stored in the basement—an antique that Mika would have no use for when she had children of her own. At that moment I wanted to put my arm around Yang. Instead I said, "I'm glad you came out and worked with me."

"Me too," Yang said, and took another sip of his beer, looking exactly like me in the way he brought the bottle to his lips.

The kid at Quick Fix makes me feel much more at ease than Russ. He's wearing a bright red vest with a clean white shirt under it, and a nametag that reads HI, I'M RONNIE! The kid's probably not even twenty-one yet. He's friendly to me, and when I tell him about Yang, he says, "Whoa, that's no good," which is at least a bit sympathetic. He tells me they're backed-up for an hour. So much for quick, I think. I put Yang on the counter and give my name. "We'll page you once he's ready," Ronnie says.

I spend the time wandering the store. They've got a demo station of Championship Boxing, so I put on the jacket and glasses and take on a guy named Vance, who's playing in California. I can't figure out how to dodge or block though, and when I throw out my hand, my guy on the screen just wipes his nose with his glove. Vance beats the shit out of me, so I put the glasses and vest back on the rack, and go look at other equipment. I'm playing with one of the new ThoughtPhones when I hear my name paged over the loudspeaker, so I head back to the Repairs counter.

"Fried," the kid tells me. "Honestly, it's probably good he bit it. It's a really outdated model." He's rocking back and forth on his heels as though impatient to get on to his next job.

"Isn't there anything you can do? He's my daughter's Big Brother."

"The language system is fully functional. If you want, I can separate the head for you."

"*Are you kidding*? I'm not giving my daughter her brother's head to play with."

"Oh," the kid says. "Well, um, we could remove the voice box. He can still talk to her, there just won't be any face attached. If you want, we can recycle the body and give you twenty dollars off any digital camera."

"How much is all this going to cost?"

"It's ninety-five for the check-up; voice box removal will be another hundred and fifty. You're probably looking at about three hundred after labor and taxes."

I think about taking it back to Russ, but there's no way. When he'd told me Yang was beyond saving, I'd given him a look of distrust that anyone could read loud and clear. "Go ahead and remove the voice box," I say, "but no recycling. I want to keep the body."

George is outside throwing a football around with his identical twins when I pull in. He raises his hand to his kids to stop them from throwing the ball, and comes over to the low hedge that separates our driveways. "Hey, how'd it go with Russ?" he asks as I get out of the car.

“Not good.” I tell him about Yang, getting a second opinion, how I’ve got his voice box in the backseat, his body in a large Quick Fix bag in the trunk. I tell him all this with as little emotion as possible. “What can you expect from electronics?” I say, attempting to appear nonchalant.

“Man, I’m really sorry for you,” he says, his voice quieter than I’ve ever heard it. “Yang was a good kid. I remember the day he came over to help Dana carry in the groceries. The kids still talk about that fortune telling thing he showed them with the sticks.”

“Yeah,” I say, looking at the bushes. I can feel the tears starting to come again. “Anyway, it’s no big deal. Don’t let me keep you from your game. We’ll figure it out.” Which is a complete lie. I have no clue how we’re going to figure anything out. We needed Yang, and there’s no way we can afford another model.

“Hey, listen,” George says. “If you guys need help, let us know. You know, if you need a daysitter or something. I’ll talk to Dana—I’m sure she’d be up for taking Mika.” George reaches out across the hedge, his large hand coming straight at me. For a moment I flash back to Championship Boxing and think he’s going to hit me. Instead he pats me on the shoulder. “I’m really sorry, Jim,” he says.

That night I lie with Mika in bed and read her *Goodnight Moon*. It’s the first time I’ve read to her in months. The last time was when we visited Kyra’s folks and had shut Yang down for the weekend. Mika’s asleep by the time I reach the last page. I give her a kiss on her head and turn out the lights. Kyra’s in bed reading.

“I guess I’m gonna start digging now,” I say.

“Come here,” she says, putting her book down. I cross the room and lie across our bed, my head on her belly.

“Do you miss him too?” I ask.

"Mm-hm," she says. She puts her hand on my head and runs her fingers through my hair. "I think saying goodbye tomorrow is a good idea. Are you sure it's gonna be okay to have him buried out there?"

"Yeah. There's no organic matter in him. The guys at Quick Fix dumped his stomach canister." I look up at our ceiling, the way our lamp casts a circle of light and then a dark shadow. "I don't know how we're going to make it without him."

"Shh," Kyra strokes my hair. "We'll figure it out. I spoke with Tina Matthews after you called me today. You remember her daughter, Lauren?"

"The clone?"

"Yes. She's home this semester; college wasn't working for her. Tina said Lauren could watch Mika if we need her to."

"I thought we didn't want Mika raised by a clone."

"We're doing what we have to do to make things work. Besides, Lauren is a nice girl."

"She's got that glassy-eyed apathetic look. She's exactly like her mother," I say. Kyra doesn't say anything. She knows I'm being irrational, and so do I. I sigh. "I just really hoped we could keep clones out of our lives."

"For how long? Your brother and Margaret are planning on cloning this summer. You're going to be an uncle soon enough."

"Yeah," I say quietly.

Ever since I was handed Yang's voice box, I feel as though time has slowed down. The light of the setting sun that evening had stretched across the wood floors of our home for what seemed an eternity. The sounds have all become crisper as well, as though, until now, I'd been living my life with earplugs. I think about the way Mika's eyelids fluttered as she slept, the feel of George's hand against my arm. I sit up, turn towards Kyra, and kiss her. The softness of her lips makes me remember the first time we kissed. Kyra squeezes my hand. "You better start digging, so I can comfort you tonight," she says. I smile and ease myself off of the bed. "Don't worry," Kyra says, "It'll be a good funeral tomorrow."

In the hallway, on my way towards the staircase, the cracked door of Yang's room stops me. Instead of going down, I walk across the carpeting to the doorway, push it open, and flick on the light switch. There's his bed, perfectly made with the corners tucked in, a writing desk, a heavy oak dresser, and a closet full of black suits. On the wall is a poster of China that Big Brothers&Sisters Inc. sent us and a pennant from the Tigers game I took Yang to. There's little in the minimalism of his décor to remind me of him. There is, however, a baseball glove on the shelf by his bed. This was a present Yang bought for himself with the small allowance we provided him. We were at Toys R Us when Yang placed the glove in the shopping cart. We didn't ask him about it, and he didn't mention why he was buying it. When he came home, he put it on the shelf near his Tigers pennant, and there it sat untouched.

Along the windowsill sits Yang's collection of dead moths and butterflies as though ready to take flight. He collected them from beneath our bug-zapper during the summer, and placed their powdery bodies by the window. I walk over and examine the collection. There's the great winged Luna Moth, with its two mock eyes staring up at me, the mosaic of a Monarch's wings, and a collection of smaller non-descript brown and silvery gray moths. Kyra once asked him about his insects. Yang's face illuminated momentarily, the lights beneath his cheeks burning extra brightly, and he'd said, "They're very beautiful, don't you think?" Then, as though suddenly embarrassed, he segued to a Fun Fact regarding the brush-footed butterfly of China.

What arrests me, though, are the objects on his writing desk. Small matchboxes are stacked in a pile on the center of the table, the matchsticks spread across the expanse like tiny logs. In a corner is an orange-capped bottle of Elmer's that I recognize as the one from my toolbox. What was Yang up to? A log cabin? A city of small wooden men and women? Maybe this was Yang's attempt at art—one that, unlike the calligraphy he was programmed to know, was entirely of his own creation. If this is the case, then there was much more to Yang than his programming manual could ever have told us. Tomorrow I'll bag his suits, donate them to the Goodwill, and throw out the Big Brothers & Sisters poster, but these matchboxes, the butterflies, and the baseball glove, I'll save. They're the only traces of the boy Yang might have been.

The funeral goes well. It's a beautiful October day, the sky thin and blue, and the sun lights up the trees, bringing out the ochre and amber of the season. I imagine what we must look like to the neighbors. A bunch of kooks, burying their electronic equipment like Pagans. I don't care. When I think about Yang being ripped apart in a recycling plant, or stuffing him into our plastic garbage can and setting him out with the trash, I know this is the right choice. Standing together as a family, in the corner of our backyard, I say a couple parting words. I thank Yang for all the joy he brought to our lives. Then Mika and Kyra both say goodbye.

When it's all over we go back inside to have breakfast together. We're sitting eating our cereal, Mika dribbling milk down her chin, when the doorbell rings. I get up and answer it. On our doorstep is a glass vase filled with orchids and white lilies. A small card is attached. I kneel down and open it. *Didn't want to disturb you guys. Just wanted to give you these. We're all very sorry for your loss—George, Dana, and the twins.* Amazing, I think. This from the guy who paints his face.

"Hey, look what we got," I say, carrying the flowers into the kitchen. "They're from George."

"They're beautiful," Kyra says. "Come, Mika, let's go put those in the living room by your brother's picture." Kyra helps Mika out of her chair, and we walk into the other room together.

It was Kyra's idea to put the voice box behind the photograph. The photo is a picture from our trip to China last summer. In it Mika and Yang are playing at the gate of a park. Mika stands at the port, holding the two large iron gates together. From the other side, Yang looks through the hole of the gates at the camera. His head is slightly cocked, as though wondering who we all are. He has a placid non-smile/non-frown, the expression we came to identify as Yang at his happiest.

"You can talk to him," I say to Mika as I place the flowers next to the photograph.

"Goodbye, Yang," Mika says.

"Goodbye?" the voice box asks. "But, little sister, where are we going?"

Mika smiles at the sound of her Big Brother's voice, and looks up at me for instruction. It's an awkward moment. I'm not about to tell Yang that the rest of him is buried in the backyard.

"Nowhere," I answer. "We're all here together."

There's a pause as though Yang's thinking about something. Then, quietly, he asks, "Did you know over two million workers died during the building of the Great Wall of China?" Kyra and I exchange a look from the odd serendipity of this Fun Fact, but neither of us say anything. Then Yang's voice starts up again. "The Great wall is over ten thousand li long. A li is a standardized Chinese unit of measurement that is equivalent to one thousand six hundred and forty feet."

"Wow, that's amazing," Kyra says, and I stand next to her, looking at the flowers George sent, acknowledging how little I truly know about this world.

Cuts

Jennifer Griffin Graham

Her blood is so noisy she can't even think. She comes in the house and goes upstairs before anyone notices her. She heads straight to the bathroom, shutting the door and then twisting the doorknob—one, two, three times—to make sure it's secure. Success. She's slid past her family how many days of her life already? One more is not a problem.

The bathroom is pale around her, paler than her own pale skin. Grey floor, white walls, the porcelain all around scrubbed twice weekly by her mother. She turns on the fan. With the fan running the bathroom is emptied out of any other sound. It slices off the boundaries of the little room. The sizzling animal fat in the kitchen, the thumping bass from her brother's room, the commercials and clinking bottles in the living room downstairs. The rustle of the newspaper. Noise on top of noise on top of noise. The fan surrounds the perimeters, lets no decibel by.

If she has to hear one more word, if anyone utters a word to her, it'll be the last word. It'll kill her. There's been enough noise already today. Noises pushing out at her skin from inside her organs and arteries. Noises pushing into her ears. It's exhausting. She wants it all to shut up shut up shut up.

She opens the medicine chest and it swings forward so fast she stops, inhales. Slower now she pulls out an old metal Band-Aid tin. They don't make metal tins anymore but she likes the cool solidity of the object in her hand, so she keeps reusing it. Inside the tin is a bundle of gauze. Underneath the gauze are the razor blades. Increasingly hard to find, razor blades. She uses exacto crafter blades these days, because all she can get at the drugstore are those plastic safety razors.

She's been shaking all day. After the nightmare hour in choir she put herself in a stall in the school bathroom—dirty green walls covered in Sharpie lines: Jessica's a dyke, I heart Dylan, The Truth is Out there—and raked her blunt nails over her arms, trying to break the skin. It didn't work. She raised some welts, but it didn't help. It wasn't the same. All the rest of the day the words piled up, stopped meaning anything, clattered around her ears. She trembled and trembled and it felt like her organs were maybe coming loose inside her. She trembles now, laying out the gauze and the blade next to each other on the counter.

Her sweatshirt has holes near the cuffs where her thumbs hook in and tug the sleeves more firmly down. She didn't cut the holes. They wore themselves in, after a year of tugging and pulling and clutching and fidgeting. The bathroom is cold—it's October, snow on the ground outside, and the heat low since her Dad runs hot—but she takes off the sweatshirt. She folds it carefully and places it on the toilet seat.

In the mirror her face floats over her white tank top. Skinny white chest. Hair bleached white-yellow, brittle as straw, one more chemically clean thing in the room. Skin white and soft and arms criss-crossed with scars.

She opens the mirror again, this time the center panel, and pulls out the hydrogen peroxide. She likes its obliterating smell. She pulls the wrapping from the exacto blade. She is so careful. Exacting. Exacto. Then she puts it back on the counter. She pulls the tank top off over her head and folds it carefully and places it on top of the sweatshirt. She's not wearing a bra. She doesn't really need to. Her boyfriend likes to tell her she's on the Itty Bitty Titty Committee. She's like the chairwoman of that committee, he says, when he's tweaking her little pink nipples. They—the nipples—are the same color as the tributaries of scars, and it's sort of pleasing to the eye. She's color-coordinated! The scars run over her arms and shoulders and some down on her trunk, but there are none across her chest. That would make it a sex crime. She's not a deviant.

She sits down on the toilet seat, on top of her shirts. She wants to see how long she can wait before grabbing the blade. She feels like grabbing the blade right this minute. She feels like lunging for it but then just who would be in charge here? So she sits on her hands and lets the noise turn over and over: up one side of her body and down the other.

Her boyfriend saw the scars the first time they had sex, and he ran one gnawed fingernail over the longest ribbon of pink on her arm. "Look everyone, it's a walking cliche!" he said. "You going to special SI-sleep away camp? Is Daddy paying enough attention?" She didn't say anything, just let him trace the scars. His words were mean, but his fingers were gentle, and something about that contradiction was almost as good as cutting.

She'd had a boyfriend previous to this one who had wept over her wounds. As in, literally, pressing his face over her arm and letting his tears ooze into her. "Why do you do this to yourself, angel?" he'd asked her. Even she couldn't take a boy like this seriously. But she couldn't bring herself to break up with him. She opened her mouth to do it a thousand times, but she couldn't release the words. Words, she knew, could fly out into the world like winged monkeys and break everything in their path. Words were weapons, and it was too hard to hurt him. Instead she'd just gotten quieter and quieter. She'd stopped responding to anything he said. She hoped eventually he'd give up and break up with her, but he was stubborn. "Why won't you let me in?" he wailed on the phone. He made her mix tapes that claimed that Boys Don't Cry, that declared him her Personal Jesus. It was only the new boyfriend who finally forced the issue, the current boyfriend.

Her fingers are numb when she pulls them out from under her bottom. She lays them on the blade. At first it's cold, but it warms as she holds it pinched between thumb and forefinger. She makes the first cut on her bicep, right under the round curve of her shoulder. The moment before she presses the blade down, every inch of her skin wakes up and shivers and reaches up for the metal. She uses a soft touch. The blade creases her, makes a light dent. Then the line turns red. Then her flesh falls open and starts to sing.

"Doot doot doot doot doot doot doot doot..."

The lipless mouth of the cut flaps, the song blasting through the porcelain quiet.

"Doot doot doot doot doot doot doot doot." It's the scat from "Tom's Diner." She'll have it stuck in her head all night now, but it's better than stuck in her veins.

The cut flutters wildly. The wind moving through it feels hot and ugly, but as it starts to move out of her a scintillant and glittering relief settles around her. The blood runs down her arm and into the fluffy blue bathmat. She'll have to get it to the laundry room without her mother noticing. For now she doesn't care.

"Doot doot doot doot..." She watches her body in the mirror and looks for another bit of blank skin to cut.

The new boyfriend is eighteen. He works at the video store where she rents horror movies every Thursday night. A few months ago he started to flirt. Every time he gave her a movie—*Texas Chainsaw Massacre, Black Christmas, Hellraiser*—he pinched her wrist, grinned like he knew she'd never call him on it. He was tall and skinny and moved with lanky aggression. She went in every week, imagining him as a Viking who would carry her off from the weepy boyfriend. She imagined that he would hollow her out. That he would fill her with something, some force that might finally rip her to bits.

"Doot doot doot doot doot doot doot doot..."

She hadn't broken up with the old boyfriend so much as replaced him. She and the video-store boy ended up making out in the stockroom, surrounded by teetering piles of VHS. He put his fingers in her hair and cupped the back of her head as if it were something fragile, even while he bit her neck hard enough to break skin. When the old boyfriend called her after that, it was as simple as hanging up on him. As simple as gliding past him in the halls at school and ignoring his pleading voice. She knew this was meaner than just telling him to take a hike. But this way she just didn't have a choice. She couldn't have two boyfriends, after all. It wasn't her fault the new one had moved in.

But thinking of the old boyfriend, his face lost in the crowd of the hallway, her blood starts roiling again. Without even thinking she quickly slashes at another spot on her arm, lower down. It gurgles for a moment, the mouth of the cut filling with blood, and then it puckers and spits the blood out and starts to lilt. The puckering, the spitting, it hurts in a different way than the cutting. It bunches up her skin like a pinch.

"I think we should just be friends," says the cut in a hollow girlish voice.

"Doot doot doot doot doot doot doot doot!" belts the first cut.

Here is a list of things that have never happened to her: she has never been raped or molested, never been beaten, has never gone to bed without supper, was never picked last for dodgeball, has never gone without a meal, has never slept in the rain, has never been slapped by her mother or father, has never even been spanked (except by the new boyfriend, once, wonderfully thrown across his lap like a helpless child), has never been abandoned or mutilated (well, aside from the obvious) or neglected, has never been prostituted for drugs or money, has never been called a name worse than bitch by an adult, and that only because the adult in question was drunk. This is why the boyfriend thinks it's all a sham, an attention-ploy, this cutting. A way to add drama to a banal life. She lets him tell her all these things and maybe they're true, or part true. She doesn't really know anymore. She doesn't like to argue with people.

"I love you like a brother," says the second cut blandly.

Ankle next. Ankles always bleed so much. It's the spot she always nicks while shaving, usually by accident. She sits down on the toilet seat again and pulls her foot up over her knee. The cut makes her shake, makes her feel sharp and clean. There's a moment where she's not sure she's punctured, and then the blood starts pouring down her foot. The voice is deep and male. "Uomini fummo, e or siam fatti sterpi: ben dovrebb' esser la tua man piu pia, se state fossimo anime di serpi."

Everything is so bright. The porcelain is pure and white and the metal faucets sparkle. It all glitters and the colors, those few colors, are profound: the cornflower blue of the towels, the now-purple-flecked bath mat, drops of blood soaking in the fibers. She knows the chemicals involved, the endorphins unzipping the colors of the world to be better and brighter than they are. But what it feels like is that with all the noise finally flooding out of her she can take a moment to slow down and realize: this is what blue is. What silver is. What white should be.

“I just need a little bit of space,” says cut number two.

There are still a few pink welts on her forearms from that afternoon in the school bathroom, the failed attempt. She hadn’t even been thinking. All day she hasn’t been able to think. In the deli where she worked after school she just watched the electric meat slicer. She wasn’t allowed to use it yet. But she watched the college girl who shared her shift whipping the block of roast beef back and forth, the cuts of meat wrinkling silkily out the other end. Chopping tomatoes with the little hand-held knife, she came close a few times. But she really needed the bathroom for it to be right. Not just the privacy, though that was part of it; what she really craved was the way the bathroom would make its own world. How for just a little while she could be the only creature alive.

She traces one of the welts with the blade. “God damn shit fuck,” it blurts. It seems they’re finally to the meat of things. Her skin gapes open pinkish red. It spews curses, though she’s not sure to whom. “Fuck damn asshole.”

“Doot doot doot doot...”

A sudden knock rattles the door. Her entire body flails like a spastic marionette, the blade flying up into the air. Small streaks of blood splatter across the mirror and the counter. She sprawls across the floor of the bathroom, shaking.

“Hey, how long you gonna be in there?” asks her father’s voice. It’s loud and rumbling, a little sloppy.

“Quando si parte l’anima feroce dal corpo ond’ ella stessa s’é disvelta...”

“My magazine’s in there. Do you think you could pass it out for me?”

“Doot doot doot doot...”

He laughs, a tangled knot of phlegm. “Burrito day at lunch or what? All right, fine, I’ll go get your mom’s Readers’ Digest.”

“World class son of a whore motherfucker.”

His steps thud along the hallway, shaking under the fan’s roar. She lies on the floor, shuddering. There’s fear. She can’t place the fear. She doesn’t know if it’s for herself or for him. For a moment she tries to imagine what would happen if he jimmied the lock, opened the door. If he saw her in her own blood. The things that would have to be said out loud. The things her tongue would have to push out of her mouth.

“And the motherfucking horse you rode in on!” calls out the last cut. “And the horse you rode in on!”

She lies on the floor. The world’s been invaded, the fan over-shouted. Now that she’s listening she can hear her brother’s music pulsing underneath the fan. She can hear faint clunks every now and then, pots and pans in the kitchen downstairs, the water turning on and then off. She can even hear a television theme song if she strains her ears very hard: Jeopardy! For just a moment she feels constricted, confined, strangled. She feels the web between her and her family stretching all through the different rooms, its tensile strength holding her shoulders tightly. She writhes around, flops her arms around. Blood splatters all over the floor with every movement. The one on her ankle is a real gusher and a tiny puddle is forming by her foot.

"...e dinne, se tu puoi, s'alcuna mai di tai membra si spiega."

The world invaded, she suddenly can't stop thinking about the choir test. The stupid fucking test! Everyone had to sing a solo, in front of the whole class, as part of the mid-term. She loved choir because she could sing, belt out, but disappear into the crowd. She could join her voice in with a lot of other voices and not even hear herself, but could feel the vibrations in her throat, could feel the stereo sound of harmony surrounding her. But she hated solos. She never auditioned for solo parts, for higher choirs, for any of that. She was happy where she was.

But Ms. Nelson was new this year and seemed to think it was important for them to sing solos. It was a requirement. Ms. Nelson was very young but very strained all the time, a crease in between her eyes that made her look miserable. Her sticky kindness was unbearable.

She'd practiced for three weeks straight, alone in her room with the door shut and locked. Every time she thought of the test her stomach felt hot and pinched. More than once after practicing she'd slipped into the bathroom and into the cabinet to get the exacto blades. More than one of the fresher scars on her arms were from rehearsals. But she practiced over and over and when the door was shut her voice came out strong and clear. She thought maybe it would be fine, this once, that she could stand in front of them all and sing the words she was supposed to say and sing them well.

The ex-boyfriend was in choir, a tenor, and his eyes never left her face as she stood up before the class. She tried not to look at him. He'd finally stopped pleading with her in the hallway and calling her on the phone. He'd stopped shoving notes through the slats in her locker. These days he was wearing all black and painting swirls on his face with kohl, but it was pathetic because he was plump and acne-patched and was never going to be Brandon Lee no matter how hard he tried. She didn't blame him, though. She understood the instinct to hide.

Her hands shook so hard. Not everyone looked at her. Lots of people were bored, passing notes, whispering. There were forty kids in class who had to sing solos over the course of the week. Plenty of them had sounded terrible. There were catty conversations in the hall after, but no one really payed much attention. She wasn't nervous what they'd think of her. She was nervous to hear her own voice out there in front of them. She was nervous about what would happen when she opened her mouth.

The piano started, and she sang. The words fluttered in her mouth. She started singing a little bit louder. Stood up straight and reached down into her diaphragm.

"Let all mortal flesh keep silent, and with fear and trembling stand," she sang. At first she felt like a music box, throwing notes out carelessly, but as she kept singing she felt a faint glow in her mouth. The words stripped themselves down of meaning and she put other meanings onto them.

"In the Body and the Blood, He will give to all the faithful His own self for food," she sang. She felt the melody on her tongue, in her throat, in her chest, in her lungs, in her skin. She sang it as an apology to the boy in black, who she loved in a way, even though she couldn't stand him. She sang it to her family, who always tugged at her everywhere she went, even when she wasn't in the house with them. She sang to the boyfriend, the current boyfriend with steel toed boots. She said different things to all of them.

Then the song ended. Everything was very quiet for a moment, and she heard a giggle from the sopranos. She tried not to look at her ex-boyfriend. She glanced at Ms. Nelson, who was scribbling on a clipboard.

Finally Ms. Nelson looked up. It looked like it pained her to have to say anything at all. "Didn't you notice that you were a half step off through the whole song? I kept pounding the right note on the piano trying to steer you back."

She shook her head, mute again. She stumbled her way back to her seat.

The ex-boyfriend leaned over towards her. She tried not to look at him. Her blood was screeching inside her ears. But he would smile at her, maybe. Maybe he heard what she was telling him, even if it was done wrong, a half step off. Maybe he understood and was looking at her to smile, to pass a note saying don't worry, I know what you really sound like.

But when she looked up and made eye contact, his mouth crumpled up in a smile.

Cunt, he mouthed, across the third row.

She slashes again at her side. Her blue jeans are purple in spots from the dribbles of red. Down the hall her brother's bass thuds dully. Downstairs *Jeopardy!* seems to be over. Downstairs she imagines her mother burning herself on a casserole dish, pulling it out of the oven. Downstairs is Dad's coffee table, covered in empty brown bottles. If they're right there on the table, in front of everybody, no one can say anything, because it's not a secret, it's not a problem, it's right there on the coffee table for all the world to see. You just can't say anything about something so clearly not a problem.

The last cut finally speaks out.

"I'm saving your lives."

Groping her way up to her knees, she clutches the edge of the counter. She pulls the gauze and the hydrogen peroxide down to the floor. She opens the bottle and pours the liquid onto the gauze, and one by one she starts to daub away the blood.

The stinging gives her another wave of shock, another round of glittering colors. She daubs the first one first. It's still singing, but quieter. She clutches it closed and presses a Band-Aid down onto it. It mumbles around the bandage for a moment and then falls silent.

She works slowly, patching them all up, shushing them gently.

"You're lucky I'm a half step off."

The last cut is calm, serious. Deeper than the others. She pours a stream of hydrogen peroxide directly down into it and gasps, throws her head back.

"Next time I'll find another way, a better way, and what I say might destroy you."

Tonight is Thursday, and she's going to the video store, as soon as she gets cleaned up. She feels cool and empty and ready for the boyfriend's calloused fingertips to shape her into something new. She steps into the shower and turns it up as hot as it will go. She wipes herself down. She has to ask her father for the car keys. Sometimes he gives them to her. Sometimes he doesn't, just to prove they're his.

When she comes out of the bathroom, the bath mat wadded up inside her towel, her mother is in the hallway putting clean ones into the closet.

"I want a tattoo," she says.

"Not under my roof," says her mother, not looking at her.

Phantoms

Vishwas R. Gaitonde

Row, row, row your boat
Gently down the stream;
Merrily, merrily, merrily, merrily,
Life is but a dream.
Popular Children's Song

The vague boundaries of the neighborhood around her home had always been the limit of her world. Now she had circled half the globe to see her uncle. She hadn't seen him in years and didn't know what he would look like—especially with the troubling news that his mind was dissipating like cotton candy in a greedy child's mouth.

The mist that shrouded the mountaintops crept down the slopes in patchy disarray. She wondered if her uncle's mind was like that. Through the gaps in the mist, Connie saw that the mountains close by were lush green, their slopes covered with tea shrubs; those in the distance were blue. The mist covered more than just bushes—here and there, lights twinkled behind the hazy veil, hinting that hardy souls lived on those heights in some fantasy world nestled on the mountaintops. Connie's eyelids were heavy with sleep; she had to keep yanking them up again with an effort. Then she was wide awake as the car lurched precipitously around a hairpin bend in the road. The crazy driver had nearly gone off the road—they could have tumbled to their death in some uncharted ravine in the Himalayas.

But the jolt was good for her. She would not nod off now. They had told her it was important to fight off sleep and remain awake when the sun was shining, that was the only way to beat jet lag.

Connie had no idea what that meant. She had rarely strayed far from her home in Connecticut. She had not even seen the Pacific Ocean. And here she was, on the other side of the world. When it was noon here, her family and friends back home were snug in their beds, the pale moon shining through their windows. It gave Connie the creeps to even think of it.

Calcutta (they called it Kolkata these days) was a nightmare from the moment she landed. The chaos at the airport was a fitting preamble to this vibrant but disorderly city, the milling crowds, the blazing colors, the crowded streets, the half-dead beggars, the swirling dust, the steady heat. Oh, Kolkata! But the air became more pure and cooler once she left the plains behind and ascended the mountains in her rental car—an old jalopy, but it came with a driver. Connie was glad about that; she could never have driven a car in this mad place.

A muscle in her cheek twitched as she thought of Uncle Clarence. She hadn't seen him now for more than a decade. He lived in India, and as the years rolled by he had become increasingly cut off from his relatives, who were dying one after another. Now there was only his sister Ruth, Connie's mother, who was frail and housebound.

They had been shocked to receive a letter from people they had never heard of—the Ambadis—who introduced themselves as Mr. Clarence Marble's neighbors. Mr. Marble, they wrote, had not been himself for several months, had recently taken a twist for the worse and been admitted to a nursing home near Darjeeling that provided mental health care. Mr. Marble lived alone, and they were trying to track down his relatives.

Connie spent the night with the Ambadis. The Ambadis were an elderly couple and were indeed Uncle Clarence's nearest neighbors, though not in the usual sense of the word. The houses were isolated here, and the Ambadis and her uncle lived at either end of a lane with nothing but trees and shrubbery in between.

"Such a sweet man, dear Mr. Marble," Nilima Ambadi told Connie, "And always so full of military discipline; but these last few months, he really lost his mind, really lost it, could not even take care of himself, so his servant told us. And after we got him into the nursing home, we searched through his papers, neat little piles all over his cottage. He kept all his old letters, that's how we got your address. So confusing it was—some letters from England, some from America but both from the same city."

"We moved to America ages ago," Connie said, surprised. They had moved from Bristol in England to Bristol in New England—it must have been a good eighteen years back. Her uncle was a real pack rat to have saved such old letters.

The next day, it was off to the nursing home where her uncle had been admitted.

Connie looked out of the window as the car rolled down the drive and stopped by a squat yellow building with bright chintz curtains fluttering in every window. She was ushered into the doctor's office. The doctor's desk was burdened with precariously balanced heaps of manila folders bursting with paper, medical journals, and newspapers with yellowing pages. But the most unusual feature in the room was the doctor himself.

"Good morning, Miss Constance Moss, have a seat. We've been expecting you. I'm Dr. Ngodup."

Connie could not take her eyes off him. He had a deep olive complexion but he looked so Chinese, so out of place here. In India, one expected people to look, well, Indian.

“Have you been informed about your uncle’s condition, Miss Moss?”

“Not really, no,” Connie said. “All I’ve been told is that he has—er—lost his mind.”

“Lost his mind.” The doctor looked at her sharply. “We’re so adept in coining these vague terms, aren’t we? Lost his mind—what does that really mean? Where does the mind reside? I mean, if you found a lost mind, Miss Moss, where would you return it to?”

“To the brain, I suppose.” Connie said, taken aback at the question.

“Think so?” The doctor looked at her gloomily as he drummed his fingers on the small space of desktop in front of him that was not covered with paper. The staccato rhythm was mesmerizing. “A lot of people think that, but I don’t. It’s like thinking of the ocean just in terms of waves beating on a shore. The ocean is more than just waves. I think the mind lives everywhere, in every cell of the body.

“But you didn’t come all the way to listen to my ramblings,” he continued. “You came here to see your uncle. After you’ve seen him, we can talk some more.”

He slapped his palm smartly on a hand bell, which emitted a shrill ping.

Connie followed the nurse down dim corridors to the room where her uncle lay. The nurse was a prim woman in a pristine, starched white uniform, and she wore a headdress that looked like a large white linen napkin meticulously folded and then fastened to the hair with pins. But thoughts of how a cloth could be folded like that disappeared when she saw her uncle, in his pajamas, curled up in his bed, softly sighing and moaning. She had not seen him in years and was unprepared for how much he had aged, how much his hair had thinned, how many new ruts and wrinkles had creased his face.

Memories of the old times with her uncle now trickled back to her one by one, some stronger than others. Her uncle was in the British army and had been posted to India during the days of empire. One of his favorite sayings was "Row your boat." Britannia would rule the waves only if each man rowed his boat and rowed it well, he said. Obviously, there were many lousy oarsmen and the empire had ended. But her uncle had chosen to stay on in India and not return with his regiment to England.

She remembered how baffled her family had been. A few others had also opted to stay behind, but they were senior officers in the army who had served in India practically all their lives. One could make allowances for them, but Clarence? He was not even thirty when India became independent. His parents had pleaded with him to return. He would be viewed by the Indians of the new India as one of their former oppressors. He would not be safe there. But Clarence had disregarded all of them and stayed on. Connie remembered how she and her cousins used to giggle and chant, "Uncle Clarence has lost his marbles!" knowing well that he was too far to hear them and that nobody would tattle either. Now she felt guilty as she saw her uncle's thin frame and tortured face. Well, Uncle Clarence, she said to herself, I've done my duty. I've rowed my boat. I'm here.

"He keeps drifting in and out of his sleep," the nurse told Connie. "All you can really do is wait here and hope he comes to soon."

Connie leaned towards her uncle to catch what he was saying. It sounded like 'Untie me.' She threw a suspicious glance at the nurse and repeated what she had heard. The nurse, who was on her way out, looked horrified at the thought.

"We never tie our patients to the cots," she said earnestly. "That only happened in the bad old days." Then, from the door, she threw a backward glance at Connie, and said, "These days, we just use sedatives."

"Untie me!"

Clarence shouted his request again as he almost bounced off the horse, which had broken into a sharp trot with the other horses. He found it hard to keep his balance, though he was sandwiched between the teenaged boy who sat in front and a small pannier strapped behind him that dug into his back. The boy grunted, tugged at the reins and growled, "Wait. Coming to camp soon."

Clarence grimaced. The ropes cut into his wrists with every jolt. The horses were galloping downhill now. All around him were majestic mountains, red, purple, brown, towering high. They were wild and desolate, all boulder and stone and rock and not a blade of grass. They rushed headlong down a rough trail. The horses in front of him kicked little puffs of yellow dust and scattered small stones in their headlong rush. Clarence was pushed against the boy and almost fell off. All the others in the group wore thick coats and turbans or skull-caps. They had thrown a blanket around Clarence, but he had no covering for his head and the wind blew his silver hair every which way. The sun was setting behind their backs, its dying fire reflected on the mountains. Ahead of them, the sky was blue-gray and the moon had appeared, flat, pale, anemic, somewhere between crescent and half.

Nila, nila, odi va. The words popped up into Clarence's head. He wondered where they came from. Something told him that they didn't belong here, that they were from another time and place, but he couldn't figure out why he thought so. *Nila, nila, odi va.* The phrase repeatedly fizzed up through his brain.

In the valley ahead of them, he could see clusters of tents set up in a circle, in the middle of which a large fire crackled, with men and horses gathered around it. The air filled with shouts and greetings as they thundered into the camp. Two men untied Clarence but his legs were wobbly and would not bear his weight, and he almost fell to the ground. The men pulled him up and supported him, and it was in this ungainly position that he once again confronted the leader of the party, a thickset man with a heavy black beard and heavier eyes.

"I'm asking you again: why are you in Afghanistan?"

"I told you the first time," Clarence said, weakly. "I was posted in Kabul in the old days of the British Raj. I loved it here, and wanted to visit the old haunts again."

A crowd had gathered around them. Somebody made a coarse-sounding comment and a shout of laughter swept through the crowd. The leader translated the remark for Clarence.

"For someone who lived here before, don't you know which road leads to Kabul, and which to Kandahar?"

The same man made another comment, and the laughter was twice as loud.

"The Americans must be in real trouble if they're sending tottering old men like you to spy on us."

"I'm British, *not* American."

"What's the difference, old man? I can't understand why the Americans keep up this pretence of two separate nations. They should just annex Britain and be done with it. Now, spy, vomit the truth or we will take other measures."

Clarence felt himself going cold, though the wind no longer whipped his face and he was near a roaring fire. He had read that the tribal warlords who now commandeered Afghanistan were not above using torture. He was an old dog now. He would not be able to withstand whatever the fiends inflicted on him.

They dragged him to a large tent. His feeble attempts at resistance were ignored as though they had been never offered. But his eyeballs spun around when he was inside. Several comfortable-looking silk bedding rolls were spread around the floor, with long tubular pillows to recline against. The silks were of gorgeous colors, their kaleidoscopic patterns alight from the many hurricane lanterns hanging from the poles. Between the bedding rolls were large pans of glowing embers, adding warmth to the glitter. They left him there, standing foolishly.

Then a plump man in flowing black robes and a golden turban entered the tent. His face was not like the hardened, weathered faces of the men who had captured Clarence; it was soft and fleshy, and his sleek beard looked oiled and combed. He beamed at Clarence and gestured towards the beds. Clarence hesitantly lowered himself, luxuriating in the brush of silk against skin. He saw the plump man do likewise at the adjacent bed, then clap his hands authoritatively. His eyes looked crafty now.

As if on cue, a scrawny young man came in with two contraptions, which he set up between the reclining men. Clarence's eyes lit up when he saw what they were. Hubble bubbles! This was high style, the posh life. The man set up each hookah expertly, filling the vases with water, fitting the heads and smoking pipes, deftly packing in the tobacco with skilful pinches, and finally lighting the coals. The hookahs themselves were exquisite. The vases were painted delicately with beautiful floral patterns, and the metal parts were made of burnished silver and gold.

"In the old days, the British generals would puff on the hubble-bubble at the court of the Afghan king," Clarence blurted out, as much to himself as to his companion. "I was, of course, too low in the ranks ever to have the privilege."

"Ah, yes." The plump man's eyes lit up. "Every commoner becomes a king when he smokes the hookah. A royal ritual this, smoking the hookah. When the Ottoman Sultan did not offer the hookah to the French ambassador, France almost declared war on Turkey. We want no such trouble with America, and so—we will smoke together, my lord."

Clarence looked up quickly, sensing he was being mocked, but the other's face was impassive. He continued to speak softly, after he took a pull on the stem, "We are the kings of Afghanistan now. We, the Pashtun. We are proud, we are noble, and we fight well. Nobody can take our land from us. The British tried it and failed. We sent the Russians packing with their tails between their legs. The Americans will not succeed, either. Tell that to your masters, my lord."

Clarence nodded, then wished he hadn't. The nod could be taken as an acknowledgement that he was a spy, that he had masters. He had nodded unthinkingly, having just taken a long pull on the hookah, enjoying the soft bubbling of the water as he drew up the smoke through the long serpentine tube. His head was feeling light and airy.

"Why were you wandering on your own in these mountains? What did you hope to find, my lord?"

To delay answering, Clarence took another long, slow pull. This time the bubbles seem to rise up in his brain and noisily pop, one by one, against the vault of his skull. His eyelids turned into heavy metal as they slowly and inevitably lowered themselves.

In all my years (and there have been a great many of them) I had never known the sun to be so hot as it was that day, when I tramped down the dusty road that led to the small village. The road had been paved once; now it had cracked up into cavernous potholes bridged by patches of asphalt. It was late afternoon, I felt close to collapse and I must have looked ghastly. Perhaps it was this that prompted the woman who walked briskly ahead of me to stop and ask me where I was going.

"To Trincomalee."

She almost dropped the bag of vegetables that she was carrying.

"What? On foot? It's a long way, and you don't look fit enough. Besides," Her eyes narrowed. "Don't you know there's a war? That it's dangerous to go there?"

"I know, but it's something I must do." I gave a long sigh. "My name is Clarence Marble. I was in the British administration here many years ago. I want to see some of the places I loved before my days are done."

"British service? Are you an Englishman?" She pulled up a fold of my skin, which hung loose on my forearm, and rolled it between her thumb and middle finger. "Hmmm, I'll say this much for you – you were white once. The sun has roasted you well."

I pulled my hand away, greatly annoyed and a little amused. Look who was talking! She was a dark woman, somewhere between the color of chocolate and charcoal, and the sweat glistened on her brow around the red dot on her forehead.

"You look tired and hungry—you must be, if you've walked all day. Why don't you rest in our village for the night? You can start again at dawn when it is cool."

I had my own misgivings about this but I was in no state to pass up her offer. We entered the village but we did not walk down the main street. Instead she took me along the perimeter, walking along a muddy trail sandwiched between the backs of huts and clumps of trees interspersed with dense brambly undergrowth that drew blood from my arms. Her hut was a one-room dwelling made of mud walls and thatched coconut fronds, a different corner of the room serving a different purpose. I had thought that my army barracks had been Spartan, but this was truly bare bones living, every shred of flesh stripped off the skeleton. The woman rolled out a straw mat on the floor and tossed an old, soiled and torn pillow from which the cotton stuffing protruded. She asked me to rest while she picked up her child that had been left with a friend.

She returned with a skinny little thing all of two years old, with a mucus-encrusted nose. The child was asleep, and to my consternation, she placed it by my side and then busied herself cooking at an earthen stove over a wood fire in one corner of the room. We made a strange threesome.

"The British left long before I was born." The woman struck a conversation as she deftly diced a bunch of tomatoes. "So why did you come back?"

"Oh, I never left." I said. "I stayed behind. I love it here. You know, I've done it many times over but I still cherish my first memory on the verandah of the Galle Face Hotel, sipping a *chhota* peg and watching the red sun sink into the sea—a splendid, splendid sight. And the little boys playing cricket or flying kites on the green. And shopping at Cargill's."

"Mister, you did all that in Ceylon. Ceylon is no more."

"Then you haven't been to Colombo lately. The hotel, Cargill's, they're very much there. As grand as they've always been."

"You misunderstood me, mister. They may be there, but they belong to Sri Lanka now, not to Ceylon." She paused, and patted the ground. "And some day, this may not be Sri Lanka anymore. This may be the soil of Eelam."

Eelam! It reminded me again that I was in a country that was tearing itself from within. The Tamil minority, tired of being discriminated by the Sinhala majority, now believed that they could live in honor and dignity only when their ancient Tamil kingdom reincarnated itself as the modern state of Eelam. The Tamil Tigers were the fiercest guerilla army in the world. And Trincomalee was slap-bang-wallop in the danger zone. An intense sadness crept over me as a few lines of poetry floated into my mind:

Our world has passed away,
In wantonness o'erthrown.
There is nothing left to-day …
…Only ourselves remain
To face the naked days
In silent fortitude,
Through perils and dismays
Renewed and re-renewed.

I wondered whether I should give up my trek to Trinco. But oh, just to stand there on the cliff top in front of the Temple of One Thousand Pillars and gaze down upon the expanse of the Indian Ocean, to let the mind soar free in the air and across the miles of warm turquoise water stretching on without end, no land interrupting, all the way to the snows of Antarctica at the bottom of the world.

"Eat. You must be hungry." The woman gave me an earthen bowl of hot, steaming rice porridge with some tomato chutney on the side. There was no cutlery so I would have to eat it by hand as these people did. The porridge was too hot to put into my mouth anyway, so I set it down to cool and lay on the mat again.

I must have dozed off, for when I opened my eyes, it was dark except for a patch of pale moonlight that streamed in from the rear window. There were shouts of glee and tinkling laughter coming in with the moonlight, so I crept to the window and looked out.

"Nila, nila, odi va." The woman called out in a singsong voice and the child, now awake and giggling and gurgling, repeated it, and then they were laughing. *Nila, nila, odi va.* They were inviting the moon to join them. The moon was bright, full, lustrous, shining through the leaves of the trees and seeming to alternately move towards them and away from them as the branches of the trees swayed in the breeze. The air was thick with a sweet smell, and I noticed that white orchids had bloomed everywhere, each stem bearing several star-shaped blossoms. It was as though the stars had come down from the heavens for the little child, and now it was calling out to the moon. I was touched.

Eventually the gnawing in my stomach pulled me back. The porridge had gone all cold and lumpy, and it reminded me of the gruel that we were served in the army. I remember how we had to line up in the cantonment of Wellington after our morning drill, holding our bowls, and Sergeant-Major Winkler would dish out the kedgeree with a fat ladle. "Fancy food won't toughen you up, lads, but this will!" he would say, as he plopped our breakfast into our bowls with a grim smile. We would scowl, imagining him eating his fried eggs with sausage and bacon and buttered toast and marmalade in the officer's mess. Good old Winky-Winks, he wasn't a really bad sort. My eyes misted again.

When I woke up the second time that night, the moon had vanished and the darkness was cold and stygian. A man and a woman were speaking outside, their voices urgent and low, but loud enough for me to hear snatches of their talk.

"What else could I have done? I wanted to talk to you before I told anybody about him." The woman's voice was defensive.

"And he said he was on his way to Thirukonamalai?"

"Yes, but he still called it Trincomalee. He sounds genuine, but he can't be, can he? Do you think he is a Sinhala agent?"

"He could be. He must have made up that story—only a madman would walk all the way to Thirukonamalai. Look, I must be off now to the meeting at Sinnathambi's place. Make sure the stranger does not leave until you hear back from me."

This was ominous. I decided to stay awake at all costs and leave right at dawn, but I nodded off again, and when I awoke, the sun was up. Cursing under my breath, I slunk out of the hut and headed out the way I came. As I walked out of the village and onto the main road, several people saw me and threw curious glances my way, but nobody stopped me. I couldn't understand a word they said to each other. Scary. How was it that yesterday I conversed with that woman, who was little more than a peasant? Was she really fluent in English? Or did I speak to her in Tamil, only to have totally forgotten the language the next day?

When I had gone a little ways off from the village, I heard a great commotion and glanced back. A crowd had gathered by the village entrance, and the woman was pointing at me and gesticulating. When they saw me, a shout went up. Just then, an open jeep trundled down the road, with many dark men in battle fatigues holding rifles. All the people began to shout and point at me, and the soldiers also shouted something at me. The next minute, they began firing and bullets spattered in the ground around me. There was a little girl, her hair in braids, riding a bicycle alongside me. She shrieked and fell down. I thought she had been shot. Then I saw she had flung herself off her bicycle and flattened herself on the ground. Swift reflexes! I could hear the jeep gather speed behind me. Where could I hide? I was such a conspicuous target and I was getting out of breath.

The road was on an embankment and the sides sloped down to rice fields. I quickly started to move downwards. The little girl had raised her head from the ground and was yelling at me, mortal fear on her face. I sensed she was warning me, but then I lost my footing and slithered down the slope, straight towards an odd piece of metal sticking out of the ground. A landmine! That's what it was!

The explosion was tremendous and I could hear nothing after that. My whirling mind could feel pain that quadrupled by the second, could smell charred flesh. Then suddenly there was only a deathly silence that seemed eternal.

The first slivers of dawn had begun to brighten the eastern sky. The men stood by the prone figure lying on the floor of the tent.

"We'll have to move along shortly," one said. "Should we leave him here on the mountainside to die or strap him onto a horse and take him along?"

The plump man trembled with suppressed anger.

"That imbecile, Hanif. He deserves a hundred lashes for this. He put too much opium in the hookah. I wanted just enough to loosen up the old man and make him talk. Hanif should have known that a small quantity for a young colt is a large quantity for a horse on its last legs. Have you people no common sense? Must I teach you everything?"

"But what do we do now?"

In reply, the plump man swung his leg in an arc into the prone man's side. There was the sickening sound of cracking ribs.

Clarence woke up with a gasp, rolling on the bed and clutching at his side. Large drops of sweat stood out on his brow. Connie immediately rose from her chair, dropped her book and was at her uncle's side. He looked up at her in disbelief.

"Hi, Uncle Clarence. You're not dreaming, it's not a ghost, it's me, Connie. Your niece." Connie held her uncle's clammy hand to demonstrate that she was flesh and blood. "I know I've changed a lot since you last saw me, so I'm glad you recognized me. The Ambadis wrote to us that you had taken ill and were in hospital, and I got onto the first flight to India. Don't worry, Uncle Clarence, it's going to be all right."

But Clarence Marble was only half-listening. He was deep in thought. Finally, he spoke up solemnly.

"Connie dear, it's wonderful to see you. But how can you be sure that I'm not dreaming? Or for that matter, that you're not dreaming? Whose dream, whose fantasy are we part of? And what happens when that person wakes up?"

Under the Weather:
Record Reviews from a Warmer World
Susannah Mandel

Riddle Sieve, *Rain Shadow:* Both cooler and darker than *Sunshower,* the omnipresent party hit of two summers past, *Rain Shadow* marks a return to their roots for the Birmingham-based moodmizzle group. This understated rubba speaks to the kind of afternoon when everything just feels scorching and awful, even with the Lens on at full, and you want to sit under a Traditional English Drizzle and have a bit of a mope. (We've never seen a real Drizzle, either, but we've heard your Grandpa go on.) At 2B/W, the Wind Scale rating is low enough that you can play it outdoors in a clearance zone as small as 3x3x3m—no need to check with the neighbours! Knowing the band, expect a creepy surprise or two to manifest out of the fog.

Nymph Load, *Warm Occlusion:* The ladies (and gent) of NL are at it again, this time putting out a wet and sensuous late-summer experience. Plenty of cheap but sultry exoticism here, with a tinkly backing and high humidity index bringing the smells and bells of that South Asian monsoon holiday you never got around to taking. Probably best enjoyed in the Weather Room; at 3M/XX you could take it outside without drowning the zinnias, but the Moist Succubi are better in private. (We know, no subtlety at all, but what would a Nymph Load jam be without them?)

The Thousand Natural Shocks, *Intertropical Convergence Zone:* This one will be big. The long-awaited magnum opus from the masters of symphonic-system mayhem, ICZ promises to wreak chaos, equatorial-style, in cloud ballrooms across the nation when it finally drops this weekend. We could tell you all about it, but we don't like to tease. So we'll just say that you're going to love it. Violently, tornadically, hurricane-force. Pull any strings you need to get into a riding party: this is one you can't play at home without shorting the systems and probably your lungs—that 19V rating is there for a reason. Bring your waterproof, and hold on to your skin…

Pansy Blade Cassandra Moko

Andrew Hook.

It starts with the desire to achieve more than her current existence. For her, this means it begins with boredom.

On the 12th November 2008 Pansy Blade lies on her back and holds her right arm aloft for a period of five minutes. After this time, she becomes desensitised—her arm dissociating itself from her body. Without motion, it becomes something other.

She repeats the practice every hour until she is ready for more.

During the day she saves lives.

She wears a tight-fitting red lycra suit. A gilded mask covers her eyes. Black knee-high boots complete the ensemble. An everyday girl in superwoman's clothing. Whilst she can't leap buildings in a single bound, she can scale them faster than most of us. She takes some pride in rescuing an old couple from the crush of their crashed car. Remoulding the vehicle, reversing the crump. Firemen ask for her autograph. She shrugs.

What's a girl supposed to do?

Unlike the comic book hero she has no alter ego.

She can't do anything socially.

She wipes the minds of those that she fucks.

Her costume is held together with a single zip that runs down the front. The top section comes apart easily, but she has to peel it away from her legs. A yellow strip hides the zip, resembling a go-faster stripe.

She has no memory of her past and no knowledge of her future.

On the 13th November 2008, Pansy Blade holds aloft her left arm. She stares at the ceiling. A single crack attempts to divide the room yet stops at mid-point, going nowhere. She anthropomorphosises the crack, gives it an identity that it doesn't possess. She imagines its frustration at being unable to progress any further, unless acted upon by an external force. She wants an external force to act upon her.

After five minutes her arm no longer feels part of her body. It hangs suspended in the air, with as much identity as the crack. At that precise moment, Pansy Blade gains some relief from her individuality, becomes one with inanimate objects. When she wriggles her fingers, the illusion collapses. She realises it was no more than illusion.

In her suit she traverses the city. Liverpool is quiet. So many new buildings, so little to see.

She finds a small boy, lost, crying. She reunites him with his parents, fights the urge to lose the three of them. Why do we seek completion instead of confusion? This is what she is really fighting against, her desire to undo the world, to unravel rather than ravel, to create questions rather than answers. The father shakes her hand and she can feel the tension within him. Even though she cannot see into the future she knows the future here. He holds her hand for a second longer than he needs to.

From there she climbs the Liver building, overlooks the Mersey. This is her common seat of rest. She finds comfort knowing that the two birds which sit atop the building are looking in opposite directions, one to sea, one to shore. Local legend has it that the birds face away from each other, as if they were to mate and fly away the city would cease to exist. There are times when Pansy Blade wishes to face herself, to find out *what* would cease to exist.

On the 14th November 2008 Pansy Blade holds both arms aloft over her head. Without needing to concentrate they *appear* no longer connected to her, but she knows it is only an appearance. Ten minutes later she can't believe she can move them. So she tries it, does, and once again the moment passes.

She sighs. Rolls over onto her stomach. Slides a pre-cooked meal into the microwave and eats it out of the aluminium tray after the beep.

There's nothing on television. There's rarely anything on television.

She holds out her arm after her meal, but the food in her stomach distracts her. She gets up, takes a bath, changes into her suit, conceals her nakedness. Searches for trouble because there is nothing else to do.

The City Records first mention Pansy Blade in '97. She has examined those records and the date holds little relevance. Her act of heroism prevented a rape. The man drowned in the Mersey. The female watched him fly through the air in awe. A simple jerk from Pansy Blade's hand and he was away. A legend was born.

Like an atom which suddenly appears from nowhere Pansy can recall nothing other than this. She exists. She has purpose. Yet she is so fucking bored.

From the top of the Liver Building she regards the city under cover of darkness. Lights populate her vision. From here they illuminate nothing other than themselves, constellations of star-like sparkles. Her suit keeps her snug. She feels neither cold nor heat. Neither frigidity nor passion. Sometimes, she just needs to die.

People don't even point up at her any more.

She wants to use the extraordinary to improve the ordinary.

She sits there awhile, contemplating the city and everyday lives. Then she returns to her apartment, extends her hand again. When she senses that her arm no longer feels part of her body she closes her eyes. She imagines her soul. She imagines her soul floating through her chest and hovering over her body. She views it askance, detaches herself. Until her soul no longer feels part of her. Until it *is* no longer part of her.

She names herself Cassandra Moko. She has nothing to wear other than the clothes in Pansy's wardrobe. The suit isn't a good fit. She is curvier in this body, which surprises her because she thought she'd be intangible.

She runs from one end of the room to the other. Is out of breath. She loves it.

She bounces on the bed. Creaking reminds her of fucking. She wonders whether she can have a proper romance, given time. Part of her wonders if she wants to.

She takes a bath. The water is sweet on her skin. She alternates the temperature from almost unbearably hot to certainly unbearably cold. She wants to feel those extremes.

"Hello."

She says the word aloud. Her voice is clear, doesn't waver. She has a conversation with herself which feels like a conversation with other people. Words tumble out of her. She laughs and the sound refreshes. She catches her smile in a mirror and it is real. The shock pulls her out of herself and when she wakes on the bed she is Pansy Blade again.

Emotions are brittle inside her. She opens her mouth but can't speak, has no one to speak to.

Holding her head in her hands her existence is heavy.

After a night without sleeping she goes shopping. She accumulates clothes easily, stores are only too eager to service Pansy Blade. She overhears speculation. It is well-known that her wardrobe is limited to red lycra, latex, and pvc. She holds a dress up and has to wipe the memory of the shopgirl who serves her. She can't break the myth because it would taint Cassandra Moko. She is unsure how she chose that name.

Back in her apartment she places the packages on the bed. *La Senza, Karen Millen, Oasis, USC*. Doing her duty she rejoins the city. Alerts the police to a man dying at home, his angina spray inches from reach. Rescues the proverbial cat from a proverbial tree, the feline's nose pushing against her palm in wet relief. Prevents a minor drug deal out in Knowsley Park without wondering why she bothers.

Above her the hot sun strips males out of t-shirts, places women in short skirts, creates children with ice-cream running through their fingers. She doesn't quite see it.

Yet in her apartment. Naked. Her back on the bed, the clothes safely away, she closes her eyes and holds out her soul. Visualises everything displacing, shredding away. Once, when she slips into self-awareness, she falls backward and becomes Pansy again. She opens her eyes. Sees the crack. Closes them again and resumes the discard. Within twenty minutes she is Cassandra Moko.

She made good choices. The clothes fit. She pulls on French knickers, feels the silk against her own silky thighs. The bra cups perfectly. The dress is light, understated. It's mid afternoon and she decides to walk.

The heat hits her as she hits the street. Her room faces north whilst the sun's in the south, but even so the difference is palpable. She gets to enjoy her surroundings, gets to love her freedom. As she walks she can feel the passing of air, her senses heightened. She journeys down to the docks, slips into the Tate. In a sculpture room she regards John Davies' work, *The Redeemers*. The posture of the two men is suggestive, slightly sinister. Their hands imply menace, their closeness implies collusion. Their lack of hair, creepy. And the brown silk shawl worn by one of the men unnerves her. It appears natural yet alien simultaneously. It reminds her of herself.

When she enters a bar no one looks at her. Without her mask she isn't remotely beautiful. Just an average girl with an average body doing average things. She sips a glass of wine, regards the street, wonders what would happen should trouble occur.

At that moment, reminded of her other self, she wakes on the bed and cries.

She becomes conscious of her voice. She sings in the shower. Buys music, books, art. What was once a bare room, a bed, a costume rail, the minimum of cosmetics, becomes a paean to existence. Before she was saving other people's lives, now she is saving her own. As time progresses she spends fewer moments as Pansy Blade. Having shed that skin she wants to hide it. Secrete it.

She invites herself into the houses of others, and doesn't have to wipe their minds when she leaves. She creates friends through her own creation. Lies about her job, her seemingly limitless income. Lies about where she lives. Lies about her past, her parents. The more she integrates into society the more she finds she has to lie. Eventually, she *does* wipe their minds when she leaves.

"I like you when you sleep."

She gasps.

"I fell asleep?"

He nods.

She considers the possibilities.

"Can I call you Cassie?"

It is her turn to nod.

He nestles into her. She feels a closeness previously unknown to her.

Now when it's hot she wears an extra layer of clothes. When it's cold she removes them. She wants to feel those extremes, not to become used to anything. She understands that everything can be snatched away at any time.

Occasionally, Cassandra can no longer recall her past. She sees newspaper cuttings about Pansy Blade and wonders whether she collects them. Other times, she sees the line retreating backwards, from herself to Pansy Blade to someone else who had once lain on their bed with their arm in the air. But she can't quite see the face of creation.

Surrounded by the new buildings of *Liverpool One* she eats a chilli chicken wrap bought at *Pret a Manger*. The taste peppers tiny explosions in her mouth. Sitting at the top of a series of stone steps she can spy an edge of the docks, the swell of the Mersey, the female of the Liver birds. She suddenly desires an overview of the city—

not only from height, but from past present and future. She wants completeness.

She knows the Liver Building is reputed to be the Gothic inspiration for both the Manhattan Municipal Building in New York and the Seven Sisters in Moscow. She realises knowledge doesn't add completeness but makes her understand how impossible it is to be complete. Sometimes, even in this existence, she realises that the more she knows then the more she realises there is to know.

But if sometimes Cassandra forgets Pansy, Pansy *never* forgets Cassandra.

She peels on her lycra skin, pushes her feet into her boots, arranges her mask with a quick glance in the mirror. Beside the bed yesterday's newspapers query her existence. She begins to query her own existence. Was she born from the collective imaginings of the city's population? Did their desire for a crime-free climate create her as their saviour? If they start to forget her, will she start to fade?

She knows she is raising more questions than there can be answers. There is ever only one answer.

But another question: if Pansy Blade ceases to exist would Cassandra Moko also cease to exist?

She knows the answer to that one.

She takes the hand of a blind man as he crosses a busy street in the knowledge that he will never realise it was her who had helped him.

There is anonymity and there is anonymity.

She wonders whether she could climb the Liver Building and have the strength to turn the birds to face each other, to see if the city would cease to exist.

Pansy has residual Cassandra memories. She seeks out her lover. Fucks him. Wipes him.

Afterwards she realises with a hollow laugh that she was jealous.

She is no longer bored. Considering she is only herself for ten per cent of the day she finds there is much to do. There is greater satisfaction when she helps the public. She no longer regards them with the disdain which had started to seep into her heart. Pansy reclaims herself as a superhero. People wave to her again. She sees smiles alight on their faces. Can sense the joy bursting out of them as they regard her with the knowledge that something is greater than they will ever know. She recognises the hope which that brings. The possibility of something wondrous acquitting the surety of their deaths.

Pansy decides to be sociable.

She enters the bar where Cassandra regularly takes a glass of wine. The barman smiles, doesn't know he's already flirted. She orders a coke, doesn't want to trash her reputation. A group of young men shyly approach. She signs beer mats. They return louder than they came, one of them touched her costume when he thought she wasn't looking. A tremble of excitement rushed through her body faster than a speeding bullet.

She knows more than ever what it is to be alive.

In the evening she fights the urge to close her eyes, but through repetition alone habit dominates. When she rises as Cassandra she has no knowledge of her alter ego.

She wanted to use the extraordinary to improve the ordinary, but instead found she used the ordinary to improve the extraordinary.

She has no memory of this.

Cassandra chooses clothes for a summer evening. Wonders why she fell asleep in the afternoon, wonders why she often cannot recollect moments in her day. Is she narcoleptic? Should she see a doctor? She can't decide whether it would be a good or bad thing to find out.

At her lover's apartment he seems distant. They eat in a restaurant with a solid reputation, but the food tastes bland, without extremes in flavour. Background music is trite, spoils the atmosphere rather than improves it. When they share a kiss in his doorway she doesn't want to go inside. When he cites work as an excuse she sighs in relief. She knows it will be the last that she sees of him.

She walks back to her apartment. She wants to run but doesn't want to look stupid. She flinches when a group of males pass her, turns her head to one side when a gaggle of girls does the same. Her shoulders hunch inwards, there's a cool breeze in the air. When she looks up at the Liver Building she thinks she sees movement.

A bird stretches its wings. Looks from east to west and back again.

Another bird does the same.

On the ground, Cassandra shields her eyes against the dark. Searches for a flash of red. She has heard about Pansy Blade but has never seen her. She has read some of the newspaper cuttings that scatter her apartment, wonders about this obsession which she can never recall. She wonders what it would be like to be her.

The birds face each other. The city shimmers as if a mirage.

Cassandra shakes her head. Continues walking. Continues.

Pansy Blade scans the city from the top of the Liver Building. She sees a woman watching her from a distance. Is tempted to wave. Something about the woman attracts her attention. Possible suicide? She always finds those harder to avert. Everything kept inside.

Nevertheless she follows the woman, first with her gaze and then on foot. She watches her traverse the dock; attempt to locate her reflection within the black water. Does a circuit before heading residential. Looks from side to side before entering an apartment. Pansy scales the wall, her fingers dislodging fragments of brick onto the pavement. When she reaches a window she regards the woman as she undresses, showers, climbs onto the bed. She watches as she raises a hand in the air.

She knows her.

On the 6th August 2009 Apex Gale performs her first ever rescue. Afterwards, she wonders how she came into being. But not for long. There's work to be done and a life to be lived.

The Norton Simon Museum of Art

John Brantingham

Theresa studied the bronze Degas ballerinas, craning her neck to get a view of one of the girls' faces, and Hart watched her absently. Susan said something, and the two women laughed together in a chuckle that included them but not Hart.

"They look happy enough," one of the paintings said. It was Van Gogh's green portrait of his mother. She had the straining smile of a woman who worked hard to see only the things she wanted to see.

"Do they?" Hart asked. He supposed really that they did—from the outside anyway. Both women were smiling and talking to each other. Both in their middle forties and successful in their way, married, professional. Susan had three children which was a blessing, and Theresa and Hart had none, which was possibly a greater blessing. Maybe Van Gogh's mother was right. This could, after all, be the picture of friendship and happiness. Maybe it was only Hart's world that was off.

"She's your wife, yes?"

"Yes."

"Oh, it's *nice* to be married, isn't it?" Hart nodded. "And the other woman, where is her husband?"

"Over there," Hart said. "Admiring some of your son's work."

Van Gogh's mother strained her neck to see Kevin. Her "Oh" was one of contentment and happiness. Mostly that's how people reacted to Kevin, a man who wore suit jackets to museums and could explain the wine list. He was the type that mothers liked. "He's a *good* one, isn't he?"

"Yes, he is."

In a moment, Theresa was standing next to Hart. She nodded toward the statues. "They remind me of me."

"Oh my yes, those little girls are awfully sweet," Van Gogh's mother whispered.

"Do they?" Hart asked Theresa. "Degas sculpted them because he felt sorry for them. They were working out ten hours a day so they could go to the ballet where they were displayed and used as child prostitutes. Their parents pushed them into that life because it was either become a whore or starve."

"Oh," Van Gogh's mother said, but it was a different "oh" than she'd made when she'd seen Kevin.

"I thought you were looking at their faces. Didn't you see anything there?" Hart asked. "There's pain there."

Theresa scowled. "Jesus, Hart. I'm going into the next gallery."

When she moved away, Hart asked Van Gogh's mother, "Nothing more from you? No? Nothing rosy to say?" But the woman was staring out into the gallery, smiling blankly and ignoring him.

Kevin and Hart moved together into the next room following their wives.

"Whores? Really?" Kevin asked.

"Maybe 'prostitute' is the right word if you feel sorry for the person."

Kevin nodded and laughed and shook his head at some private joke. In and amongst the Picassos, Kevin got a phone call.

"You don't *like* him, do you?"

Hart looked around for the voice and found it coming from the brochure in his hand. There was Van Gogh's mother on the cover.

"No, actually, I do like him, and I admire him too."

"*Isn't* that nice?"

"Sure, he retired last year at forty, and he's helping runaway kids full time. That's his job, and he works fifty hours a week generally."

"Isn't that *nice?*"

"Sure, he's the best."

She cleared her throat. "But you don't *like* him. You should be nice to a man like that."

Kevin was laughing on the phone. He was probably directing an underling to bail a kid out of jail or counseling someone to stay off drugs. He was almost certainly doing the one thing that would help that person fight the good fight and change his or her entire life. After talking to Kevin, that person would become a priest or a lawyer who fought for the downtrodden.

Hart said, "He a good enough guy. The problem is that he's having sex with my wife."

Van Gogh's mother was silent for a moment. Hart assumed she was trying to locate the correct platitude. When she did, she said, "Oh, I can't believe that."

"Yeah, neither could I for a month or so. Then I actually saw them at it. They didn't see me, but I saw them." Trying to block the memory out of his head, Hart stared at the Picasso, a figure with some kind of instrument.

"I always found this kind of talk distasteful."

Hart cocked one eyebrow and looked at the woman in his left hand. "So do I. Frankly, I think I find it a little more distasteful than you do."

The green on her face went a little pink, and she bit her lip. But then she brightened a little and said, "Do you know what I find distasteful? These Picasso paintings. They're always about people being killed or bad women. Why not haystacks or a starry night or something *nice*?"

Jesus, Hart thought, maybe he would have cut his ear off too, so he wouldn't have to hear this woman any longer.

"Beautiful, isn't it?" Hart pivoted on his heel to see Kevin.

"Sure, everyone loves Picasso."

A noise came from his hand, something between a grunt and a cough.

"What was the call about?"

"Oh," Kevin looked at his phone as though it might contain some information still. "It was an old client of mine." He smiled shyly and blushed.

"He offered you money to get back into the game, didn't he? He did it because you were so good at the game, didn't he?"

Kevin's eyes found the ground. God, Hart thought, you're willing to save kids, to bring them off the street, but not if someone offers you a lot of money to go back to work.

"Yes," Kevin said. "They offered me more than double what I used to make. I couldn't believe it. I mean financially, it flat out makes no sense, and I told him so."

"But you were the best, right? They needed you to be there with them, right?"

He shrugged modestly.

"And now you're torn, but it's become clear to you that you'd have to be a fool not to work with them for another couple of years at least. You know, that way you could really make sure that you're comfortable."

"No."

"I mean it's no big deal. The kids are always going to be there, and you can come back to them in another couple of years."

"No," Kevin said again. "I'm not going to go back. I mean, there's the temptation, but exactly how rich do I need to be, you know? How many steak dinners can I force feed myself? How many trinkets do Susan and the kids need?"

"You said no?"

Kevin stepped back, surprised that Hart would even ask.

"Of course, I did. I keep telling you, you need to come down and see what we're doing at the center. When you see these kids change, I swear to you, it changes you. You think to yourself that you're going to dedicate yourself to them forever."

"Ah."

"I mean, I know you've done that sort of thing for years now yourself. You can't be a teacher and be a bad person, right?"

Hart shrugged. "Professor, and I don't do that kind of work."

"It's changed me. I'm never going back to that life."

Later, in front of a Klee, Mrs. Van Gogh said, "You know, maybe the best bet would be just to ignore the whole thing. They're *good* people. They'll see the error of their ways."

Hart shrugged. He liked Klee the best. Why couldn't a Klee figure have been the one to give him advice? At least he hadn't lingered in front of a painting of Jesus.

"I have been ignoring them. I've been hoping things would just get better."

"Oh, you're not so *bad* are you? You pretend to be cynical, but deep down, you're a good boy, aren't you?"

Hart laughed.

"And it will turn out all right. Take my word for it. There are so many things that seem like problems, but if you just ignore them, they go *away.*" She sighed. "In the mean time, you should take up a hobby. Something outdoors and healthy. Get away from all those books you read."

"Well, I have taken up bourbon as a sort of hobby. Sometimes I branch out into gin or vodka."

There was a beat or two and then, "Oh. You don't want anyone to like you. That's it you know. You don't *want* Theresa to like you." And then she was silent.

The two couples congregated in front of a Kandinsky and listened to Hart who told them about the Blue Rider period. He didn't know much, but he knew more than they did. They talked about art and wine and books until they stopped looking at art and were just sitting on benches. Eventually, they were hungry and left for dinner. On the way out, while passing Van Gogh's mother, she called Hart over. "You're a mean man, you know that? But I think it's the *alcohol*, and not you. It isn't healthy. *Promise* me that you won't drink tonight."

Hart smiled at the woman. She was so much like his own mother. Hell, she was everyone's mother. "Tonight," he said, "I'm going to kill Theresa, kill myself, or kill a bottle of bourbon. You choose."

The woman's eyes became misty with tears, and Hart took a step back, surprised at how touched he was. It actually felt good to have someone care. "Be safe," she said.

"Thank you, ma'am."

Hart followed his wife out of the museum. He followed her to dinner. He followed her home where he drank far too much. That night he followed her into his bed, and the two fell asleep touching each other.

The Circus of the Body

John Zackel

Does it mean, as I seem to be saying, that the subject is condemned to seeing himself emerge, in initio, only in the field of the Other? Could it be that? Well, it isn't. Not at all—not at all—not at all.
—Jacques Lacan

I.

As a young boy, Odilon Viellot believed that the inside of his body looked very much like a circus. It was this old memory of a supposition that Odilon shared in bed with his wife, Veronica. In the hollow of his skull, he said, a small clown car orbited his consciousness; in his arms, tiny painted elephants marched back and forth over the hill of his elbow; in his chest, acrobats performed dangerous leaps over the net of his intestines. Skin was merely a circus tent, and his heart, a sort of ringmaster.

Years of adult sense, education, and contrary scientific research notwithstanding, Odilon wondered aloud if he was but a thirty-three year old boy for whom jugglers caused headaches and snake handlers erections.

He told this to his wife but spoke to the dark light bulb at the center of the ceiling.

Veronica, who knew her husband delighted in remembering his boyhood, nodded at appropriate times, raised an eyebrow at others. She listened with the half ear given by those half asleep. When he was finished, she turned over, put her hands in between the knobs of her knees.

They slept ass to ass for comfort's sake.

The next morning, Veronica Viellot, sitting on the crowded subway below the city, thought again of her husband's childish dreams and tried picturing the inside of her own head. Passengers stepped on. Nothing came. Londoners rushed past like blood cells. Empty, empty, empty. She concentrated and focused and strained, until, at last, she felt defeated by the impossibility of completing her own autopsy. The sinking in her stomach was nothing like a falling tightrope walker. It was nothing like that at all.

2.

It appeared silly for what it was; for the technology of it all, it looked like a young girl's headband, forest green and plastic. Its surface had a dull sheen but was still shiny enough for the spotlights in the laboratory to reflect off the headband, an effect that caused an unfortunate halo to appear around the wearer's head. The first test subject, Coolidge, a pygmy chimpanzee from the Congo, looked like a subject in a Renaissance church painting, solemn, pious even as it scratched its privates. A nearby janitor, a strict Catholic, intervened after seeing the chimp with a halo: it took all of Dr. Odilon Viellot's lunch hour to convince him otherwise: "A trick of the light. Do you understand? Not a saint. A monkey."

(In secret even Odilon thought the halo substantial, and he momentarily reconsidered the headband's design. Perhaps a bicycle helmet design. A baseball cap. A top hat. An upside-down metal bowl. In the end—the end being a minute and a half of consideration—the device was so full of potential that he could not be stopped by aesthetics or tricks of the light, and so Odilon did nothing. The janitor grew bored and returned to work. Odilon bought a chocolate candy bar, which, much to his surprise, entirely sated his appetite. The monkey clapped its hands at nothing.)

3.

What had started with electroencephalography quickly progressed into wireless neural mapping. When the design of the headband first entered Odilon Viellot's brain a year ago, it did so like a long needle: he stopped making love to his wife, Veronica, and, still erect, ran to his office in the adjacent room. Pasty, hairy, soft cookie dough body, the naked Odilon sketched out a few equations on a yellow notepad, wrote the words "head-band" and "don't forget" at the bottom of the page, underlined the words twice for effect. Already he was seeing this yellow page as if framed and hanging in a museum.

From the bedroom, Veronica called out. "Odie?"

"One moment one moment."

"What the hell's going on?"

"Can't talk."

"Are you masturbating out there?"

"Yes no sort of."

He flipped to another sheet on the yellow legal pad and wrote so quickly he could barely keep up.

4.

"Are we ready, Hermes?"

Herman, the bulky yeti-of-an-intern, lifted up his ruler of eyebrows. "Herman, not Hermes," he corrected, his voice a soft mismatch to his appearance. He rubbed a drop of perspiration out of his eye. "Are you sure I'm wearing this right? It's very tight."

"Do not worry, Hermes." Odilon moved behind the intern's metal chair and peered down at the green headband on Herman's head. "Try to clear your mind."

"What if I become a monkey?"

Odilon shrugged.

The room was shadowed except for the spotlight on the chaired intern and, about twenty feet directly across from him, a spotlight on a short cage. In between the metal bars of the cage, Coolidge the pygmy chimpanzee used its big toe to scratch its opposite foot. The chimp's eyelids drooped like sagging Venetian blinds. It yawned like a father in the afternoon.

"I'm wearing the receiver, right?"

"Yes, yes, yes." Odilon, hunched over a nearby computer, hit the PRINT key. The printout was twelve pages long: each page was all ones and zeroes in black ink. He quickly scanned it. "I think we're ready," said Odilon. "I think. The chimpanzee is fully sedated."

"I'm not sedated. Can I get sedated?"

"Don't be such a worry-baby," said Odilon. He approached the chaired intern once again, took a deep breath, then tapped the top-center of the man's headband, tapped it twice, with his index finger, a double tap of casual impatience, testing a piano key, flicking a cigarette. Immediately the green headband on the intern's head started blinking with an internal light; it started humming a baritone. "Here goes everything," he said.

Across the room, the chimpanzee's headband started flickering in synchronization, its halo flashing on and off like a saint in limbo: almost immediately after the flickering started, the chimpanzee collapsed in a pile of mammalian hair and whimpered. The spotlight above Herman and the spotlight above Coolidge blinked out.

Everything went pitch black.

5.

Arriving home three hours earlier than normal, Odilon crept up the stairs to surprise his wife. He tiptoed toward the bathroom at the end of the upstairs hall and, the door wide open, saw his wife, Veronica, wrapped in a towel, staring at the fogged-up bathroom mirror. She looked sadder than he remembered. “Look at you,” he heard her say to her reflection.

“Look at yourself,” said her reflection.

The house was too quiet and too spacious and even his sock-feet walking across the carpet seemed to annoy the silence. He cleared his throat.

She turned as if expecting him. As if he wasn’t real.

“There you are,” she said.

“Hello, bunny,” he said. He was still in the hallway.

She glanced back at her reflection. “I think I look sick.”

“You look like a million glittering protons.” Her hair was wet and bunched together in superstrands. He felt a surge of bliss and bit his tongue to calm down. “We had our first test today.”

“With what?”

“The headband. *You know*.”

“Is Herman OK?”

“Who? Oh, he’s fine. Listen: the headbands worked *perfectly*. For thirty minutes the chimp’s consciousness was transmitted into the intern’s head. The chimp just slept. We have it all on tape. The only problem and it wasn’t really a problem-problem was that the intern took off his clothes at one point and spoke in a mix of grunts and broken English. But electroencephalography be damned, because my headband worked! Perfectly.” Odilon moved into the bathroom and felt some water under his socks. He stood behind her in the mirror. The condensation was evaporating on the glass. Her towel was bright pink. “*And* I had a call from Colonel Ainsworth today, high up in the military. He wants to give me a contract, about using it to interrogate. A *contract*. Bunny, this it!”

She took a pause which seemed to lower the ceiling. Odilon could hear his own breathing; he sounded like an animal on a respirator.

"I called a lawyer today," she said.

"Come again." He was in the bottom of a well, speaking up. "What now?"

"I'm moving out Friday."

"I thought we were done with that." He took a step back. "I thought since…with the headband, you know? I'll have more money and we won't have to fight about that and we can move and it was supposed to be better. I'm not being crazy here we did have that conversation, didn't we? I'm not being crazy here."

She tilted her head. "You never understood it."

"Sure I did. Sure I *do*. I know what it was about. Don't think I don't know what it was about."

"I need to get dressed."

Veronica slipped past him and left the bathroom. She walked toward the bedroom and gently closed the door behind her.

Odilon watched her wet footprints materialize on the carpet; he tried to think of something to say that wasn't spiteful or prickish. Droplets of water that had briefly run down her skin. Now on the carpet. Footprints. Water marks. Say something. Say something.

6.

At the laboratory, the military interrogator, almost as short as Odilon, stood up so wooden straight that he seemed to be the tallest in the room. His first or last name was Craig. Craig was shaved bald and wore camouflaged fatigues that hid nothing in the white workroom.

Craig gripped Odilon's hand. "I've heard so much about you, Dr. Viellot. Colonel Ainsworth recommended I come to test out your device."

"Ok, well. Ok. I thought Ainsworth himself was coming here."

"The Colonel sends his regrets."

"Have you brought somebody to test it on? I mean my headband works *perfectly,* of course, of course, but you need a consciousness to be sent, you know."

Craig nodded like his neck was lifting weights. "We have a prisoner coming in."

Looking around, Odilon spotted a number of tools that could be used as weapons. "How dangerous?"

"About a four out of ten."

"So on the scale is one murderous psycho-killer and is ten safe puppy, or is ten—"

The lab doors opened. Two fatigue-sporting men brought in a handcuffed prisoner in a bright orange jumpsuit.

The prisoner had a burlap bag over his/her head.

"You don't need to know its name, Doctor. Just that this is an evil person." Craig motioned with his hands, directing the guards to bring the prisoner over to the nearest chair. The prisoner sat, bag still on head. Across from the prisoner was an empty chair. "Let's get started."

Odilon handed Craig two seemingly identical green headbands. "The first one is the transmitter. The second is for you."

Without waiting further instructions Craig put his headband on his baldness. "How do I look?" he asked.

"Like a million glittering protons," said Odilon without thinking, and felt sick.

Craig ignored it. He approached the prisoner's chair and placed the other headband overtop the burlap bagged head.

"Shouldn't you?" asked Odilon.

"Take off the bag first? No."

The prisoner squirmed a little in the chair, but didn't seem to fight. Tufts of the burlap bag stuck out on either side of the headband. The bag looked more like a pillowcase or a sagging bag of dog food.

Odilon cleared his throat. "Tap your own headband. Tap it twice softly somewhere near the center. I'll tap him. Her. It. The prisoner."

Craig took a seat across from the prisoner. He sat up straight. "If this works, Doctor, you'll be a national hero."

"Whatever." Odilon tapped the prisoner's headband twice. "Here it comes, Craig. Here comes someone else."

7.

Thursday evening, a night before she left. His house felt more frigid than normal; he could almost see his breath. Dark matter filled his torso with nothingness and a sucking void. He moved as if the air had been taken from him.

The walls were littered with sketches, ideas for other inventions, notes to himself about thermodynamics, human psychology, brain waves. Most scraps of paper were taped up hastily. Obviously torn from newspapers, notebooks, magazines, each ripped-edge seemed more important than anything else in the world, himself included. He felt like a snowman made of stressflakes.

Finally the inventor went up to his bedroom, where he would not be sleeping, and looked in at his wife, taking up the bed.

An orange glimmer from an outside street lamp carried in the room and fell across her face and throat, the soft waves of her hair, and Odilon in all his imagination could not have created such a picture.

He stood in the doorway, holding two green, plastic-looking headbands, and thought about what to do next.

8.

As soon as the prisoner's consciousness was sent to Craig, Craig began weeping: in that moment of headband transference, Craig lived the prisoner's entire life, thought every thought the prisoner had considered, thought every thought the prisoner couldn't articulate, had an imagined future as every human being does, died an imaginary death and attended his imagined funeral. Craig saw Craig capturing the prisoner, saw himself through the prisoner's eyes and realized his own ugliness. Finally, it was when Craig saw the prisoner see Craig see the prisoner that Craig lost himself, and tipped over in his seat. Odilon rushed over to him, threw off the bald man's headband, but it was too late: Craig was both Craig and the prisoner. His mind, unable to settle on a decision, gave up, and not knowing what else to do, Odilon had Craig transported to a nearby psych ward for study. If nothing else, he thought coldly, Craig's insanity might prove useful for science.

The military contract was terminated. A military tribunal would later declare that the headband was too valuable to allow for public use but too dangerous in its increase of real empathy. It would be taken to a storage facility, along with all of Odilon's notes, and kept secret for an indeterminate future.

9.

Yet standing in the doorway to his bedroom, Odilon Viellot thought none of this, for his wife was sleeping in his bed for the last night of their life together, and time would undoubtedly be so cruel as to progress from moment to moment until his wife would undoubtedly awaken, pack her final things, and leave, forever. He felt this loss in his chest, like a bullet ricocheting inside a hollow room, like someone had taken a melon baler and stolen-scooped his soul. The headbands in his hand clinked together like wine glasses. Again he looked at them: the green surfaces attracted the nearest light as if to say, "Be an optimist, Odilon. Try it out."

But he considered the ethical implications of placing a transmitter headband on his sleeping wife. To an extent, it would be a violation of her consciousness, a mental rape, almost, and this threat of psychic violence greatly disturbed him. Was he capable of such a thing? Probably. To know his wife, to really and truly know her, something nobody in the history of the world had accomplished, to close the infinite separation between one person and another. Why was she leaving? What had he done that was so abhorrent? Did she love him? Did she know that he loved her? Was there a chance for him to fix it?

Odilon took a deep breath and walked over to his wife's resting form, and he fought every urge to kiss her, to stroke her hair, to smell the side of her face. He put the receiver headband on his own head. He stared at the transmitter, the other headband, and it seemed to speak.

It would fit on her head, fit nicely, as if she wanted to wear the headband, a style choice. He'd tap each headband in their centers, watch them glow, and then blink. And then he'd receive his wife for the first time in their marriage.

He would see her fears of depression, of failure, of living an unhappy life with Odilon; he would see hopes of abstract sunsets and unnamable celebrations. Perhaps he would see only images, each flashing over another, without explanation and without logic. He would see an oak tree, its dried wrinkled bark; a light switch; a plastic bag of candy corn; her favorite book cover, a hardcover edition of *Kafka on the Shore*; a nun shuffling down a forest path; an overcast sky and the first drop (smell) of rain. He'd see her childhood cat, Rugrat, the velvet of her fur; an oxidized penny; smudged ink of a piece of notebook paper; a sponge hanging half-off the kitchen counter, dripping water on the floor. He'd see her see him, on their first date, at the circus; his overeager eyes and his despicable fashion sense; the sight of an elephant; a blur of primary colors; people in a crowd, looking as if they were a single person repeated over and over again; the red tent overtop them; the wind ripple through that tent; the chocolate brown dirt in the middle ring. He'd see his own hands trembling, then fisting to hide it; he'd see the stubble on his face and the empty space above his head, because he'd see how short he really is.

He'd see her in the house, by herself, at all hours; he'd see the sad looks in the mirror; the phone being answered with excitement, as if it might be somebody who listens, who wants to hear; he'd see her look at her wrists; he'd see a hairbrush full of clogged hair; nylons hanging over the shower rail; he'd see her purposefully tilting the paintings hanging in the house just to reflect her mood; he'd see the bottom of the bedroom door from inside the bedroom, that angry hallway light that meant Odilon had come home in the middle of the night, again, that he hadn't bothered to call her or let her know, to let her know he still loved her, which wasn't much to ask. He'd see himself see her look at her reflection, and he'd see her reflection, too; the desperation in the eyes; the drops of water from the shower; the fogged up mirror and Odilon standing behind her; he'd see his own desperation; his own fascination with himself; his notes left on counters, C U LATER and WHO KNOWS WHEN I'LL B BACK; the sloppiness of his writing; the indifference of his prose. Perhaps he'd even see him leaning over her sleeping body; the foolishness of what appeared to be a blinking headband atop his head; and he would see himself cry, because he wouldn't know what else to do; he would see his own violation of the woman he supposedly loved.

Intimacy, a tightrope walker crossing a chasm of infinite space. Odilon stared at the transmitter still in his hand. He stared until he decided what to do next.

The War of the Gnome and the Mountain Devil

Thoraiya Dyer

Rain doused the mountain town, swift, silken and sibilant.

Shoppers at the Saturday morning market vanished like smoke from a pinched wick. Christine Caley, caught without an umbrella, stood miserably under a cherry tree wiggling her toes in her wet stockings.

It was a long way uphill to the train station. The pension pass in her pocket was wet. The ache in her hip had predicted the storm earlier in the morning. Regardless, a shaft of sunlight striking the mulch-spattered earth where the hollow tree had stood had spurred her out the front gate.

She clutched her single purchase, a potted shrub in a plastic bag.

Perhaps she could wait in a shop until the worst had passed. She peered across the street. Everyone had their black, trench-coated backs turned toward her. They always had. They always would. There was no need for the rain to pull a grey curtain between Christine and the world. It was ever-present. The wind touched her and the wet, the light and the shadow, but no human hand, except for the fists of that young man.

They had shackled those long, pale wrists. She remembered his black running shoes at her eye level, leaving bloody prints on her floor. In a sickening moment of confusion, she had opened ruined lips and tried to call him back; she didn't want to be left alone, not even by him.

She looked down at her sensible shoes and wriggled her toes again. At such moments, only the physical barrier she posed between the crying skies and the pavement proved that she existed at all.

Movement drew her gaze back up. An umbrella blossomed above her. Streaky yellow light fell over the lumpy features of Brian Hacking.

Brian was her neighbour. Like her, he lived alone. Christine had waved to him before, but they'd never spoken. Christine was careful about who she spoke to.

"Mrs Caley," he said seriously. "You're drenched. Please allow me to escort you home."

Christine stared at him, wondering if she was dreaming.

"I came on the train," she said at last, looking away. She placed one cold, surreptitious palm against a branch of the cherry tree. It was solid; if it was real then so was he.

"So did I. But I'm going home in a taxi. Seems a waste not to make use of the back seat, don't you think?"

If she hadn't tentatively lifted her gaze again, she would have missed the mischievous smile that shrank his wide mouth into a pinched, provocative pucker.

Had she thought him ugly? He wasn't so bad. Her eyes skittered away again; they lit on a garishly painted garden gnome in his other hand. Immediately, she wanted to laugh. Had she thought him serious? Perhaps, just this once, it would be safe to let someone take her home. After all, there was capsicum spray in her pocket, and there would be the security of a witness; it was unlikely he was in criminal collusion with the taxi driver.

"I think you're right, Mr Hacking," she said. "It would be a shame."

They set off together for the village centre. The colours of autumn swirled in rivers of rain, down gutters and over the black backdrop of bitumen street. In nearby eucalypt gullies the bellbirds had not stopped calling; their song was a reminder of the cracked sandstone canyons cradling the towns, the green and gunmetal labyrinth lurking beyond the Federation architecture and European gardens.

Christine hadn't always lived in the mountains, but the Great Western Highway and the state railway still connected her to her birthplace in the Sydney basin, forming a paired umbilical cord of snaking tracks and hairpin bends.

"Call me Brian," Hacking said, making her jump.

"And what's his name?" Christine ventured bravely, indicating the gnome.

For a moment he seemed baffled by the statuette in his possession.

"I don't know why I bought this," he admitted eventually. "It just kind of jumped into my hand. I love to lose myself in a garden."

Abruptly she remembered the day Brian Hacking moved into Toilworthy. He'd taken immediately to the roses and box hedges with assorted pruning implements, even though a trail of movers still wriggled like a cardboard centipede through his front door. It was as though he'd been waiting a long time to see green and growing things, to be able to move freely, to shape in some places and shelter in others.

"I love gardening, too," Christine gushed, feeling her face turn pink. She lifted the pot in her hands and peeled back the plastic so he could see.

"*Lambertia formosa*," he said. "A mountain devil. Wonderful."

"A hollow tree in my back yard came down last week. I wanted to fill the space."

"Oh, would you like some help cutting and removing the dead timber? I have a sharp axe."

"No," Christine said, scandalised. "Habitat for the native animals."

"Of course," Brian replied, and she risked another look at him, anxious she'd spoken too sharply. But the hand holding the garden gnome was just shy of her shoulders and he angled the umbrella to keep the drips from the back of her neck, even though she was already wet.

He was protecting her. Christine's heart skipped a beat. She was close enough to feel the heat from his body and she recklessly imagined him in her living room, building a fire from sweet-smelling bluegum he'd cut with his axe, smiling at her in that mischievous way.

"I watch your verandah," she blurted.

"I'm sorry?" Brian laughed. It was a kind laugh.

"I watch your verandah," Christine tried again, feeling her colour rising, "in the mornings when the king parrots drink from the puddles. You have a wonderful sprinkler system. The way it pops up and does its job and then pops out of sight again."

"I made and installed it myself. All controlled remotely from the garden shed. I'm a retired electrician."

"Sounds like you're very handy to have around."

"You should have me around more often and find out for yourself."

Christine tittered but then she fell silent. She wasn't sure.

She still wasn't sure when he seated her on his jacket in the back of the taxi and got into the front seat himself. He chatted amiably with the driver and she still wasn't sure. She wasn't sure while the sunflower umbrella opened above her a second time, or as he pressed her proffered money back into her hands.

"Mrs Caley," he said, "I wonder if you'd come with me to the folk music festival tonight."

Christine stood in silence for a moment. It was like the silence when she came upon a wild animal. Like the moment before it disappeared into the bush, leaving her alone.

Brian Hacking did not disappear. Finally, finally she felt sure.

"I would like that, Brian."

She took her mountain devil through the front gate of Tanglethicket, thinking that she should plant it before she got changed into dry clothes. There was no telling when it might rain again.

At last, I was in the earth.

It clung wonderfully wet between my toes. Life filled me. A wild sweetness cavorted inside. The enemy; I smelled them in the market. Dozens of them. Ever since awareness had come to me, I'd felt the itch inside which was the drive to defeat the enemy. One of them or a hundred, it didn't matter.

One of the ones from the market was still close, but I had the advantage, for he was trapped inside the walls of the Kingdom they gave him to rule, slave to the straight line, while I was free to come and go as I pleased.

In the earth, I waited for the woman to turn her back so I could peel away, grin through moss-green teeth and skitter along branches. I longed to dance the dance of the scribbly gum and kiss the whiskers of the wattle. Out of season, I'd wake the seeds and draw their shoots into the sun, commanding them from the feathered backs of saddled songbirds.

Before night, before the enemy had time to make his first move, I'd have the mountainside alive with my magic. So long I was forced to watch and wait, while I bloomed and my scarlet petals fell. Now I had a foxy face, two wicked horns, a long, twining tail. Now I'd been set loose. My roots were unravelled.

All I needed was the absence of human eyes.

Brian Hacking's heart skipped along a winding stave, each step a crotchet, each toe-tap a quaver.

He grinned at his date—much drier, now—and she grinned at him. He savoured her happiness and his spirits lifted even higher. How simple it was, to uncage a sparrow and yet how many had stopped to do it before, how many had felt the light pressure on their wrist and the satisfaction of seeing Christine Caley test her wings?

Her husband, he supposed, but there had been no husband, she whispered over the creamy head of her poisonous-looking Guinness, for forty years.

"Did he die?" Brian murmured respectfully.

"No," was the curt reply, and Brian sensed a retreat behind bars and racked his brains for a change of subject. Something safe. Something he knew would win another smile.

On stage, the guitar and the cello, both honeyed by the dim light, were separated by six or seven metres, and yet they held hands in the darkness overhead; they struck sparks in their audience's eyes and ears and marinated in their mouths. Invisible were the backdrop and the white plastic chairs, the fluttering flaps of the marquis and the rubbish underfoot.

"Tell me about your garden," Brian said.

"Tanglethicket is more of an idea than a garden. It's a haven. I like to sit and listen. I imagine I can hear green things growing."

Brian nodded enthusiastically. His garden was his refuge, too. While he worked there, while he wrangled that small piece of wilderness, he could sometimes forget the horizontal rain of fire; the hurled, splintered, flaming fists of wood flying through exploded windows.

He could forget the bright, tear-filled eyes of his screaming children as he buckled them into the car. The dog; the dog was still inside the house, barking. Brian turned, plunging into the smoke; dragged the mutt outdoors by the scruff of its stupid neck. Hurling it away from him under the ash-smothered sky, he turned again.

The car was burning. The children were silent.

The children were burning.

Brian blinked and they were gone. Christine Caley sat beside him, dreamily sipping her stout.

"I like the battle," he said slowly, recovering, "for perfection. The overall plan sits in the gardener's mind's eye. Nature has no plan. Nature is mindless. The geometry of a garden, the way the water flows in the fountains or the moss forms a checkerboard with the paving stones, it's a way to celebrate the majesty with none of the mess. None of the ugliness."

"There is no ugliness in nature," Christine reprimanded him.

"Oh, there is. Nature is a bitch."

She was a murderess, throwing her dead boughs around the house, holding it in arms of flame. She was a sadist, cutting up the access roads with blazing trunks, blowing smoke into the eyes of helicopter pilots and firemen, pulling her black and orange shawl over all of them. In the outback, she had the upper hand, but not here.

Not here, where her wanton ways had been civilised, where the bush had been pushed back and the towns planted with the jewels of northern hemisphere manors.

Too late, he noticed Christine Caley's fingers close around her elbows and her eyes return to the floor. And he couldn't help but feel angry. She was too sensitive. He was tired of watching his every word. And she was just like the greenies who'd stopped the fuel reduction burns in the National Park. It was because of them that Brian had buried two small black bodies – and one larger one, its soft and secret places desecrated by fire – in an unfamiliar graveyard.

"I want to go home," Christine said.

"After this song ends," he replied, tight-lipped.

I was through the gate.

The gate; the Man had given me a plot. A plot to make perfect. A plot to rule. I felt the fences, my new boundaries, unbroken. My willpower bounced off the barriers, the ripples striking ripples. All the time it grew; fed; multiplied.

As soon as the sun went down, I saw what the enemy had wrought. The roses had embraced and native seeds in the lawn had erupted, despite the poison laid down by the Man. The trees had sent stray tendrils out to test the wind, rebelling against their glorious symmetry.

No matter. I was here now and the enemy was sleeping. From the very first moment I came out of my mould and the magic awoke in me, I knew I would have the advantage of darkness. I knew I must strive to bend the green things to my will.

The tendrils of those trees curled away from me as I approached. They knew I was come to cure them, to teach them right from wrong. They were reluctant, my lambs, my wayward flock; they found me hateful but they'd be grateful in the end.

There would be order. I had a plot to rule.

First, every gardener had to sharpen his tools.

Crooning, I cast the Workspell. It drew the Man from his bed into misty moonlight. He shivered in his thin singlet and drawstring trousers. I looked on him with scorn. Perhaps he didn't have the strength, but he was all I had.

"The weeds," I instructed him. "The weeds must be pulled out by hand. And then the grass must be cut."

The Man bent to his task, glassy-eyed, single-minded. The seedlings were destroyed by his digging, determined fingers. The grass was tamed by his hungry machine. I cast the Silence over Man and machine, so that the enemy would not be forewarned.

"The birds," I hissed at the Man when he stopped to rest. "The birds that brought the seeds. They must be dealt with."

The Man cast his blank gaze over the fence. On the other side was a wretched tangle of incestuous vines and native scrub. That was where the foul creatures roosted. I cast the Deep Sleep on them. I couldn't pass the fence line, but the Man could. It was within his power. I cast the Darkness over the Man, so that he passed unobserved.

He climbed, awkward as a sick snake. He scrabbled amongst the thorns for the sleeping birds. His hands stretched their necks and he let them lie where they fell. It wasn't enough. The proximity of that shameful snarl repulsed me.

"It is an abomination!" I shrieked impulsively at the Man. "Do something!"

Night was running thin. The Man did not have much time. He took another machine into the demesne of the enemy and sheared away at the madness until there were straight lines. There were flat planes. There was order. My sensibilities were soothed.

On his return, the Man was bleeding; exhausted; barely able to stand.

I released him from the Workspell and he collapsed into his house. Sprawled on the carpet, he slept, just as light touched the treetops. I turned to stone with a satisfied smile on my face.

Christine Caley woke with the smell of wet leaves in her nostrils.

She was comforted by it. Her dream of flying over waterfalls still lingered; it merged with the song of lyrebirds in the dells.

But then the smell was too strong, and she sat up in bed, unlocked the security shutters, unbolted the sliding sash and cracked open the window with a frown. Outside was a scene of devastation. If she hadn't known the clouds had cleared long before Brian Hacking brought her back from the jazz festival, she would have sworn there'd been a destructive thunderstorm in the night.

Leaves. Branches. Debris everywhere.

It wasn't natural. Somebody had done it. Fear and fury warred within her.

Christine undid the seven locks on the front door and crept outside, bare-footed, her pepper spray in hand in case the intruder was still there.

Intruder, she thought, but she was terrified that she knew who had done this. Brian Hacking, who thought gardening should be a battle for perfection. When their night at the festival had turned uncomfortable and they'd retreated to their separate homes, he must have waited for her to fall asleep and then taken his psychotic revenge on her garden. He couldn't bend her to his will, so he had bent Tanglethicket instead.

But why hadn't the sensor floodlights come on? Why no alarms, no summoned police cars? Somehow, he had avoided the system – or sabotaged it. He was an electrician, after all. It all fit perfectly.

The banksias were maimed. The waratahs had been beheaded. Sprays of button grass had been shorn into cubes and all the tender growth of the flowering eucalypts was gone; they'd been turned to balls on sticks, forming an appalling row of prescribed horticultural standards.

The strangled bodies of king parrots littered the driveway.

Christine's knees gave way at the sight of them; she vomited into a clump of grevilleas. She had allowed that man to touch her. She had dared to think they might be friends. But of course he was capable of murder. Of course he was made to do harm. All men were made to do harm.

And Christine was made to be taken in by them, to trust them right up until the moment they struck out, whether it was with words or fists.

I don't love you, Matthew had shrugged. *I don't think I ever loved you. Marriage just seemed like the right thing to do. But you've lost the baby, now. There's no reason to stay together any more.*

But you said you loved me, Christine's youthful self had whispered, feeling as though her chest had been opened with a hacksaw and salt water poured inside.

I lied.

Shivering uncontrollably, she went back into her house and locked the seven front door locks. She set the pepper spray down on a padded chair in the kitchen. Closing and bolting her bedroom window, she curled into a ball under the covers. How gentle Brian had seemed. Her gazelle-heart had kicked up its heels when he knocked on her door, when he took her hand and kissed it.

But he had left a bloody trail behind him; pieces of his madness. How had he appeared so normal? How had his depravity been so completely hidden?

Christine wept.

There'd been a battle in the night.

I smelt the blood. I glimpsed the fallen, lying in the soft, feathered graves of their own skins. The enemy had somehow been here. My place had been desecrated.

I closed the wounds in Old Man Banksia. My magic drew out the slashed spines of kangaroo paw til their tremulous tips swung whole and rolling in the wind. I couldn't replace the lopped limps of the sap-seeping gum trees, but I could kink and knot their trunks to break the curse of their sameness.

Perched on a twig, I let the sun seep into me. It warmed my thoughts. It kindled my plot for revenge.

Over the fence, the alien plantings shed dead foliage. Autumn colours, an admission of weakness, an admission that growth was to be stopped for a season. Soon, the trees would be bare. I sensed the pipes the Man had laid for them under the earth. Pipes to feed them water. They who were pampered strangers, helpless to fend for themselves in our harsh home.

My plan crystallised. I called a steed from inside a tree hollow. The glider came grouchily, unfurling its furry membranes. Together, we leaped; we flew over the fence, and I saw the stone face of the enemy, frozen and helpless while daylight, ally to the trees, filled the natural world with movement and life.

The glider stuck it snout under a layer of straw, locating my entry point. Thinning myself to twigness, I slipped into the pipes. Some were full of water, but I didn't need to breathe. I followed them to a dark, musty, manure-smelling place with wires and switches and I bit through plastic and metal with my pointy green teeth.

There was lightning in some of the wires. Most of it escaped to earth, jittering through me. It would have stopped my heart if I had one, but I was no beast; it would have burned me if I was a branch, but I was no tree. Instead, flame blossomed in the manure.

Fire would destroy the intruders. Fire would cast them out. House and hickory, pickets and pines. Building and birch bower, outhouse and oak. Only the soil and the blackened stumps of grass trees would remain, but fire was known to us. We embraced it. The native trees would put out fresh growth.

The foreigners would die.

And the enemy? His hated, painted visage would peel like snakeskin. The bubbles inside of him would burst. He would fly to pieces and golden guinea-flowers would cover the grey dust of his evil innards. He was only one of an army of enemies, but still, there would be one less.

I sent the glider to warn the animals.

Brian Hacking fought for consciousness.

His leaden limbs wouldn't obey him. His nostrils felt clogged. Behind his closed eyelids, child-sized skulls accused him with blackened teeth. He was supposed to take Nick and Helen to the dentist. Too many sweets, but Brian couldn't help indulging them. They wouldn't stay small forever. One day they'd have jobs, partners, children of their own, and they wouldn't need Brian to buy them chocolates.

Don't spoil them, Athena scolded, hands inky from doing an oil change on the paddock-basher. She wiped her greasy hands on her overalls, but the blackness wouldn't come off. It covered her like a spreading stain. She sank into darkness under a cascade of bricks.

Tumbling masonry rocked the foundations of the earth. The collapsing garage wall was more momentous than the Berlin Wall or the Great Wall of China; the fire crackling over the car was more disastrous than the Great Fire of London. Three people held the whole of creation for Brian Hacking.

They were his whole world, and they were burning.

He opened his eyes and found himself spread-eagled on the carpet, covered in garden clippings. It was early morning, but something was wrong with the light; it glowed dirty scarlet at the back door. There were cuts and bruises and bloody smears on his hands; there was dirt beneath his fingernails and he distinctly remembered scrubbing them raw before taking Christine Caley out to the festival.

The festival. It had all gone wrong.

They had shut each other off. He remembered that much, and was ashamed by it. In a bout of impatience, he'd taken her home when he should have smoothed over the disagreement and kept trying to get to know her. She was a little fragile. So what? Nothing worthwhile was ever easy.

Brian tried to stand, and staggered. Every muscle felt like it had been pummelled with a meat tenderiser. He couldn't understand what was wrong with him. What was he doing on the carpet, anyway? Hadn't he watched a little TV in bed and then had an early night?

It struck him that the eerie light was the light of a bushfire. He staggered to his feet, his senses cleared, skin prickling at the imminent danger. He heard crackling and realised the house was full of smoke. It wasn't his lingering nightmare. It was reality.

Impossible. The rooftop sprinklers would have come on. His system was infallible. Backups after backups had been installed. Timber frames and shutters had been replaced by aluminium and steel. The petrol generator and the pumps were all state of the art. He'd tested it and tested again. Fire could never touch Toilworthy.

An invisible beast burst out of his chest. Howling, it flogged him out through the back door and into a wall of smoke. Disoriented, he tried again to comprehend how the fire could have gotten past his defences.

Someone had to have inactivated the sprinkler system before they set fire to the shed. Brian had only told one person about the garden shed.

Christine Caley.

Maddened, struggling to breathe, to see, Brian snatched up the axe that lay in the woodpile. In the haze, he saw the ghostly silhouettes of charred skeletons. Their teeth dropped out of their heads as they laughed. Flame dripped out of their hollow eye sockets as they cried.

And Christine Caley danced with them, pulling their puppet strings, laughing.

I was trapped.

Baking; boiling; scorching. I felt the pressure building. The sandy loam beneath me turned to glass and the loathsome sun kept me bound and helpless to retaliate. Where was the Man, whose mind was so attuned to mine that the Workspell fit him like a glove?

Where was the Man? Could he not defend my kingdom?

It wasn't knocking that brought Christine out of her self-pitying stupor. It was a chopping sound.

Glass splintering. Chains rattling.

Christine flew out of bed for the second time, only to find an axe embedded in her front door. As she watched, the metal wedge wriggled a retreat. It vanished momentarily before driving again through splinters. The sixth of the seven bolts fell to the floor, adding to a scattering of impotent screws and bent tin plates.

Before she could scream, she saw through the rent in the door that Toilworthy was burning and her crippling fright subsided. The axe belonged to the fire brigade. They were coming to get her out. She took a step forward as if to undo the final lock, reconsidered in light of the axe-wielder's enthusiasm and sank instead into a padded chair to wait.

Funny, that there had been no sirens. And that the bulky shape of the fireman was not clad in reflective yellow and orange, but a dirty singlet and brown, drawstring trousers.

Brian Hacking burst into her house, covered in soot and with black holes for eyes. The axe shook in his hands.

"You think you can destroy me?" he bellowed, raising the axe over his head. "You think you can take my soul? My soul's already lost!"

Christine's fingers found the pepper spray behind the cushion of the chair. Her throat was closed with fear. She couldn't breathe. She couldn't speak. She raised the can and sprayed it into the merciless set of Brian's features. He arched his back and fell, clawing, at his face.

She watched him thrash, still frozen in her chair. Half-entangled in the long strip of oriental carpet, he pulled the hallway mirror down onto himself. It dealt him a cracking blow to the head, and he was still.

Christine rose from the chair and took the axe from his hands. Shaking, she set it against the wall. Outside, flame licked at the dagger hakea by the front step, and embers wafted in and settled in the carpet backing.

He was a madman, he had come to kill her, and yet, unconscious, he was non-threatening. Unconscious, his crease of a mouth and pudgy cheeks took on the kindly cast she recalled from the market.

Christine couldn't move him. He was too heavy. She imagined herself leaving him in the house, running down the street with her flyaway hair and soiled nightgown. Perhaps someone would come to help. Perhaps they would take Brian away to hospital. Or perhaps no-one would come, and she would watch Twigthicket burn, a blazing tomb for Brian Hacking. Either way, she would be alone again, always alone.

"I am tired of being alone," she said softly.

She closed the splintered front door. It was no barrier to the thickening smoke, though the heat from the flames was somewhat lessened. Lying down on the floor next to him, she pulled the carpet over them both. She took his warm brown hand, held his palm to her cheek and closed her eyes.

In her mind, he smiled at her in his mischievous way.

Mrs Caley, he said, *I wonder if you'd come with me to the next place. We can go together. You won't be alone.*

Christine felt lightheaded. Her chest hurt.

"I would like that, Brian," she whispered.

I followed the wild things along the bank of the stream.

It wended and it wound. Past horny bark and brittle autumn flowers. Past patchworks of broad, serrated leaves and woody seed pods. All were toughened survivors. All had the power to rise from the ashes.

We poured into the gully, where the open, exposed forest of the clifftops turned to a pocket of jewel-sprinkled rainforest.

The smoke had not come this far; not yet. The stream disappeared underground, beneath a stand of man-sized tree ferns. I scuttled along the roof of the damp tunnel, upside-down on the water-slicked stone. Careening around a side wall of the cavern, I scaled a vine and reached a collapsed part of the ceiling where interlaced foliage formed a dark green web.

I spent the last of my magic on an upwelling of water. I wove it through the litter and suspended it in a glittering seal of crystal across the opening. The plants did not fear death, but the animals did. They could be utterly finished by a river of fire. I reassured them. Here, they were safe.

Leaping, I landed in the fork between two brown branches. Strength waning, I tucked my four legs and my tail into my thin body. I curled around the branch and vanished.

The branch was not the branch of a Mountain Devil. Today, nonetheless, it bore a little green seed pod in the shape of a two-horned, foxlike face.

Nature had triumphed, today.

It was the end of the enemy, the gnome from the market.

There were more, always more. Where did they come from? They were not natural bush creatures like me, to reproduce by flower and seed, water and light. What was it that entered into stone and turned it so vengefully on my kind?

In the distance, two houses burned. I heard the sound of sirens, but I knew they were too late.

Brian Hacking had never felt so cold.

It was in his bones. Bones? He had no bones. Frozen in the twilight, he felt all of a sameness, a bland grey sameness with a thin veneer of paint.

Strangely, he did not mind. He was made of magic and stone and he had a job to do. As the last of the daylight faded, he found he could wriggle his concrete fingers. He could tap his concrete toes. He couldn't start the work until he was given a plot of land to rule, but that would be soon, surely. The battle for perfection, that was what made time amongst unruly growing things so satisfying.

Unruly growing things? That was defeatist thinking. They would be his henchmen. His soldiers. He would be their commander and they would obey him. But how?

As knowledge seeped into him, memory faded. He learned the Workspell and forgot he'd had a wife and children. He learned the Darkness and forgot his own name. He learned the Deep Sleep and forgot he'd ever been a man.

And with forgetfulness came a wonderful lightness, a blissful release.

Certain odd facts, he didn't forget. The nursery, he knew, was a busy one, on the edge of the Great Western Highway. Every tourist on the way back to Sydney had to pass it, and some would pull over, and of those that came close, some would resonate with him. Some would feel the urge to pick up the garden gnome, and soon, very soon, he would leave the nursery.

Nicholas Went Looking for the Mayor's Right Hand

William Alexander

Nicholas found his mother blocking the front door of his house. He didn't know it was her. He pushed harder.

"The door's stuck," said Nicholas's shoulder.

"I know it's stuck," said Nicholas. He tried again.

"How do doorknobs actually work?" Nicholas's hand asked him. He ignored it. Both of his hands were constantly asking questions about watches and feathers and how every small thing did whatever it did. Everyone contained a chorus, but Nicholas in particular was a series of endless dialogues, inquiries, and contradictory sounds. His ankles liked to sing.

This was before he found his mother.

Nicholas gave up on the front door and went around the back. His ankles hummed a tune to the beat of his running.

The dead may finally take up their half of a very long conversation; aliens or deities may answer all those radio messages we send; the great apes may someday teach sign language to parrots and squid and everyone else, but today, in this place, the *interesting* conversations are between ourselves and pieces of us. Ask your stomach why it hurts. Ask your eyes what sunlight is like before optic nerves make interpretive decisions. Ask your friend about that bruise. Now ask the bruise.

Blood covered most of the living room floor, and continued to spread.

Nicholas's feet had nothing to say when they backed away from the stain. His fingers said nothing when he dialed the phone and called for help. He sat on the floor and waited for help to come.

Only one part of him spoke. The voice was small and lodged somewhere in his chest, underneath a lung. It sounded like his father. Nicholas tried to ignore it. He tried asking it to stop. He tried beating his hand against the side of his ribcage. His hand did not complain. Neither did his skin. The voice continued.

They found Nicholas's father, miles downstream and with blood still underneath his fingernails. They found him by the noise his fingernails made. "Wash us again. One more time. Just one more time. She's still here." They found him crouched down on the river bank, scrubbing his hands and digging underneath his nails with a twig.

He left some of his own blood under her nails, too, though her nails had nothing to say about this. Neither did any other part of her.

Nicholas wanted to talk to his hands, and he wanted his hands to talk to him. He wanted to hear reassurance that they would not ever be bloody. His hands were silent, his mother was silent, and his father was very far away, and the voice lodged somewhere in his chest still sounded like his father. Nicholas tried to drown out the sound of that whisper. He sang the tunes his ankles used to sing. He broke things, just to make more noise than that fragment of his chest.

The aunt and uncle he stayed with couldn't help him. Their own voices were empathetic, comforting, and nice, but both her knees and his elbows made suspicious, skittish noises every time Nicholas moved, so Nicholas went looking for the mayor's right hand.

The town stood on the side of a hill, and the mayor owned a bar on the downhill end of town. The slope brought everyone to the mayor's bar eventually.

Nicholas pushed the door open and went in. Every surface of the bar was made out of wood—some polished, some not—and every part of it creaked when touched and creaked when left alone.

Nicholas left messages with the bartender, and he waited. He was only half as old as he needed to be to set foot in the bar, but no one asked him to leave. The bartender gave Nicholas free sodas while he waited. His mouth loved soda. His stomach hated it. Neither one said anything.

The voice in his gut spoke in an undertone, and not about the soda. Nicholas held the bottle and tried not to think about breaking it.

The mayor and the mayor's right hand walked in. Cold air came in with him, and moved through the bar like a big dead dog licking faces. The mayor wore a duster and he wore a hat.

Everyone and everything stopped talking. The mayor stood beside the bar. The bar creaked under the weight of his elbow.

Nicholas watched the bartender lean in, mumble, and point. The bartender passed a short, clear drink to the mayor's right hand, and the hand took it with him as the mayor came over to Nicholas's table.

"May we join you?" asked the mayor's right hand. The mayor said nothing.

Nicholas nodded, and the mayor sat down. He sipped his drink. The fingers of his right hand tapped the surface of the table as though each fingertip had something separate to say.

"What would you like to discuss?" asked the hand.

"My parents," said Nicholas. "Do you know what happened?"

"I do," said the hand, "and you have my sincere condolences."

"Thanks," said Nicholas. He meant it. The condolences did sound sincere, coming from the hand. "My father's locked away, but there's a piece of me that talks just like him. Nothing else talks. Just that piece. I think it's somewhere over here." He touched his side, and flinched where he had bruised himself. "Sometimes it moves around, and then I'm not sure where it is. I can't talk to it, or pin it down, or get it to stop."

The hand tapped a drumbeat on the table. "It is almost a sovereign thing, the piece of you which does not keep still. You have wandering wrath inside."

"What can I do about it?" Nicholas asked. "How can I get rid of it?"

"Try to coax it into some extremity, like a toe or the tip of your nose. Try to keep it still. You might be able to reason with it, then."

Nicholas scrunched up his forehead and stared at nothing. He frowned. He tried to focus. "I can't find it," he said.

The hand tapped Nicholas's chest, hard. He rocked back in his chair, glaring and trying not to. The skin around his eyes tensed with the effort. He tried to breathe in a calm and normal rhythm. The hand poked him again. "It's moving. It's here now. Focus. Coax it." The hand continued to jab, herding rage around inside his chest. Then the hand knocked Nicholas underneath his chin, and slapped him backhanded against his right cheek.

Nicholas took his empty soda bottle and swung it at the mayor's right hand. The hand moved aside. The bottle broke against the table. The hand reached across and gently pinched Nicholas's left earlobe.

"Got it," said the hand.

"Ow," said Nicholas. He could feel the whispering piece squirm in his earlobe. He tried to take a very deep breath. "Sorry about the bottle," he said.

"Don't worry about the bottle," said the hand. "Just pinch your ear. I am going to stop, and you need to keep it trapped."

Nicholas pinched his ear, hard. The hand withdrew.

"Do you have it?" asked the hand. Nicholas nodded. "Good. Now you have a choice. We can cut off your ear in the hopes that this will remove the wrath from your body entirely. It will hurt. It will disfigure your features, and I am not actually sure that it will work. I do not recommend this, but it is one of our options."

Nicholas swallowed. "Have we got other options?"

"We do," said the hand. "We can try fixing that fragment in place, where you might be able to deal with it, reason with it, and deny it access to the rest of you."

"Let's do that," said Nicholas. His fingers were starting to hurt as much as his earlobe.

"Excuse us a moment, then," said the hand. The mayor stood up, tipped his hat, and went back to the bar. He bought a glass of wine for a woman in a blue dress, and held his hand up to her ear. The hand asked questions, and her ear answered, but Nicholas couldn't hear what they said to each other.

The two of them came back to the small table. Nicholas watched them approach. He didn't understand how the woman moved according to such different rules than the ones his own feet knew.

"Hello," said the woman with her own voice.

"Hi," said Nicholas with his.

The woman sat down. The mayor continued to stand. She took out one of her many earrings, a silver ball welded to a very small spear. She dipped it in the mayor's drink, sterilizing.

"Are you ready?" she asked.

"I'm ready," Nicholas said, though he didn't really feel ready.

She reached over the broken glass on the table, stabbed the earring stud through Nicholas's earlobe, and slipped the clasp over the back.

Nicholas shut his eyes, shut his mouth, and didn't make a sound. His earlobe, however, screamed.

"There," said the woman. She stood, leaned over and kissed Nicholas's forehead. "That should help. Keep it clean until it heals."

"Okay," said Nicholas.

The mayor's hand tipped the mayor's hat in gentlemanly thanks. The woman took the mayor's right hand in her own and gave it a courtly kiss. Then she went back to the bar.

"You can still try to cut your ear off if it refuses to parlay," said the mayor's right hand. "Come to me if you need a sharp knife for it. And do not ever take off that earring."

"Okay," said Nicholas. He noticed that the mayor wore an earring of his own. He wanted to ask about it, and his hands also wanted to ask, but everyone somehow restrained themselves. "Thank you."

"You are most welcome," said the mayor's right hand, and the mayor took his leave.

The bartender came and cleaned up the broken glass. Nicholas pinched his pierced ear, and winced.

"Ow," said Nicholas.

"How does the clasp work?" asked his own hand.

"Do you think it'll slip off when we're sleeping or swimming or something?" asked the other one.

"I don't know," said Nicholas. "I hope not."

His earlobe said nothing at all.

Little Star

Daniel Brugioni

Stepping out of a supermarket and not being hit with a cold blast that freezes your nostrils and tears the air from your lungs—that's a surprise I haven't gotten used to—and don't mind in the least. Tonight, like all nights on Marathon Key, is lovely. A warm, soft, fragrant breeze blows in off the Gulf, raises the tassels adorning the light poles in the parking lot, greets me, as the sliding glass doors open, like an old friend with news to tell.

I've bought only a few things—I didn't really need to go to the store, but I just love strolling down the aisles in such a far off, wonderful place: it makes me feel at home—even at the edge of the Tropics. And I'm leaving on a cruise tomorrow, and thought it'd be prudent to stock up on some supplies.

I can see why people my age move down here. I've been here a week, and the pain in my hip is all but gone. (And I think most of what's left is just me expecting it, and overcompensating.)

Stopping at the edge of the sidewalk, I look out over the lot. A grove of palms sways before a sodium arc tower, like a troop of dancers in silhouette. Behind it, the white span of my hotel looms miragelike in the newly-full darkness. And behind that, the Gulf Herself. I look forward to lying abed tonight, listening to Her whispering in the curtains.

Millsville, Indiana seems so far away, and good riddance, so far as I'm concerned. The day I left, it was one degree below zero, with a wind that made it feel thirty degrees colder than that. Tonight, according to the flashing yellow numerals atop the Caldo Largo Bank Building, it is 77 degrees at 7:13 p.m. I feel an urge to pinch myself when I think that this is February. Instead, I say another quiet prayer of thanks for my grandson...such a good boy, though everyone had written him off. Everyone but me, that is. To think, it was my son who let me down, and my grandson, whom I had not seen in years, who picked me up. The Lord works in mysterious ways—and also beautiful.

I start across the lot, relishing the way my hip doesn't hurt, relishing the way the wind feels on my old winter-white skin, relishing the way being able to walk to the store on my own, to buy a bag of ground coffee and a carton of creamer and a bunch of bananas makes me feel—good, like there's still some life left in my old body, like there's still a ways to go. I can't get around very well back home, and where I live, in the Sticks (my grandson's word) there really isn't much to get around to, unless one wanted to walk through empty fields and trees full of deer stands at the edge of the Cloud River.

Tomorrow morning, at just before nine, I'll be leaving. I've never been on a cruise before, and I'm eighty-four years old. Just thinking about it makes my knees shaky, like they're full of water - but in a good way, like I'm a girl, getting ready for her first trip. I am, I decide.

"Evening ma'am," a tall black man in a uniform says as I pass. "May I help you with those." I smile and tell him that I'm just fine on my own. I think of my son then, and a wave of bitterness rolls over me.

"Have a good night," the man says. I tell him to do the same.

Above me, the stars gleam like searchlights, wavering, big as grapefruits. The palms make whisper music. There are no cars on the road, and I cross easily, to home. "My," I whisper as I make my way through the bright lobby, tipping the doorman a wink as I pass, "how quickly I've come to think of this place as home." I stop before the gold doors of the elevator and, as I wait, realize that I've left my cane in my room. The elevator dings and the doors swing open. I laugh. "Going up," I say to my reflection in faux gold. I'd not forgotten my cane in fifteen years.

There's something in the smell of the air here, so clean and warm, that makes me sleep deep (and fall asleep fast). Dreams of the most wonderful sort light my nights, most of which involve my husband. He died when I was fifty-seven, and, after a few years, I found I couldn't remember him that clearly, and so I didn't really think of him that much. But down here, on Marathon Key, as soon as I touch my pillow, it's as though he's waiting for me, holding a light aloft, beckoning. On the night before last, he and I walked down by the Gulf shore, watching the clouds of a distant thunderstorm illumine the faraway horizon. In the lightning, he looked as he did when we were married, a young, clumsy, crushingly-handsome boy just back from the war.

"Mary," he said. "My little Mary."

"Let's move here," I told him. "I don't think my old bones can take another Indiana winter."

"Still living in cloud cuckoo land, I see."

That's what he always said to me when we were courting, though he never would explain what it meant.

"Why do you say that?" I asked.

"You've already moved here," he said. "With me."

This made me so happy! We embraced, looking across the expanse of water. Strangely, there was no thunder.

In another dream, last night if memory serves, he led me across the sand to a rowboat tied to a rickety jetty (on the Ocean side this time) and beckoned me, lantern in hand, to climb aboard. "Don't worry, Little Star, this craft is seaworthy, and I won't let you drown."

"Where are we going?" I asked.

Instead of answering, he pointed towards the stars and water. My eyes followed his gaze, lighting on a huge, gleaming ocean liner. Lights lit up the decks and the masts, every window ablaze with warm liquid fire. When the wind calmed, I could hear music, and though I couldn't make out the songs, the strains moved me in a way I can't define. "It's like angel music," I said. George nodded and took me by the hand, helping me into the rowboat. "For an angel," he said.

The dreams ended with my awakening in the predawn, basking in air that smelled like fresh laundry, George's last words reverberating in my ears: "See you tomorrow, Little Star."

My last night on the Key, I think sadly as I dim the light and lie atop my covers in the Gulf's perpetual sighing breeze. My room smells like coffee. I sigh, and cannot sleep. I don't want to leave.

Waves slosh upon the shore in rhythm with my thoughts, and they turn happier: what, I wonder, is keeping me in Millsville? I loved to wake up early in the morning to feed the animals, sure, but what of that? Weren't there hungry animals down here? Yes. The Key Deer, so cute and small, even the adults looked like the adorable baby white-tails that came to the edge of my field in the dawntime, to forage. Raccoons, too, and squirrels, and cats…they are everywhere. I had no friends in Millsville—they'd all either died or moved away and died. Only my son, and he never came…and my grandson, he lives down here.

I think of Casey, then, and my heart swells with sorrow. Of course, Casey—I could never leave him. He's been a friend through thick and thin, always there to greet me in the morning, happy to see me no matter how bad I'm feeling.

"But I could bring him down here," I say to the room, the waves, the wind. They seem to sigh in agreement: *yes, do come.* Thus, it's settled. I rise, and snuff the lamp, and the room fills with stars.

George scarcely waits until I am asleep—here he is, holding his lavender spirit lamp before him, beckoning me to join him, face alight with a smile that makes my heart skip. *How* I wonder *was it that I couldn't remember him clearly? He is* divine!

"Good evening, Little Star," he says. "How are we tonight?"

I tell him that I am fine, that I have decided to move down to the Keys, once and for all. He merely smiles, waves his lamp across our path, and takes my hand.

"I decided I'll bring Casey down, too. He's an old dog, but I think, like me, this air will be good for him."

"It is an elixir," George says.

He leads me to the short space of boardwalk at the back of the hotel, beneath a spray of palms that loom remarkably against the star field, through sea oats and tufts of grass stalks that whisper like paper as we pass, on to the beach, where the tide laps obediently.

"Where are we going, George?"

As he had on the previous evening, he does not answer, but points.

The ship I had seen last night, bobbing like a tea light on the ocean, is now at anchor, just a short distance away, so big it dizzies me. (Could one swoon in a dream?) I let out a short gasp and George kills the lamp, tightening his grip on my hand.

"It's so beautiful," I say. We move across the sand to a long pier (I hadn't seen it before) and down it, to where a smiling black man in uniform waits, illuminated before the gangplank—the man I'd seen in the parking lot of the store only a few hours earlier.

"Good evening, Mr. and Mrs. LaBounty," he says as we approach. "Your room is ready, and we'll be setting sail shortly."

"Thank you, Derek," George says, and I nod as I pass. "Where are we going?" I ask, but George only smiles. "It's a surprise," he says. "And I think you know." I think about telling him that I'm booked on a real cruise leaving in the morning, and that I don't, indeed, know, but I don't. Instead, I sigh and kiss George on the cheek. We climb the gangplank onto the fore deck, which has been festooned with colorful bunting and streams of lights.

Another man in uniform meets us—Harold; I recognize him from the deli counter at the grocery—and signals us to follow. We can hear a great deal of commotion and conversation from somewhere, but the deck, save for the decorations, is entirely empty. Harold leads us all the way to the front of the ship before turning off the main throughway and down a small flight of stairs. A short, dimly lit hallway later and we have arrived. Our door (complete with small novelty porthole) stands ajar and my breath hitches in my throat.

"It's beautiful," I say again. It is. Though the ceiling is low, the room is wide and spacious, ornamented with dark oak paneling and intermittent wall sconces that light the space brilliantly in a dreaming yellow hue. An enormous bed lies below a row of starfilled windows, turned back and ready. Across the room, a couch and two dim-glowing floor lamps wait, before a small foyer giving on the bathroom; I can't believe what I am seeing. "Is that a hot tub?" I ask. Both George and Harold say, simultaneously, that it is.

This is some dream I think but do not say. Harold stands in the doorway, backlit by the stars. "Dinner is ready when you are," he says, tips his cap, smiles—and is gone.

George leads me to the bed and we both sit. Looking at him, I have the odd impression of time and dimensions overlapping; at one moment, he looks just as I had last seen him, gray and wrinkled (though still handsome)—old, and at the next, it's as though he's been discharged from the War that very afternoon.

A shiver tightropes my spine. George notices and looks at me inquiringly. "It's nothing," I say.

"Oh, but it is," George says, oscillating before my very eyes, smiling warmly. Once, I am sure, for the most transient of moments, that his face is that of a corpse, the way it looked on the morning when he'd gone to the bathroom to shave and had had a heart attack.

"Why am I suddenly so cold?" I whisper. As if in answer, the ship's myriad engines shudder and then hum to life, vibrating through every pore of wood, through every fiber of my being—a noise so big it is a feeling, and vice versa. George stands and walks to the closet, removes a large bundle from the shelf at the top, and turns back to me, holding a blue blanket, which he unfurls and wraps around my shoulders.

"Our grandson is here," he whispers. "We'll see him at dinner."

I try to tell him that that's wonderful news, that I'm delighted, but I cannot still the shivering. It feels as though someone were sticking pins into the ends of my fingers. I know that I am dreaming. I cannot awake. George stands, hands clasped before him, his eyes dour, his mouth turned down.

I try to tell him that I must close the windows of my hotel room… obviously the night has turned cold, as is its wont (so I've heard) in the wintertime, obviously the warm Gulf breeze has become a gale…but it's as though my lungs were frozen, my throat as ice.

"In all those years, you never fixed the latch, Little Star?" George asks, smiling ruefully (though quite sympathetically).

I cannot ask him what he is talking about.

"Living alone, so far from everyone…"

I try to tell him that I had Casey with me, that I was not alone.

"Open your eyes, Little Star." Again, his face is that of the dead man I had seen last, lying prostrate beside the toilet, face half-covered in shave cream. "Open your eyes, my love."

I do. Sun fills them, and frosty wind. My eyes, focusing to agonizing coherence, light on a span of wasted field ringed by bare trees and, beyond them, the quicksilver flash of the near-frozen river. "What?" I try to say. I can. I am no longer cold. I am lying on the ground beneath the stairs – *my* stairs. A blur of brown tears across the field's edge: Casey, roaming the span of bare corn rows and crisscrossing grooves of frozen tractor tracks. My hand…it all comes back to me now.

I had arisen to feed the animals, had let Casey out to use the bathroom. When I tried to get back in, I'd found that the door had locked behind me (on account of the broken latch I hadn't time to fix). Blood, freezing, lay everywhere…I'd cut my hand.

And then my grandson, whom I had not seen in many years had come, had taken me by the hand, had delivered me…my grandson, such a good boy, though everyone had written him off for leaving us. Where was my son? He was supposed to have come, but he hadn't.

I close my eyes.

George is beside me, in the sunlight of a ruined winter day, in the windy moonlight of an old gulfside hotel, lit by sconces in a low-ceilinged cabin on our gleaming ocean liner. "No, Little Star," he says, and here is the George I knew last, older but lovely nonetheless, composed, still crushingly handsome. "Our son is with you… he just arrived too late. Don't think ill of him."

"What happened?" I ask.

But I know. I have come home. To a small Key in Florida, on the edge of the Gulf, where my ship has been waiting, where George has bidden his time in the perpetual summer moonlight, where my grandson has lain ever since he ran his motorboat upon the rocks of a small island in northern Lake Michigan ten years ago (how we thought he'd left us, for he was of that age, and restless, and had never really gotten along with his father). But here he is, now, filling the doorway with his smiling shadow, dressed beautifully in tux and tails. For a moment, his face goes the soft color of seawater, but only briefly, and then he is smiling again, hurrying across the low room to me, ducking to embrace me. "Thank you for coming," I say, and he smiles and soothes my hair. "We should go, Grandma. They're about to take anchor up."

I rise, surprised to find that I am dressed in a sequined gown that touches the floor, which reflects the lights radiantly, which appears, to my dazzled eyes, made of light. With a handsome man on either arm, glad in my heart, we cross the room. Ascending, I see that the deck is no longer empty. I gasp. My friends are all here, smiling for me, clapping for me, singing an off-key though weirdly moving song that raises the hackles on my bare arms for me. A clank from the starboard, and the anchor climbs.

Someone says, "Welcome home, Mary." It's my best friend from grammar school, Jeanie, whom I had not seen in fifty years.

A chorus then: "Welcome home, Mary!" The crowd parts for the three of us, and we make our way to port, descend another flight of stairs, and enter a long, glowing room, lit brilliantly. My eyes fill with tears as I see the long table, the many, many dishes, the crystal glasses gleaming. They've saved me a place next to my husband, next to all my friends.

I sit. Many miles away, on an already forgotten morning, my son is kneeling beside me, laying his hands upon my face. "Mom," he says. "Mom!" Casey, sensing movement at the far edge of the field, bolts towards it, barking happily.

February 3-February 16, 2008
Hyde Park (Chicago)
Madison, Indiana
For Mary LaBounty

The Man Who Lives in My Shower

Dallas Woodburn

There is a man who lives in my shower. He was here when I moved into my apartment three months ago, so I didn't have much choice in the matter. When I asked what he was doing lounging in the tub, he said, "First come, first serve." Which didn't really answer my question, but the man who lives in my shower is an enigmatic sort of fellow.

He leaves when I need to take a shower. (He's not *that* kind of man.) I don't know where he goes—the living room, I suppose, or the kitchen. Perhaps he simply sits on the counter beside the bathroom sink, waiting for me to be done. But he hides from me outside the bathroom. I only see him when he's in my shower.

The Realtor Woman—"Call me Kym"—who sold me the apartment wore maroon lipstick, smudged slightly on her top lip, and electric-yellow high heels that emphasized the drab paleness of her skin. As she led me from entryway to dining alcove to bedroom she seemed to stomp down each foot with angry emphasis, but when she turned to relate some crucial point about window lighting or square footage her smile flared at me like the flashbulb of a camera. We both knew she was asking too much for the apartment. She spoke to me in the tone of the celebrity chef assuring the audience how simple it is to make triple-layer cheesecake with seedless raspberry sauce—trying to convince the audience that they, too, can add meaning to the chaos of their lives by baking a perfectly textured dessert. In this case, my dessert was the liberated possibility of my life if I chose to live in apartment 3B at 2697 Twenty-Ninth Street.

The apartment was above a Mexican/Greek/Ethic restaurant, where I imagined myself trying exciting new foods and becoming friends with the owners (undoubtedly a friendly old immigrant couple who would throw in free sides of baklava or bean salad and call me *mija*); the kitchen window looked out onto a quiet street, just a block or two away from a tree-shaded park, where I could take walks in the evenings or mornings or afternoons, if I became the type of person who takes walks. Maybe I would get a dog, and then I would have a reason to go on walks. A dog would probably do me good. Some company.

"I'll take it," I told the Realtor Woman. Her smile slipped for a moment into a round "o" of surprise at my abruptness. After all, we hadn't even reached the bathroom yet ("Just wait till you see the gor-ge-ous tile work the previous owners put in around the tub!"). But, like the celebrity chef turning back to the cameras after a commercial break, she quickly regained her composure and rebooted her smile. *Say cheese!* I was momentarily blinded by the flash, and stars still twinkled in my vision as I signed the lease agreement.

It's been two months, and I think the man who lives in my shower is becoming more comfortable with my presence—my slippers in the doorway, my bathrobe on the hook behind the door, my face lotion and toothpaste on the bathroom counter—because lately he's started talking to me. Actually, he remarks on nearly everything I do. All from the bathroom, of course. He stays in the shower and shouts out commentary. Like this morning, as I walked past the bathroom —*My bedroom,* he reminds me, *please show some respect and knock first*—on my way down the hall to the kitchen, he yelled something I couldn't hear.

I paused, turned. "What?"

"Where are you going?" he asked, peeking out from behind the plastic shower curtain. (He thinks the plastic curtain is tacky. "A floral-print cliché" he calls it. I told him I happen to like clichés. He responded by turning on the tap, soaking his head, and shaking water all over me, which I found very childish. When I told him this, he said, "I happen to like children.")

"I'm going to make breakfast," I said.

"What are you making?" he asked.

"Toast."

"What kind?"

"Peanut butter. You want some?"

"No, thank you. I'm not very hungry." (He's never hungry. That's another good thing about the man who lives in my shower. He's not like my freshman college roommate, who ate my food but then pretended not to know what I was talking about when I called her on it. There are few things worse than going to the fridge expecting to see the leftover chicken curry you'd carefully boxed up and carried home the night before, only to find the second shelf has an empty place between the milk and the mushrooms and your white take-out container is in the trash.)

"To be honest," the man who lives in my shower continued, "I don't like the way you make toast."

"What? I make toast fine. How can you ruin toast?" I slipped a slice into the toaster and retraced my steps to the bathroom, standing just outside the doorway so he couldn't see me in my faded flannel pajamas.

"It's not your toast, exactly. It's your bread. Why do you freeze your bread?"

"How do you know I freeze my bread?"

"I just know," he said. "But I don't understand it. Nobody likes frozen bread."

"I freeze it so it doesn't get all moldy. I can never eat a whole loaf by myself without it growing moldy."

"Can't you just buy a smaller loaf? Or split a loaf with a friend?"

"That's ridiculous. Who would I split it with? And why do you even care that I freeze my bread? It works for me."

"I hate to think of you prying frozen bread slices apart with your fingers. And then sometimes the crust gets all under your fingernails. Nobody likes that."

DING! The toaster chimed. I padded back to the kitchen.

"And besides," he shouted after me, "toast doesn't taste as good when you make it with frozen bread."

"I can't even tell," I shouted back. "I think it tastes de-lish-ous."

"That's only because you've gotten used to frozen bread," he said. "You forget what real toast tastes like."

"Why do you freeze your bread?" Ryan asked me in the last conversation we ever had. Actually, it wasn't the last conversation. We had one more conversation, later that night, but I don't like to think about that one.

I was making a sandwich for dinner, phone wedged between my chin and shoulder, and I complained about getting pieces of crust stuck underneath my fingernails when trying to pry two frozen slices apart.

"It gets all moldy if I don't freeze it," I explained. "I can't eat a whole loaf by myself without it getting moldy."

"That is the saddest thing I've ever heard," he said.

"Well, I'm pretty sad without you."

"I miss you too, babe," he said. "But someday we'll have a place of our own. And we won't have to freeze the bread. I'll make you fresh-bread sandwiches."

"Promise?"

"Promise."

The next day, he hung himself from his shower rod with his necktie.

It was the tie with the goldfish on it, the one I picked out for him right before he left for Detroit. I bought it because Ryan and I had a pet goldfish named Sparky. Most couples buy dogs, I know, but Ryan had horrible allergies. I didn't really mind. I liked watching little Sparky in his glass bowl beside our tiny kitchen sink. I liked the way the sunlight came in through the window and reflected off the water, and the way he swam to the surface and darted at the flakes of food I carefully shook out for him each morning and night.

When I found out about Ryan's accident—that's the word my mind still clings to, *accident*—I thought, of course, that there must be some mistake. Ryan was happy. It was a farce, a fake, a framing.

Later, when the detail surfaced about the goldfish necktie, my stomach tightened and something inside me congealed into recognition. Ryan left no note. But I know the goldfish necktie was meant for me.

Exactly one week later, I woke up to Sparky floating belly-up in his little glass bowl, surrounded by uneaten food flakes. I couldn't bear to flush him down the toilet, so I buried him in the tiny backyard, underneath the hydrangea bushes. The hydrangeas, with their bunches of tiny white star flowers, were what you saw when you looked out the kitchen window. I liked to think Sparky had enjoyed his view of those bushes from inside his little glass bowl.

Before the hydrangeas had lost their blooms, my life was packed into boxes. I said goodbye to that tiny house on Hayward Avenue and moved into a tinier apartment on Figueroa and Twenty-Ninth. I came home from work one evening to the unmistakable sound of shower water running.

"Yoo hoo, is someone home? Excuse me? Do you have any shampoo?" a voice called from the bathroom. "I'm all out."

And that is how I met the man who lives in my shower.

The man who lives in my shower is shaving his moustache. I'm glad; I'm not a fan of moustaches. It looked okay on him, because he always kept it neatly trimmed. But shaving is definitely an improvement. I tell him so.

"Thanks," he says. "I think."

I watch the whiskers fall into the bathroom sink. Some drift sluggishly across the counter. "You're going to clean this up, right?" I ask.

"Of course. What kind of roommate do you think I am?" He turns to face me, half his moustache gone and the other half covered in white foam. I am about to laugh, but then I see it.

The goldfish necktie. He's wearing the goldfish necktie.

"Wait ... you're ... the necktie." I point.

He looks at it, holds it up between his thumb and index finger, lets it flap back down. He shrugs.

My tongue is itchy. "The necktie. Where'd you ... where'd you get that?"

He smiles. "You gave it to me."

"That's ridiculous!" I'm shrieking now. "I never gave that to you! Where'd you find it? Huh? Where?"

He shakes his head. "I won't be here much longer, Bee. Please, let's not waste time arguing." He turns back to his half-shaved moustache. His eyes, in the mirror, flit towards mine; he holds my gaze for a moment, as if to see whether I understand.

I don't.

He looks away.

I stumble to my room, shut the door, and crumple into a heap on the bed, thinking of the way he would lazily run his finger around the lip of Sparky's fish bowl when we were talking in the tiny kitchen after dinner. I'd be washing the dinner dishes and watching him out of the corner of my eye, his finger lightly making circles around and around and around that fishbowl, and it was all I could do to keep my knees from shaking. Usually I managed to set the last dish on the counter to dry, rinse the soapsuds off my hands, and smooth my hair flat before I calmly took his hand and led him to the bedroom. Once, though—the day he finally shaved his god-awful moustache—I hadn't washed but one wine glass and a frying pan before I couldn't take it any longer. I grabbed him in front of Sparky, right there in that tiny kitchen.

Tell me, isn't that what happiness is? A shiny goldfish in its bowl, hydrangea bushes in bloom, someone to love who can't even wait to finish washing the dinner dishes to love you right back?

When people used to ask about my engagement, I liked to tell them that it was both the happiest and saddest day of my life. Happiest because it was the day Ryan asked me to be his wife. Saddest because in the next breath he told me he was leaving.

“Jerry chose me to go to Detroit, Bee,” he said.

I blinked. “What?”

“He needs to send someone, and he thinks I’m the best candidate. He told me after work today.” Ryan looked up at me, still awkwardly perched on one knee beside the bed. His hands, lying palm-up on the bedspread, seemed lonely without the satin ring box cradled in them.

“When?” I asked.

“Three weeks.”

“Wow. That’s soon.”

“I know—I know it is. But listen, Bee—it’s only for a year. Just until you finish school. Then you can come out and join me.”

“In Detroit?”

“Yeah—or, you know, wherever they transfer me after that. You know how versatile sales is. Branches close and other branches open. They send you somewhere new. But that doesn’t matter. Really, Bee. Because we’ll be together. Right? Look at me.”

I looked down into Ryan’s earnest hazel eyes, at the tiny mole above his left eyebrow and the crooked part in his floppy dark hair, and the tears that had been welling up in my eyes leaked free, blurring my contact lenses. Happy tears and sad tears all muddled together. He reached up and brushed my cheek with his thumb. Cupped my chin in his palm.

“You and me, Bee. That’s all that matters. Right?”

I twisted the ring around so I couldn’t see the diamond; made a fist so it dug into the tip of my finger. Pain. It still looked pretty, though, even without the diamond winking up at me.

“A year’s not so long,” I said. “I guess a year isn’t so long.”

He hugged me then, and kissed me, and it wasn’t until he died that I realized I’d never actually said yes.

I have a new saddest day now. And though the ring still clings to my finger, I don't think of it as my engagement ring anymore. *Till death do us part.* What a silly promise, that death could part two people. Death means love grips tighter, suffocates, becomes laced with regret. And regret is messy. It clings to you.

Till death do us part. What a morbid, terrifying thing to say at a wedding. Of course, we didn't make it to our wedding, so Ryan and I never promised that death would part us. Maybe that's why it hasn't. Maybe that's why he refuses to leave.

Now, if ever anyone asks about my engagement ring, I pretend not to hear. Nobody likes a suicide, especially when they're expecting a wedding.

A golden strip of light shines beneath the bathroom door. I knock softly, twice, then step inside. The man who lives in my shower is perched on the side of the tub, a stack of crumpled white pages in his lap. He looks up and nods hello.

"I didn't know you could read," I say.

"What made you think I couldn't?"

"Nothing. I don't know."

"You didn't think ghosts could read?" he asks. "Is that it?"

"Are you a ghost?"

The man in my shower gives me a half-smile, but doesn't say anything. He simply shuffles the papers and continues to read.

I watch him for a moment—did his hair always flop over his eyes like that, the part slightly crooked? I search for the tiny mole, the one over his left eyebrow, but it's difficult to see in this light.

"What are you reading?"

He glances up. "Your short story."

Blood throbs in my temples. "What story?"

He flips back to the first page. "It doesn't have a title."

Not that one. I reach in and with one swift motion grab the papers from him. "How did you get this?"

He blinks up at me like a startled child. "You gave it to me. Remember?"

"I don't know what you're talking about. I never – "

"Who's this guy, Bee?"

"What guy?"

"Who's this guy in your story?"

I stare at him for a moment. His eyes look more green than hazel, but maybe it's just the light. I shove the papers at him and slam the door behind me.

"Who's this guy, Bee?"

His voice on the other end of the line was small and tight. I pictured his words with little curlicues of anger, scribbling their way into my ears.

"What guy? What are you talking about?"

"You know exactly what I'm talking about. This guy. In your story."

"My story—Ryan, that's fiction—"

"Who is he? Don't lie to me. I've read your other stuff. You always base your stories in real life. You even told me that, remember? God!" I heard the muffled sound of something falling in the background. I pictured Ryan's angry clenched fist. I pictured his leg kicking a chair, knocking it over.

"Ryan. Listen to me. There is no one else."

"Shut up, Bee. You could at least be honest with me." He was breathing hard and his words were slurred.

"Have you been drinking? You're being ridiculous. I am being honest, Ry!"

"Then who is this guy?"

"I based him on you, okay? You."

"Liar!" Another loud crash. I tried to imagine what it was. The first time I visited Ryan in Detroit, we went to Ikea and I helped him pick out furniture for his apartment. Metal stackable crates for his DVD and music collection. A long, narrow, glass-topped coffee table. I made him buy the tall painted vase; he kept it in the corner and filled it with sunflowers whenever I visited. Maybe that crash was the vase falling over. I pictured crushed yellow petals, water oozing into the carpet.

"Ryan, calm down. I'm not lying to you."

"I have hazel eyes."

"I know you do."

"I have hazel eyes and this guy in the story has blue eyes."

"So? I just changed your eye color – "

"Your eyes are so big, like the eyes of a little boy, blue as a perfect robin's egg –"

"Ryan – "

"Looking into your eyes, it's as if I can curl up and fall asleep inside them – "

"Stop it – "

"Safe, warm. Protected – "

"Ryan, I sent you that story because I want you to be a part of my life out here. I want to share my work with you. I want your support. I'm having that story workshopped next Thursday and I was hoping you could give me suggestions – "

"Here's a suggestion: why don't you go show it to your other boyfriend?"

"I'm not going to argue about this with you any more."

"Just because I'm far away doesn't mean you can parade around like a fucking slut – "

I hung up. I thought about calling him back right away, but decided instead to watch an episode of *Friends*. Give him a chance to calm down and sober up. Then I would call him back. It was the *Friends* episode with the fake Monica. One of my favorite episodes. After the ending theme music swelled, I dialed Ryan's home number, then his cell. But by then there was no answer.

Of all my regrets, that stupid episode of *Friends* is the hardest to keep buried.

The last two words he ever said to me were *fucking slut*. That is why I don't like to think about our final conversation. That is why I still eat frozen bread. And that is why I dropped out of my MFA program and stopped writing altogether.

I found out later that Ryan had gotten demoted at his job that day. His boss said he had been coming in late, leaving early, missing sales calls. A couple of his coworkers thought he was depressed and suggested he see a shrink, but Ryan never wanted help from anyone. Especially not from me. I tell myself that's why I had no idea, until that last conversation, that something was wrong. I tell myself that's why I didn't know how close to the edge Ryan was. He was 2,000 miles away. He was good at hiding. He gave a remarkable performance, at least until the very end. That was the only time I got a small peek behind the curtain.

And what did I do? I hung up the phone.

Midnight. I can't sleep. I slip into the kitchen, heave open the refrigerator door. Hummus, yogurt, ketchup, milk. Leftover chicken and rice in a plastic container, a condensation of water droplets on the inside of the lid. I close the refrigerator door.

Padding back to my empty room, I notice the golden strip of light still creeping out from beneath the bathroom door. I tip-toe up and press my ear against the thin wood door panel. Nothing. My heart seems to be beating very loudly. I hesitate, my fist inches from the wood, and then I knock softly, twice. Nothing. I slowly open the door and step inside. For a half-instant, I'm terrified that I'll see his body, hanging lifelessly from the shower rod.

But the man who lives in my shower is perched harmlessly on the side of the tub. Has he moved at all in the seven hours since I stormed out on him this evening? He is wearing the goldfish necktie, but it is unthreateningly loose around his neck. He is still holding the stack of crumpled white pages in his lap. He looks up at me.

"Hi," I say. My voice is dry and croaky.

"Hi, Bee," he says.

I look at my toes as I walk towards him. My nails are painted pink, the polish chipped around the edges. I don't even like the color pink. I sit beside him on the rim of the bathtub. It is filled with sudsy water, cold to the touch. Now my hand has soapsuds on it; I wipe it off on my striped pajama pants. I glance down at the page the man who lives in my shower is reading. It is the same page from earlier.

"I love you," you say. We're lying together on my bed and you turn on your side to look at me. Your eyes are so big, like the eyes of a little boy, blue as a perfect robin's egg. Looking into your eyes, it's as if I can curl up and fall asleep inside them. Safe, warm. Protected.

"I love you, too," I say. I've said it before, to other people, but nobody's eyes are as blue as yours, and I realize with a flood of piercing certainty that until this moment I've never really meant it.

I look at him, finally. His eyes are hazel. His part is crooked. He looks exactly the same as the last day I saw him, hugging goodbye at the airport. He held me so tightly, I remember thinking for a moment that I couldn't breathe. As if he was trying so desperately to hold onto something. I should have known, then. How could I not have known?

"How could I not have known?" I ask. Warm tears gather around my eyes.

"I didn't want you to know," he says.

"But why not? I could have helped. I could have ... Things could have been different."

He sighs. "I wanted to be perfect for you. I couldn't bear for you to see me in such a bad place."

He drops a page of my story into the bathtub. I watch the page fill up with water and sink. I watch the ink blur. He drops a second page, then a couple more.

"I was so mad at you," I say. "I was furious. How could you do that? How could you leave me like that?"

"It was a mistake." Another page drifts lazily down into the sudsy water. "You have to believe me. I didn't mean to leave you. I'm sorry, Bee. I'm so sorry."

My nose is running, my eyes burning with angry tears. I wipe them away with the back of my hand. "And that's supposed to make it all okay?" My voice is louder than I intended.

"You can't go on living like this forever," he says.

I don't say anything. I hug my knees up to my chin so I am precariously balancing on the narrow edge of the tub. Slight pressure, and I'll fall in.

"Frozen bread and ghosts won't do."

His hazel eyes gleam the same way they did when he told me he was leaving for Detroit. I know his next words before he says them: "It's time for me to go." Only, I realize now, there was something else there before, a flicker of fear that I mistook for anxious exhilaration. That isn't there now. His face is calm. His eyes are unclouded.

"Goodbye." He leans down and kisses my forehead, softly. Just a slight pressure, like the gentle push of an index finger against the small of your back, but it's more than I can bear. I waver and tumble backwards into the bathtub, bumping my elbow against one of the faucet knobs and sitting down hard on my tailbone. The soggy pages of my short story, unfinished and untitled—the last words I wrote—drift around me. I shiver. I pry off my sopping shirt, strip away my pajama pants. I gather the pages of my short story into a comforting weight against my chest. Only then do I glance up at the man who used to live in my shower. He smiles at me from the bathroom doorway.

"Goodbye, Ryan," I say. "I'm sorry, too."

"You have nothing to be sorry for."

"I love you."

"I love you, Bee. I always will." And then he is gone.

I have a dog now. A golden retriever. I got him from the Humane Society. His name is Fitz, after F. Scott Fitzgerald. The Great Gatsby is my favorite book, through Ryan could never get through it. I think he would have liked my Fitzgerald, though. He would have liked to see me take Fitz on walks through the park. We stop at a bench overlooking the playground. Fitz curls up on the ground near my feet. He doesn't need a leash; he won't run away. I sit sideways, with my knees up on the seat, and tilt my face to the winter sunshine. I gently open the cover of my worn spiral notebook, smooth flat a fresh page, and place the tip of my pen against the emptiness. It will take a long time to fill it, I know. But I begin.

Lady with an Ermine

Nick Jackson

Darkness, suddenly a flash of light, revealing a chamber. The blood vessels spin round – again a flash of brilliant light. Is God there somewhere, or something worse, some dreadful shadow lurking in the depths of the unknown, beyond the reach of the light?

"Nothing obvious." He snaps off the torch, I blink and the surgery returns: books, the leaves of a prayer plant, a photograph of two blond children in red pullovers.

"You've been working too hard, have you?" Dr Vincent balances the torch on his knee. "Zigzag patterns in the periphery of your vision, you say. These are all quite common phenomena." He's very courteous as he shows me to the door of the consulting room. "Do come back if there's a recurrence. But try and rest; try to keep things in perspective."

The bus drops me at the entrance to the complex of buildings. I squeeze past the lowered vehicle security barrier, amble along a muddy path to the rear of a portakabin and let myself in through a shabby door. A smell of faintly damp plaster-board and old shoes hangs in the air. There is the usual faint hum from the bank of computers along one wall. Fluorescent yellow hard hats hang in a row above a line of grubby boiler suits like a comic line-up of invisible workmen.

I open the fridge and take out a carton of milk, take a sniff and pour it down the sink with a sigh. I flick the switch of the kettle and listen to the hiss. All the mugs have a brown scum inside; I select the cleanest. People imagine our research takes place in a rarefied atmosphere of glass and steel: the soft trickle of a fountain in the background accompanied by the rustle of bank notes, freshly ironed by an army of android technicians. I clear a space among the card-board boxes and old wiring circuits. The desk top is tea-stained and gritty with biscuit crumbs (Swiss creams?) that someone has been eating.

Arriving on the scene before anyone else gives me a sense of satisfaction. I do some of my best thinking at this time of day, before the others start to arrive, bringing their own trails of consequence, their own collisions. Arriving early gives me time to adjust my buffering zones, to establish my points of impact with the thousand tiny shocks I know the day will bring.

It is our job to check the raw data: to sift the results and decide if they will be of interest to future analysts; to look inwards at the precise nature of the matter.

Last night I dreamt of going back to the museum. The building itself was unchanged but I was aware that behind the building, the countryside had been swept away by a motorway. The woods and fields, where I'd walked as a boy, were gone in this dream and this knowledge oppressed me.

I could smell the honeysuckle perfume my mother used to wear; I catch it now, a faint scent, that lingers on the edge of my awareness. She turns to look at me over her shoulder. And suddenly I am back in the dream running to keep up. With my small sweating hand held tightly in my father's, I stumble up the steps of the museum.

Is this a dream, or is it true and happening to me now? I find it more and more difficult to tell the difference. Dr Vincent tells me that this is not unusual – that many people find it hard to make the distinction.

The museum attendant was one of those shrivelled men, so tiny that the cashier's stool had been specially designed to place him at the right height to receive money and dispense little violet-coloured tickets. I never once saw him off that stool. I doubted whether he ever left it, except for mealtimes and to go for a wash-and-brush-up, for he was always impeccably presented.

It was my father who first took me to the museum, after the death of my mother. I think the museum was my father's attempt to help me begin to forget, or at least to lessen the pain of loss.

Thus, it was through a mist of tears that I beheld the shell of a stuffed leatherback turtle, sticky with varnish.

"Once the seas were full of turtles," said my father, poking at a leathery flipper with the tip of his cane.

"Please not to touch!" snapped the attendant in his high-pitched voice.

"...before the delicacy of their flesh made them a prized dish. Turtle soup was so delicious that Ibn Hussein ate nothing else."

"Did you ever taste it?" I asked.

"No."

We moved on to a mummified corpse from China: perfectly preserved teeth in a slack-lipped smile.

"In the Tang Dynasty it was an honour to be mummified, to be embalmed for posterity, so that we can look at him today, and contemplate our own mortality. The fact that we are here at this moment, with all our faculties and in a state of good health, is not something we should ever take for granted."

The empty eye-sockets gazed at us. The head, tilted to one side, seemed to enquire of us what it was like outside the prison of this building.

Any other father would perhaps have thought twice before bringing his grieving son to such an exhibition of curiosities. My father had the insight to understand the rational basis of my grief – that my mother's loss was simply a vacuum that had to be filled. And he was going to fill it: with knowledge, with facts, with the cold hard particles of matter. He knew that it was the best way to help me to understand the brevity of life, the unfathomable mysteries of the Universe and the constantly changing nature of the present.

We paused before a two-headed lizard. The heads were blunt, in seeming imitation of the tail which was equally blunt, or perhaps it was the tail that imitated the head. One of the heads peered at us, fixing us with the black bead of an eye, while the other head tore at the bloodied carcass of a chicken that had been thrown into its cage. It held it down with one claw and tore away strips of meat with its tiny, sharp teeth. The watching head was motionless, only occasionally betraying its living nature with a tiny mechanical shudder.

"The dinosaurs," murmured my father, "gazed in just the same way at the volcanoes erupting on the still-warm crust of the earth." He looked down at me but I could see it was not me he was seeing – he was looking beyond me at the spouting lava flow that had opened a great wound in the granite flanks of a mountain. "Who knows what it is that they see, these cold-blooded beasts. Perhaps they're waiting for the ice-caps to melt and for their time to come, once more."

I have always kept women at a distance. I watch them drift past, like spectres. Occasionally one approaches too closely but it takes only the slightest touch and they withdraw, hurrying away to warm their frosted fingers.

Only once, a young researcher – dark, Scottish with gold rimmed spectacles... We had begun to sit together at lunch. I think we appreciated each other's long silences. I suppose I might have brushed against her in the corridor a few times. We went on a few excursions to an art cinema and I recall an episode of indistinct fumbling on a sofa bed.

We'd kissed a few times, dryly, in the darkness and perhaps, if she'd not at that moment switched on a small table lamp, things would have taken a different course. As it was, the light illuminated her broad cheeks and on her neck a large birth mark which I'd not noticed before.

"Edgar," she murmured and then she gave a tiny snort of amusement, "You have such small hands."

I must have looked shocked, for she added hurriedly, "But very soft and gentle, like a woman's. No, not like a woman's exactly, just very sensitive."

"Why are you trying to find fault with me when it is you possess such a disfigurement?"

She looked as though I'd slapped her and coloured a deeper pink than the cushions on her sofa bed.

The next time we met she could not meet my eye and I told myself that this was precisely what I might have expected. We never lunched together again.

The next exhibit was visible only through an eye-piece in a panel of black-painted board. At first there was only an amber coloured glow with something fine and whiskery that fussed at the edges of my vision. Then the long thin lariat of an antenna whipped into view and a burnished carapace, as wide as a car bonnet. The label declared it to be a giant Asian whistling cockroach and indeed, if you placed your ear to a tiny zinc grill, you could make out a faint musical hissing – something like a rendition of a baroque concerto played upon a miniature glass harmonica, but infinitesimally faint.

Something made me recoil from the delicate music: a memory of an afternoon when I had been practising the piano – a little tune my mother had taught me. As he passed the piano, my father had accidentally knocked the lid of the instrument and it had fallen, trapping my fingers.

The attendant became impatient with our slow progress and in his cross staccato he urged us to "move along and give others a chance to view the spectacle" even though there weren't any other spectators beside ourselves.

My father strode away and I caught up with him in front of a copy of "Lady with an Ermine", the original of which, he informed me, is to be found in the National Museum in Cracow. There is a sense of stillness in the model's pose, without strain. Both she and the little white animal she is holding gaze in the same direction with an identical expression of placid intelligence, as though she were in possession of a profound, yet inexplicable truth. From the time of my first visit, I formed the idea that the woman in the painting was my mother. The impression was so strong that, even though my father had told me that the woman was, in fact, the mistress of the Duke of Milan, I couldn't rid myself of the thought that they were my mother's eyes in the painting, her lips, and her slender hand stroking the animal's fur. I wanted to curl up, like the ermine, on that soft bosom.

I ran home, after that first visit and, on a scrap of paper torn from a volume of Buchner, I drew from memory what I remembered of that face. My clumsy sketch bore little resemblance, in reality, to the woman's features but at least I had an image of my mother's face which would soften the memory of the cold waxen mask I'd seen in the casket. He had removed all the photographs of her that were in the house. So that I should not miss her, he said, or form any false ideas about her. Being a pragmatist, he wanted to impress on me the importance of the scientific view. He told me that the artist, Leonardo Da Vinci was an expert in anatomy and that the hands were particularly well-painted. He went on to explain the structure of the human hand: the network of veins and capillaries and the complex nerves and muscles. If you were to strip the skin off the human hand, he explained, it would be just like the inner workings of an intricate machine, just like those in one of the factories he owned.

When inspecting my desk drawers, as he sometimes did, he came across the sketch I'd made. He picked it up and turned it towards the light.

"You have no talent for drawing," he informed me, "Do not waste any more of your time doing it."

He carefully folded the drawing and meticulously shredded it before letting the pieces fall into the waste-paper bin.

The last case in the museum, a tall deep case lined with black velvet and illuminated by seven small brass spotlights, contained nothing, nothing at all. There was a blank space where the information card should have been. My father always passed it without a second glance, but I often stood for a moment, wondering about the exhibit that had been removed.

We made many visits to the museum. During our visits he imparted to me his profound knowledge of natural history, geology, art and philosophy in whispered lectures under the constant stare of the attendant whose eyes seemed to follow our progress around the exhibition, no matter how crowded or empty the room was.

It was shortly before I was due to leave for America that we came for a final visit. My father, by this stage of his life, was beginning to lean more heavily on his cane and his breathing had become a little laboured as we passed between the exhibits.

The attendant, more diminutive and shrunken than ever, nodded to us and slipped the coins below the desk into his cash tin. I had never ceased to feel the cold criticism of his stare and even as I stood, in a white linen suit specially tailored to my frame, I could feel his eyes following my steps.

The exhibits had changed very little over the years but on this visit we found an impressively large case occupied by a small rusty nail, though so encrusted with orange deposits it had the appearance of a twisted little grub.

"Nail from Noah's Remarkable Ark" read the accompanying text.

My father gave it no more than a cursory glance.

"God is dead," he muttered and shuffled on.

It came as a shock for me to discern the mocking bitterness of his tone. For a moment I began to doubt my father's philosophy and to suspect the signs of a crumbling and distorted faith, like the cracking in the hull of a gigantic ship into which the waters had begun to pour from the gash made by a passing ice-berg.

We had completed the full round of the exhibits and were approaching the exit. The final case which had never, to my knowledge, contained a single thing, not even a nail, was still vacant. My father had already moved past it and stood by the exit waiting for me. I glanced into the velvet-lined interior. What I saw made me smile; I'd caught sight of my own ghostly reflection, dressed in the white suit. I seemed, momentarily, to have been suspended in the case. I adjusted the angle of my hat, pleased and amused by my appearance, then noticed, just behind my head, the pale face of the attendant who was positioned behind me. Our eyes met in the glass.

On the occasion of that final visit, it seemed the time to say something to my father, to somehow acknowledge that we were approaching the end of an era. Soon, very soon I would be leaving home, perhaps forever, and it seemed fitting to say what I'd prepared. Except that when I opened my mouth I found that all the words had become wooden and meaningless.

"Father, I..."

He gave me one of his quick, sharp glances.

"Yes, what is it?"

"You've been a good father. It must have been very difficult."

"What?"

"To bring me up, after mother died."

He didn't speak, merely moved his head slightly.

"If she had lived, she'd have shown me all the things you've shown me."

"She would never have brought you here."

My father said no more; he merely looked back into the dark entrance to the exhibition hall. I half turned and, out of the corner of my eye I saw that the attendant, who I'd never before seen away from his desk, had followed us out and was standing, with one hand on the door frame.

When I turned back, my father was already striding away into the dusk.

"What are you looking at?" I rounded on the attendant.

"That's a very fine suit," he spoke in a light, soft voice, "The white looks well on you, young man." It was the first time he'd ever spoken to me.

"Don't call me that. My name is Amadeus, Mr Amadeus." I began to feel hot and uncomfortable in my suit.

"I'm to go to America," I told him. "I have a scholarship to study the physical sciences."

"The earth goes around the sun," he said and smiled, "I know that much. And people may travel great distances in their lives but they always come back to the same place."

The attendant went back to his desk and I was left alone. It was then that I became aware of a muted hum. I assumed that it came from the lighting but it seemed to follow me. Sometimes it was no more than a faint murmur, sometimes it grew to a roar, at times it seemed to disappear, then returned almost imperceptibly.

I did not sleep that night, nor would I sleep for many nights. My mind was too full. I'd seen myself, for the second time that day, as I passed the mirror in our wood-panelled hallway. At first I only glimpsed the features I'd always seen. But the longer I stood there, staring at my face, the thinner and more angular it seemed to become and the more my neck shrank into my shoulders. The tailored linen suit was no disguise for the thin torso inside.

Here I sit, monitoring the invisible collisions which occur, remotely, at the bottom of a concrete shaft. Their traces, the only empirical data we have for the operation of invisible processes, are measured in a concentric layering of gas-filled chambers.

I mentioned the tinnitus to Dr Vincent; he prodded my ears with a polished metal implement and agreed that it could be. If it gets too bad, I am to go back and see him. But the more I listen to it, the more I am convinced that it is something external – an electrical hum, quite explicable, anyone would say, given my proximity to so much equipment. Dr Vincent maintains that the museum never existed. He says it is the manifestation of an early trauma. He says the lizard represents my sublimated sexuality. Utter nonsense, I told him, but he insisted on the significance of the two heads – the one head denying the erotic impulses of the other. I'm thinking of transferring to Dr Prakash. He may be bald but he only voices his opinions when asked.

I think of my father's semen, the collisions in my mother's womb and his proprietorial paw resting on her bosom. I am my father's son. He has brought me up to analyse the data I see before me. I consider it, suck my pen top and scribble down a few lines of a programme to correct a small technical glitch. Distantly, but distinctly, I hear the strains of a glass harmonica. My mother is combing her hair after her bath, it falls down into her lap like a lithe animal and coils there.

The Buried Groom

Kevin Frazier

Yelena married a man who was dead.

She found him in a Helsinki cemetery. She was seventeen. She wandered among the graves, noticed a leaf as it fell from one of the maples and landed on a tombstone.

A raindrop slipped off the leaf's damp tip and rolled down the granite façade, across the clear acrylic edge of the tombstone's screen. This was back in the early days of virtual grave-markers, when it was still unusual to see digital memorials in most cemeteries.

Yelena squatted in front of the screen, stared at a film clip of a young man in a loose-fitting basketball uniform. The clip was out-of-focus. Still, Yelena could see that the young man was tall and lanky; his arms were all bone and no muscle. He went up for a jump-shot inside the key. The ball banged off the backboard, missed the hoop.

The wind blew harder. A soft drizzle started to pelt the grass.

Yelena would always remember how the rain gave this visit its particular character—the way the drop on the leaf had slipped towards the screen, the way the drizzle began to streak the front of the tombstone. Each drop added a new blur to the screen's thick acrylic cover. Later she would wonder if it was because of the blurs that she didn't reject Mark the instant she saw him. He was never the most obvious man for her to admire. He had big ears and a skinny neck and bright orange hair. Yet Yelena couldn't see his face clearly enough to decide how she felt about him. The rain smeared his image into something suggestive and intriguing. He was a flare of moving smudges, colored mists that her mind kept trying to resolve into a clear set of features.

The drizzle grew to a steady downpour. Yelena rose from her squat. Walking away, she already knew she would come back again tomorrow.

She started going to the cemetery nearly every afternoon.

Yelena was a Russian in a school full of Finnish teenagers, and she was too shy to push through the barrier between her and the other students. They weren't openly hostile, but they showed little desire to talk to her or overcome her natural diffidence. Her father, a Russian poet who could no longer find a publisher for his work, had stayed in Moscow after her mother had married a Finnish cardiologist and brought Yelena to Helsinki. So for the last three years Yelena had lived in Finland. Her loneliness was constant, an endless hunger for contact—even though she could never bring herself to smile at anyone on the street or speak to anyone in a café. Every day she moved more deeply inwards, further away from everyone else. Often she felt she was disappearing down a long well, with nothing but a shrinking iris of light opening out towards the people around her.

When she turned to Mark, it wasn't love she wanted so much as companionship. He was her friend for many years before he became her husband. She would go to his tombstone after school and stand in front of the screen, its small square glowing in the center of the thick gray slab. Below the screen was a modest engraving: "Mark Riley 1978-2009."

The screen showed dozens of video clips from Mark's life. It presented Yelena with thousands of photographs. It allowed her to read his diaries, study articles about his university scholarships in history and math, review the subtitled testimonials from his friends. There were several hundred hours of material, all played over and over in a perpetual silent loop.

She loved spending time with him. He had a beautiful smile, a toothy grin that revealed a crooked left incisor and emphasized the laugh lines around his mouth. He was Australian by birth, but his parents were foreign correspondents and he had grown up in a variety of places—in New York and Amsterdam, in Vienna and Istanbul, in Stuttgart and Paris. The basketball clip came from his days at a New York high school, and she watched other clips of him playing rugby in London and handball in Munich. In the testimonials his friends all seemed to agree that as an athlete Mark had been more enthusiastic than talented. "He was always ready to try any sport you asked him to try," one friend said, "and he always had a good time even if he didn't play well." Yelena, raised to consider it a grim humiliation to perform poorly at anything she did, found this side of Mark fascinating.

During the summer she went to see him whenever she could. She became addicted to watching him, captivated by sitting on a blanket in front of the tombstone and staring at the pictures and clips as they flowed across the screen. She had always been an obsessive person: her mother and stepfather both knew this about her and had long ago learned to accept it. So they probably didn't see her interest in the cemetery as being very different from the way that, in her childhood, she had spent most of one spring perfecting a certain arm gesture for her ballet class. By mid-July she knew that Mark was by far the most important person in her life.

That fall she started attending Helsinki University. She had hoped to go abroad, but her mother didn't have enough money for the tuition. Since the universities in Finland were free, Yelena agreed to stay in Helsinki.

She studied linguistics. Gradually she prodded herself into showing up at different parties and pubs. She even began going out on dates.

She credited Mark with improving her social life. He looked so happy and relaxed in most of those clips from his past…yelling and singing while someone poured a cup of punch over his curly orange hair…standing in a torn gorilla suit while he was mocked by a dozen friends in elaborate lion costumes…laughing and losing his balance while he tried to skateboard down a flight of concrete steps in a parking garage...

She felt that, because of these clips, her summer with Mark had loosened her up. With his example in mind, she quit worrying so much about whether she might throw up from drinking too much vodka, or might not know the name of some old Finnish rock group that everyone was discussing.

The discovery that she could develop friends and relationships changed her, at least in the short run. Over the next couple of years she came to feel a bit superior to Mark. She seldom visited him anymore, and looked back on her addiction to him with a certain shame. If he had helped her through a difficult period as a teenager, she was in no hurry to remember him. She associated him with loneliness, depression, shyness—all the things she had banished from her life.

Certainly she could see that he wasn't nearly as impressive as her most serious boyfriend, Hunter Wilson, a wealthy young American who worked for the Helsinki office of an international consulting company. Where Mark was pale and freckled and scrawny, Hunter was muscular and dark, bronzed all year round due to his insistence on taking frequent holidays in Southern France. And where Mark was easygoing and a bit careless, Hunter was commanding and efficient. He might spend the day saving a company from bankruptcy. Then he might spend the night organizing an art exhibition for a friend or arranging equipment for an environmental group attempting to enter China. He had many different circles of acquaintances—painters and bankers, filmmakers and architects, Danes and Norwegians and Swedes. And as long as Yelena was with him, she knew that these groups were hers as well as his. She had left Mark and his pulsing tombstone far behind.

The year Yelena finished her graduate work, Hunter asked her to move to Cannes with him. His company was opening an office there to give financial advice to independent film companies, and he would be in charge of the local operations. He found a job for her as a translator of Russian business documents, and they did much of their work outside together, on the cast-iron balcony of their old stone townhouse or beneath a brightly striped parasol at one of the shoreline cafés.

After about six months of this Yelena realized that she missed Mark and wanted to see him.

At first it was a fairly pleasant feeling. She simply wished that she could share all of this with him…could spread out a towel for him on the hot white sand…could play a set with him on one of the dusty clay tennis courts…could show him how after a thunderstorm the pinnae would open their compound leaves on the twisting limbs of her favorite umbrella-thorn acacia tree…

Soon, though, his absence began to depress her. She continued playing tennis, but all she could think about was how much she wished she could be back at the cemetery. She also continued swimming, but while the surf foamed around her thighs and the spindrift misted her face, her thoughts kept returning to Mark's death—the unfairness of it, the bittersweet sadness of his arrival in the hospital on the weekend of his thirty-first birthday.

His car had been hit by a skidding truck, and his body had been crushed between his seat and the steering wheel. He had lived for the next forty-six hours. Two different clips showed him in his hospital bed…his orange hair in disarray…the left side of his scalp shaved and smooth, with its semicircle of seamed flesh and its horseshoe of stitches…his soft brown eyes blinking in the blue-black rings of their bruises…his shattered nose under its absurd mass of bandages…and his broad tolerant smile, still there, still fighting to the surface through the distortions of his broken teeth and twisted jaw… Yelena had cried the first time she watched this, and she almost cried again now, standing on the townhouse balcony, closing her hand around a warm raindrop that had fallen from the clouds and into her open palm. Then she went inside and told Hunter she was leaving.

The next ten years were productive.

Yelena started a translation agency in Helsinki and its success was immediate. She was a hard worker and a good translator, but she gave some of the credit for the agency's growth to Mark and his diaries. He had started a business of his own when he was in his early twenties: a service center for immigrants who wanted help with the practical problems of moving to Finland. Yelena learned much from his mistakes, and observed that he had left a fairly detailed record of his business problems.

Although the tombstone didn't show every diary page he had ever written, it offered four hours of his entries, at thirty seconds per page. Most of the pages were easy to read, dashed off in Mark's clear cursive. Yelena photographed many of them and took them home to study.

She discovered that Mark's company had been in a constant crisis—always on the verge of bankruptcy, always too busy or too slow, always a bit noisy and chaotic.

His writing tended to be affable and candid in describing his various lapses. A typical entry read:

"Hired Hanna as a legal expert and Arto as a marketing assistant this morning. Almost fired them in the afternoon. Apologized when I figured out I'd given each of them the other's assignment. Made it up to them by taking them both out to dinner. The rest of the employees also came. And their friends. And the friends of their friends. Bar tab was ruinous. Fun night, though."

Yelena used the diaries as negative guidelines, as missteps to be avoided. Mark's recklessness taught her caution. His wasteful spending taught her to set strict limits on her monthly expenses. His inability to develop a core group of customers taught her to restrict her clients to those who paid their invoices on time.

When she signed her first major deal—an agreement to do all the translation work for a computer security firm—she went to the cemetery with a bottle of champagne.

She toasted the screen, raised her glass to the video clips showing a trip Mark had made to Istanbul a few years before his death. She followed him through the city. She walked along the streets. She held his hand. They went down a set of steep crooked lanes in the Besiktas district, passed some narrow furniture stores and low-key lingerie shops and a pair of secondhand cell-phone outlets. Then she sat with him at a café beside a mosque. To her right was a massive concrete soccer stadium where soldiers with machineguns marched in front of the entrance. To her left, so close that she could have bent down and dipped her fingers in the water, the Bosporus washed up against the café's wooden wharf.

"Look," Mark said. His face, a bit puffy around the eyes, was open and excited, in pleasing contrast to Yelena's reserve.

He was staring into the water. Yelena followed his gaze. She saw that hundreds of jellyfish were bobbing just below the water's surface. Their faint bulbous forms—as well as the long trails of their stingers—rocked with the motion of the current. They were so pale that they barely seemed to exist. Yelena had the sense that, if she blinked, they might turn out to be optical illusions, a trick of the sunlight on the waves.

She knew what Mark was going to say next, because she had already read it in his diaries. "They look like ghosts," he said lightly, "though floating around in polluted water isn't really my idea of a satisfying afterlife."

"What would you prefer?" she asked.

He shrugged, grinned. The breeze stirred the tight orange curls of his hair. The sleeves of his T-shirt billowed around his long, lightly freckled arms. He reached over, touched Yelena's face. The soldiers marched. The jellyfish floated. The champagne spilled on the cemetery's grass.

She married Mark on the twentieth anniversary of the day they met. The ceremony took place in front of his grave. She told no one what she was doing. She had never mentioned Mark to anybody else. His isolation from the rest of her life was part of what made him so important to her. Plus as the head of a company she had no desire to expose her feelings to the ridicule of outsiders.

She wasn't crazy. She knew that she had fallen in love with a loop of images on a tombstone and not with the actual Mark Riley, who must have been very different from the man she'd created in her imagination. Still, she wanted to be Mark's bride. She wanted a wedding. She wanted a ceremony to help bring out the full flavor of their love. If this made her ridiculous, then being ridiculous was something she could accept.

She held the wedding at night. This allowed her to start walking towards the tombstone at exactly the moment the screen showed the clip of Mark playing basketball in high school. She wore a white dress with a short train. The train dragged along the gravel. A mosquito settled on her veil. She shooed it away. Then she read the vows that she had written. She promised to love Mark forever, talked about how fortunate she was to know him.

She set two wedding rings on the tombstone. One of the rings she placed on her finger. The other ring she placed in a hole that she had dug at the tombstone's base. Then she took a spade and covered the hole with a small mound of mingled grass and earth. Some of the grass stuck to the hem of her dress. She brushed the blades off with the side of her hand.

Then she went home and ate a piece of the five-tiered wedding cake. The dress rustled as she walked. The veil grazed her shoulders, brushed the back of her neck. The ring felt cool and light on her finger. She had thought it might be uncomfortable, but instead she found its weight and tightness strangely soothing. She liked to picture the other ring in the ground, buried in front of Mark's tombstone.

With much more satisfaction than she had anticipated when she woke up this morning, she looked at herself in the mirror. The wedding was over. Mark was hers. She tried to mimic his broad grin, and was both embarrassed and pleased when his expression seemed to float across her face before twisting into the tightness of her usual self-control. She laughed at her reflection, at the odd new wife staring back at her. Then she went to bed.

The marriage had its problems, though in the end they proved minor. Yelena only wore the ring at home, and continued dating other men. This caused her some guilt, but she believed the living should be given a fair chance to usurp the dead. She looked forward to a dramatic contest between Mark and her suitors, a battle for her love.

The battle never took place. No matter how acceptable the men were—and some of them were quite nice—they simply couldn't move her as strongly as Mark did. It was the Hunter situation all over again. The last of Mark's rivals, a deep-voiced Italian pediatrician who worked at her stepfather's hospital, proposed to her three times in five years. By the final proposal Yelena knew she was locked into Mark so firmly that she could never be pried away.

As the translation business grew more profitable, she started working only three days a week. This gave her extra time to visit the cemetery, and she became increasingly confident that Mark needed her at least as much as she needed him, despite the many women who flitted through his clips and pictures. Without her he was alone—worse than alone, just a flicker of dim electric light playing to rows of headstones and markers. Every hour of every day he spilled out over the utter indifference of the graves and the maples, the grass and the groundskeepers.

She could never bear the idea of Mark as a mere corpse, abandoned to his death. If her love had unusual limits, it also offered unusual satisfactions. In a sense, she had resurrected him. She had met him two years after his burial, and decades later she was still giving him some of the life that his collision with the truck had tried to cut off. Their marriage rescued the essential Mark Riley, the one who could be salvaged from his physical wreckage. The longer she sat in front of the screen and watched him, the more of him returned to the world...the kidney-shaped birthmark on his left elbow...the slightly panicked widening of his eyes when he accepted an academic award at the University of Munich...the comfortable swivel of his dangling foot when he crossed one leg over the other...the languorous motion of his fingers rubbing the side of his neck when he was about to start yawning...

Loving Mark appealed to the side of Yelena that was always willing to throw away apparent advantages for the sake of a grand gesture. It was the same impulse that would, at one point, cause her to turn down an offer from an international translation firm to buy out her agency. The firm wouldn't guarantee permanent positions for her favorite employees, and she refused to betray her friends even though the buyout would have tripled her personal net worth. Similarly, instead of undermining her relationship with Mark, the impractical aspects of their love helped guarantee her devotion to him. Their marriage was, after all, a spectacular rejection of everything that made most relationships possible.

Besides, she found pleasures with Mark that she couldn't have found anywhere else. In compensation for his lack of a vulgar physical presence, he maintained eternal youth. As Yelena reached her late fifties—as her knees stiffened and made it a bit harder for her to bend down in front of the tombstone—Mark moved and laughed and talked with inexhaustible freshness and energy. While she had found his looks the least of his qualities when she'd met him, she could now see that his youth had a beauty all its own, and this beauty became more and more fascinating, more and more compelling. It held a special romantic charge for her, the stimulus of an illicit pleasure, heightened by the poignant progress of her personal changes—the encroaching slowness of her sprint when she chased a shot on the tennis court, the increasingly muffled shudder of the maple leaves in the cemetery as she began to lose her hearing.

One night someone shattered the tombstone's acrylic square and smashed the screen. Teenagers occasionally vandalized the graves, and little could be done to stop them.

Yelena contacted the cemetery's caretaker, asked if the screen could be repaired. The caretaker said it was possible: all the information for Mark's memorial was stored in the cemetery's digital archives. But Mark's parents, who had created the memorial, were dead. And though they had established a fund for the memorial's upkeep, the fund wouldn't cover the costs of rebuilding the screen and fixing the tombstone.

So Yelena paid for the repairs herself. She also made copies of the material from the archives. Then she began work on a project that would occupy most of her retirement. She created a new memorial, one that combined Mark's photos and clips with photos and clips from her own life. With the help of the editing program on her computer, she took the old scenes from her days of sunbathing in Cannes and replaced the shots of Hunter with shots of Mark. She made Mark the man strolling beside her along the waves, made Mark the one spreading suntan lotion on her back and shaking sand off his beach towel. In turn, she became the woman sitting on

Mark's shoulders at the New Year's Eve party. She appeared as a spectator at his basketball games. She walked with him under her favorite acacia tree. She held his hand in the hospital. She joined him at the café in Istanbul and looked over the side of the wharf, at the jellyfish floating in the water.

Through a bit of bureaucratic wrangling, she arranged to have her tombstone built beside Mark's grave, in a plot that had always held a work shed for the gardeners. Her granite slab would be identical to his, with an identical screen on the front. Both screens would show the same loop of images—the revised visions that Yelena had designed of Mark and her carrying on their relationship together. From now on, everyone would be able to see them in their love. Their marriage would survive her death.

Nearly twenty years after Yelena was buried and the twin tombstones were finished, a boy wandered into the cemetery and limped along the gravel path.

Otto was nine. He limped because a couple of kids from his school had just knocked him down and kicked him at the nearby playground. This was normal for Otto. He didn't pay much attention to his schoolmates, and some of them repaid his indifference by hurting him. It puzzled and irritated them that he didn't seem to care about the things they cared about. He didn't want to go skiing with them or gossip about their teachers, didn't listen to the music they liked, didn't help them make fun of Leena Nieminen for wearing her braids in the wrong style. So every now and then Antti Salonen and Tommi Iloniemi would taunt Otto and beat him up. They did it not with any great savagery but with the casual glee of children carrying out an acceptable social activity, the high spirits of healthy boys working off excess energy.

Otto never told his parents about the attacks. He was ashamed to admit his unpopularity. His usual method was to run away and cry until he calmed down. Then he would go on as if nothing had happened.

Limping through the cemetery, he rubbed the place on his left shin where Antti and Tommi had given him their hardest kicks. As he walked, he wiped at the corners of his eyes with his fists. The most humiliating thing about being beaten up, Otto thought, wasn't the actual hitting and kicking but the tears that always came to him. It was the tears that had sent him rushing off—hurrying away so he could prevent anyone from seeing him cry.

He looked up, watched the leaves shivering overhead as the wind moved through the maples.

He sat down on the ground, pulled his pant-leg up so he could look at his shin. A couple of welts were already forming just below the knee.

He didn't know what to do. He wanted Antti and Tommi to like him but he didn't want it enough to change anything about himself. He was looking for something else, something more interesting than the things that seemed available to him. He had no idea what it might be, whether it was a person or a game, a place or an idea, a goal or a cause—or maybe some combination of these things, a pattern that he might spend his whole life putting together. He wished he could explain this yearning to Antti and Tommi, but he knew that if he tried they would simply use it as one more proof of his strangeness.

A raindrop struck one of the leaves. Already loose, the leaf slipped from the maple and spiraled towards Otto's head.

A moment later the leaf landed on the side of a tombstone and stuck to the granite façade. This was Yelena's tombstone, but there was no way for Otto to know it. The tombstone had been ruined. Six months ago a panium addict had broken into the mausoleum on the mistaken idea that it was a morticians' studio which might contain some drugs for him to steal. Enraged by his failure to find anything useful, the addict had started a fire and burned the mausoleum down. The fire had spread to other parts of the cemetery, including the twin tombstones that Yelena had placed here. The fire department had arrived quickly, and you could see that the flames had never made it past Yelena's grave: they had stopped at the charred stump of the maple that used to hang above her slab. The maple, burning, had collapsed on top of both Yelena's tombstone and Mark's tombstone. Although the granite had survived the flames, Mark's slab had been knocked over, facedown. At the same time, the screen on Yelena's tombstone had melted into a warped ruin. The liquefied acrylic had spread down the granite and had covered most of the chiseled letters of her name.

The ruined and anonymous quality of the tombstones interested Otto. Here and there a clump of grass had managed to spring up, but most of the ground around both of the graves was either charred from the flames or dug up and overturned where the limbs of the collapsed maple had been removed.

Otto walked over the scorched rocks, the blackened twigs, the gashes of exposed earth. A glint caught the corner of his eye, a nearly subliminal gleam that might have come from a coin or a shiny scrap of paper.

He pivoted towards the glint, looked at the ground between his feet. Then he bent down and reached for a tiny curve of gold sticking out of the soil.

He took the curve between his fingers, tugged gently on it. As it slipped loose from the ground, he saw that it was a ring: a small gold wedding band.

The ring was too large to fit on his fingers, so he held it in his fist. Carrying it through the cemetery, he tried to imagine how the ring might have come to be buried here. He tried to picture who might have owned it, what kind of man or woman must have worn it in the past. He didn't know precisely what the ring meant, either to him or to anyone else. Yet he had the firm sense that this was one of the things he had been looking for—the first piece in the pattern he had been trying to find for himself, the first clue to the yearning inside him.

He put the ring in his pocket, walked home. That night, after dinner, he slipped out of his bedroom and hurried back to the cemetery. Then he spent an hour in front of the twin tombstones. Sitting, thinking, he turned the ring back and forth in his fingers and felt its weight at the center of his palm.

The Greenwich Village Cuckoo

Joseph R. Quinlan

It's a talent my father had. Okay, I can't really know; my widowed mother refused to speak of him. Let's say I strongly suspect he had it. I'm not proud of it, this talent. But we're all compelled to make use of our advantages.

I don't seek them out. I swear I don't. They find me. Moths to a flame doesn't begin to describe it—except in my case the flame is an illusion. The other night was a perfect example. Well, not perfect. A perfectly representative example. Let's say that.

She found me in a dingy bar and grill on the lower east side of Manhattan, closer to what used to be called the Bowery than to the Village. A place where I used to go a lot for supper because it had always been a kind of refuge, a place where I would be unlikely to be able to exercise my talent. I don't think I'll be going back there anymore.

Just as well. The food was nasty. As far as I ever noticed, I was the only person who ever ate there. Everyone else exclusively drank. The ancient black man who did the cooking had patches of dry, flaky skin on his face and on the backs of his hands, and he looked like he slept in the alley between shifts.

I say she found me. And that's how it often feels at the beginning: before I pursue, I'm pursued. But that's not exactly right. Fay wasn't looking for me, specifically. I doubt she was looking for anything. She was just running errands, keeping busy, trying to get through a difficult time.

She came in because her Dan owed a bar tab in the place. The insurance company was being decent about things and had already given her an advance on the settlement. She was tying up loose ends before going home: somewhere in the Midwest—Decatur, Duluth—somewhere like that. I learned most of this later.

Her Dan was a regular at the bar, but I didn't know him. He was a "day regular," and I was, more or less, a "night regular," but, beyond that, the bar was a place where unhappy middle-aged men came to drink by themselves and to hide. They didn't make conversation; they pretty much never looked up from their beers and their shots of whiskey.

I say "they" but I might just as well say "we." I'm near enough to middle-aged. I hid out there. I never used to look up from my food and my drink. I wouldn't have recognized Fay's Dan or any of the regular customers from the bar if I saw them out on the sidewalk right in front of the place.

And, of course, not a soul in the place would ever have recognized me—with the possible exception of the cook, seeing as how I was pretty much his only customer.

I was in a booth off in a corner with my back to the door when she came in. The bartender asked her to wait while he went into the office and looked up Dan's bar slip. The decent thing would have been to tell her to forget about it. But maybe the bartender was just an employee. Maybe it wasn't his call. Or maybe he owned the place but needed the cash. Or maybe he was just that much of a cheapskate. He asked her to wait.

She was worn and slumped. She'd seen better days. Obviously, life with Dan had not been easy. She probably once had a good figure. She was about forty, I would have bet, but if she'd told you she was fifty you'd have believed her. She evidently did her own fair share of drinking, probably alone. She glanced around the place with dull resentment: this was where her Dan had chosen to spend his time.

I was halfway through my food, ready for another beer. I downed the remains of the beer in front of me, slipped a ten under my plate, got up and got out of there. I kept my face expressionless and my eyes on the floor. It was a cool evening, as they tend to be in New York in November, and I had worn a jacket into the bar. I had taken it off and dumped it onto the cracked Naugahyde seat cushion when I came in. Now, rather than take any time putting it on, I slung it over my shoulder.

I felt her eyes on me then.

I opened the door and hurried out into the blare of a fire truck siren.

Did she follow me? She must have. I don't believe in fate or e.s.p. or the supernatural, don't believe in ghosts or in a life after death. I heard about all that stuff growing up, from my mother and from her family, but I don't believe it. Never did. We're creatures, like any other: no more connected to hidden realms, no more equipped for immortality than squirrels or lizards or fruit flies or houseplants. We are a product of the natural world, and there are natural explanations for everything that happens to us.

Why didn't I just go home? I was restless, probably from having my meal interrupted, and I needed to walk. I could say that; there's more than a small amount of truth in that.

Did I want her to find me? Maybe. I almost never do now, but I used to make money off these interludes—mostly given to me, but one way or another—and maybe the old entrepreneurial spirit was still at play.

Maybe what scares me most of all is the possibility that I might have dodged through the streets, given her no chance to follow, raced crookedly to my building, rushed up the stairs, got behind my double-bolted door, and later there would be a knock and she would have found me in spite of everything, and then how would I explain that from natural causes?

She found me in the East Village, in a used bookstore on a narrow street that's bent like a beckoning finger. I was standing in the furthest aisle toward the back, pretending to be interested in a stack of old biology textbooks jammed sideways onto the creaky shelves.

She came around a corner. I never heard her come in. She didn't seem to notice me at first, seemed entirely absorbed in the books.

"Excuse me," she murmured. I shuffled backwards to let her pass.

Her presence made me fidgety. Made me tug my shirt collar, tousle my hair. Made me engage in a dozen little mannerisms, none of which are common to me: usually I'm as still as a statue. Made me rap on the side of a wooden upright three times, softly. The sound was distinct in the quiet shop: TAP tap-TAP.

She froze, turned, apprehensive and hopeful, gazed at the stand of books, then at me.

That funny little tap. Just like her Dan. Who knew what the circumstances used to be? Maybe that's how he used to knock on the bathroom door to ask if she wanted company in the shower. Or how his knuckles played unconsciously against the bedpost after they made love. Or maybe they went all the way back to high school, Fay and Dan, maybe it was a private signal between them, tapped back and forth under their desks: I-(pause)-love/you.

My face ached. I felt the muscles under my skin writhing, contorting to make my features more like Dan's. I really don't know how the process works. I suspect it is somewhat similar to what a police criminal sketch artist might do. I think I throw out dozens and dozens of possibilities and look for minute responses from my —"victim" seems too harsh—let's say, from my quarry. When a particular set of the mouth or flare of the nostrils or cock of an eyebrow gets the right response, is recognized, it freezes while the other facial features keep shifting.

It's an unusual process, certainly, but still a natural one. There's a sort of communication going on. But it's subliminal, between two living human beings—it is not supernatural. Dan's gone. He is not possessing me to communicate with Fay.

Phrases came swimming into my head. Things Dan used to say. Mostly simple phrases—Dan never was very good with words, and he probably got worse as the years wore on and the drinks kept going down. Where do they come from, these words of Dan's? It must be that I create a kind of psychological portrait of Dan based on the image of him that Fay is drawing with my face. Does that make sense? Internally, I'm working out a problem: if I were a person who looked like this, what would I sound like, how would I speak?

It must be something like that.

Things didn't really work out between Dan and Fay. But I knew that already from all the time Dan must have spent in the bar. Whatever dreams they started with had long ago faded away. Whatever attraction once existed between them had slowly been consumed by a thousand trivial resentments.

But I wasn't becoming the Dan whom Fay had lost last week—or last month or whenever it was: she never told me since she assumed I already knew. I was becoming the Dan she desired. The Dan she had lost by infinitesimal degrees. The Dan that maybe only existed in some imagined future that never became reality.

And Fay was becoming the Fay whom that Dan would have desired in turn. Yes, she was changing too. She was a cup of muddy water turned to wine; a dove set free from the magician's cape; a woman sawn in half, dramatically made whole again. Every miracle is metamorphosis. But so is every stage trick.

Fay's apartment was nowhere near. She described it vaguely as being north of Columbia University, which I took to mean on some lonely avenue on the edge of Harlem. We walked to my place, off Houston Street.

Before we left the bookstore, I pulled Fay's coat closed and buttoned it for her, top to bottom, like Dan used to do a long time ago.

When I was younger I was more careful to always go to the woman's place. Obviously, escape is easier. That used to be important to me. To get out before the illusion wore off. To disappear, like a successful magician, behind the curtain while the audience is still wondering.

Fay and I went to my place. And I did my part to help Dan's soul rest easy, to depart this pale with fewer regrets. I allowed Dan and Fay to properly say good-bye.

Afterwards, my voice cracking in the dark, I said, "I'm not him, you know."

"I know," she whispered.

I offered to walk her out, to pay for a cab. She snuggled against me, wound her arms around me. Her fingers dug into my back.

The darkness of sleep leaked away into gloomy dawn, and I opened my eyes to find Fay staring at me. If I have appeared as many men to many women, they all—the ones who stay too long—show me the same face: bleak, incredulous, searching. Desperately searching for some glimmer of miracle or magic. But there's none to find.

The plainness of my face when I'm me is appalling. I'm utterly forgetful. Utterly mediocre. People turn away from me before they have looked. Not repulsed or disgusted, purely uninterested. I'm a blank. I'm worse than invisible. I'm no one when I'm me.

Fay did not turn away. Her face looked ashen in the feeble light. She saw now that Dan was truly gone. It was as if the Dan she dreamed last night was never here at all. And he wasn't. Not last night, not ever.

She didn't cry. She didn't speak. I turned away as she dressed.

She walked into my field of vision on her way to the door. Methodically, she undid the locks: first one, then the other. She kept her back rigidly straight, seemed to be forcing herself to do it. She opened the door, paused, turned. She looked everywhere else but she didn't look at me. The light was stronger in the room now. At first I thought she was trying to spot some bit of jewelry she'd been wearing, some missing object. But it was like she was trying to take in every detail of my squalid, unkempt place, trying to create some larger picture, trying to penetrate to some deeper level. I'm not sure what she was looking for.

She stepped into the hall, leaving the door open, and I heard her slowly creaking down the stairs.

The hall was empty. People were beginning to stir in other apartments; they would be passing by my door soon. I got up and closed the door. Out of habit, I flipped both locks.

Medusa

M. Lamaga de Sanchez

After you left I turned to stone: white marble woman at kitchen table. The cup of tea I'd been drinking when you looked at me for the last time cooled and began the slow process of evaporation.

This is it, I thought. Forever.

But even statues erode. Features, once chiseled, soften and blur. It began with tiny ripples from fingers to arm, gradual movements perceptible only over time. Eventually, I learned to navigate my new body.

Next I decided to scrub the kitchen floor. After eons of staring at the same spot, I'd become intimate with every spill, crumb and hair.

Routine at first, the procedure grew grave as the vinyl remained stained. I tried bleach, pine, even Comet. The scouring only highlighted thousands of small cracks and dents inflicted by shoes, appliances, feet, claws.

Deciding there must be something better underneath, I pulled up the grimy vinyl to reveal green and orange linoleum, circa 1950. Very exotic. You would have hated it.

I slipped on a slinky ballroom gown and danced the Cha-Cha-Cha, imagining a dewy-eyed couple in patent leather pumps and wingtips gliding over this floor, once upon a time.

I'm of the belief that things and places hold traces of what was. Go to a Neolithic temple where people have worshipped for thousands of years, or the dungeon of a castle where they tortured prisoners. If you're not cold as rock yourself, you'll feel it. And if those walls can hold the past, why not a floor?

For a while I enjoyed the linoleum, but then I noticed discolorations. Were they stains? There must have been a reason it had been covered with vinyl, after all.

I grew obsessed, imagining Patent Leather and Wingtip entangled in sleazy affairs and screaming matches that led to bloody noses, spilled Martinis, and drunken sex on that very floor. No wonder I couldn't get it clean.

Not to assign blame, but this house was your idea. I liked the modern one we looked at, with skylights and open rooms. You insisted on history. And where are you living now? Some chrome and glass loft without any walls, high in the sky, looking down.

Vowing to eradicate its sordid past, I tore up the linoleum with a crowbar and discovered pink tile, of all things. Was this house once the refuge of some sensitive Victorian spinster?

Maybe so. I spent the next week crocheting doilies and writing erotic poems thinly veiled by religious symbolism, content in my candle-lit solitude, wearing high-necked dresses and corsets that kept my creeping passions contained.

All that ended last night, when the wind rose to a howl. I found myself rippling through the house in a white linen nightgown, writhing against the windows and hissing at the sky. What with all the billowing curtains and flickering candles, I nearly burned the place down. The pink tile had to go.

I shed my white gown, corset and frilly bloomers. Naked, I grabbed a sledgehammer and got to work.

It took me till dawn to smash the tiles and get the slivers up, aching muscles and cut feet be damned. The longer I worked, the angrier I got at the former owners who just covered old floors with new. Didn't they know hidden influences are dangerous?

By this morning I'd reached the sub-floor: pine boards, gouged and marred. Before pulling them up, I took a last look out the window.

All around me I saw houses, bones obscured by paint, carpet and curtains like layers of veils. A knot of neighbors dressed in sleek gray suits and high-tech running togs stood whispering and darting looks at my house. I don't know what they saw last night, but there's no point in explaining. They wouldn't understand.

With the claw of my hammer I slid nails out of the sub-floor, piling them in a tangle of twisted rust. Lifting the planks I found, under the joists, a well of dark blue water, illuminated from somewhere deep below.

On the edge I dipped my ravaged feet and watched the blood wreath my reflection in spirals: red snakes, dancing around the head of a woman I'd heard of only in stories. Lies.

The last bit of stone melted to flesh. Eyes wide, I uncoiled, down into her blue light, shedding this house, this worn out skin, this apocryphal life.

Paper Airplanes

N. D. Segal

Imagine:

A woman sits in an office with walls and a door, not a cubicle, at a dark wood desk with her back to a wall of windows. The other walls are decorated with corporate art, her desk with a philodendron and one photograph of two teenaged girls. She wears a black suit, a black and white stripped blouse, black shoes and stockings. Her makeup is sensible, her earrings small. Her hair is cut in a short style that flatters her small, neat features.

She's reading the first draft of a report and tapping the eraser end of a red pencil on the wood of her desk. For a long time, the only noise in the office is the soft tap of that pencil on wood and the occasional rustle of paper.

Finally, sighing, she drops the pencil and pushes the pages away. "Shit," she says, reaches for a pad of lined yellow paper lying on the desk, and tears a sheet off. She starts folding the paper into an airplane, the standard pointy-nosed model. When she finishes folding, she looks at what she's made, smiles faintly. "Weird," she says and chuckles, then lifts the plane and throws it.

For just a moment, not even a moment, maybe half a heartbeat, she follows the plane *up.* As she makes to release the neatly creased paper, her fingers stick to it. For just that fraction of a second, she can *not* release the airplane. It starts to pull her up. For that smallest bit of time, she rises with the plane, weightless. She could fly with the plane toward the ceiling.

Except, of course, she remembers she can't fly—we all know we can't, after all—and lets go. The plane soars up on a current of air from the radiator, and she settles heavily into her chair.

"Whoa," she whispers as the plane glides gently onto the carpet near her door.

She stands up, snatches the plane off the rug where it has come to rest, and drops it tail first into her lacquered wastepaper basket. With a little shake of her head, she turns her back on the basket and settles herself at the desk.

She swivels in the chair to face the windows, studies the glass-encased buildings opposite her, or perhaps she's staring at the cloudy sky over them. After a few minutes, she speaks again. "I hate this job."

She begins to sing the words to the melody of the "Blue Danube Waltz," rapping her knuckles on the arm of her chair for emphasis. "I ha-ate this job, da-da, dum-dum, I ha-ate this job, da-da, dum-dum—"

After a few moments, she stops singing, swivels the chair to face the photograph of the children. "College tuition must be paid," she murmurs and turns to her computer. She pulls the pages she was reading earlier across the desk to the keyboard and begins to type.

The phone gurgles and she answers it, listens to the caller identify himself, and rolls her eyes. "Oh, hello, David. . . . Yes, I'm fine . . . . Work is fine . . . . The car is fine—David, I'm at work, so if you have something . . . Excuse me? I didn't hear . . . Oh, no, no, no. You *promised* Jenny you'd be there. It's her first college recital and she—No. I will not tell her for you. I am not your messenger, and now I have to go to a meeting. Good-bye, David."

Carefully, almost tenderly, she sets the receiver down on its cradle and breathes loudly before smacking her hand on the desk with a loud *whack.* She winces and shakes the hand just as someone knocks on her door and peeks in.

"Thought you'd like to know: Kromer is kicking about the cover design again," Tina says with a wry smile.

"Doesn't that manual ship in two days?"

"Yup."

"OK. I'll talk to Charley. Kromer will listen to him."

"Thanks. See you at the meeting."

After Tina closes the door, she makes a note on her desk calendar and lifts the receiver of her phone, punches some numbers.

"Hi, Charley. Sara. About the Earthquake Contingency Plan cover . . . Right. Two days. . . . No, no, it's Kromer and the cover design again. . . . Right, no, he initialed every change, including that cover. . . . Thanks, Charley." She laughs briefly. "You said it, not me. . . . Thanks." She settles the receiver back on the cradle. "Sexist, my ass. He's just a selfish bastard."

After a quick glance at the wastepaper basket, she begins typing. "Dance, little cursor, dance," she snarls.

Sara works at the computer until a soft bell sounds on the machine. "Time to make the doughnuts—which would be a better job, come to think of it," she says. "However, we will cooperate." She prints the pages she's produced, gathers them from the printer, places them in a leather portfolio, snatches up a fountain pen, and starts out her door, but stops.

Frowning, she walks back to her wastepaper basket and lifts the paper airplane out. She sets it in the middle of the desk blotter and leaves the office for the daily project review.

The Kromer issue has been taken care of, and then there is good news, bad news, a new project, no more staff, deadlines moved up.

"More late nights," someone mutters on the way out of the conference room.

"My dog doesn't remember me," someone else says.

Sara doesn't join in the complaining, just goes back to her office and sits at her desk. The paper plane sits there in front of her. She stares at it for a few minutes before fetching a cup of coffee from the machine down the hall. When she get back to her desk, she contemplates the plane some more while sipping from the paper cup.

Finally, she looks over at her clock and raises her eyebrows. "Half an hour? Whoa."

She pulls the pages from her portfolio and turns to her computer, starts typing again, while the sky behind her darkens and that plane sits on her desk.

After three or four pages, Sara grimaces. "This is ridiculous. What are you afraid of?" she says and snatches the plane up, makes as if to throw it but glances over her shoulder at the lighted offices in the buildings across the street and doesn't.

Instead, she tucks the paper into her skirt pocket and makes sure her jacket covers the part that sticks up. The she walks down to the conference room, which is windowless and has locks on both doors.

She locks those doors before she takes the plane out, shakes her head slowly at it, and throws it.

Her feet no longer touch the floor. They float a few inches above the carpet as she is carried almost the length of the room. As the plane dips toward the floor, her feet touch down and the plane again sits inert in her hand.

She stands there, where the plane let her down, and stares at the *thing* she's holding.

Can you imagine her thoughts at this point? Because paper airplanes cannot lift people, you know. She certainly knows. She also has to know that she can't tell anyone what has just happened. No matter how much she dislikes her job, the assistant manager of the publications department of a major property insurance company who is supporting two children in college does *not* tell anyone that something magical has happened. No.

She puts the plane back in her pocket and walks back to her office, slowly, thinking.

She is smiling, ever so faintly, but smiling, when she places the plane in her briefcase as she prepares to leave for the day, and still smiling the next morning when she comes back to work. She's still smiling that faint smile when she finishes rewriting the report and carries it to the photocopier herself because the unit secretary is busy elsewhere, still smiling when the printer notifies her that the files she sent over yesterday are corrupted and please send the backups, still smiling when the network goes down.

Several days pass. Her smile doesn't fade or grow, just lives there on her face as she goes calmly about her business. People notice the faint smile and whisper about it. They whisper about secrets, Maybe, some speculate, Sara is dating someone new. Maybe, others suggest, she's inherited some money.

Her secret is simply that every night when she goes home, she flies her paper airplane in the attic. She used to watch a lot of television in the evening after work, but now, after having moved all the boxes and suitcases to one side of the space, she flies every night and smiles every day.

One day, about a year after her maiden flight, as she walks through the parking garage toward the elevator that will take her up to her office, a man snatches her briefcase. The paper airplane is in the briefcase.

Imagine what you'd do if something like the magic airplane were stolen from you. You might scream or cry out, chase after the man. She does none of that. She simply stares after him. Her smile is gone.

So is a project she's worked on for two months along with the two-hundred-dollar briefcase.

After reporting the theft of the briefcase—which can be replaced with or without the insurance money, after all—and the project—which is backed up at home and in the office—she walks quietly into her office and shuts the door firmly behind her.

The pad of lined yellow paper from which that first plane came is still in her desk drawer, the one that locks, the one where she stashed that pad of paper after she flew the first time. Now, she pulls it out, tears a piece of paper off carefully, folds another pointy-nosed airplane, and sets it on her desk, just leaves it sitting there. If anyone notices, no one says anything, not to her, anyway.

For two days, she leaves the plane sitting there. Maybe she's afraid to fly it. Maybe she's afraid the gift is gone forever, gone with the thief, who almost certainly threw it away once he opened the case. Maybe she knows gifts come with a price that she's no longer willing to pay. Or maybe she wants it to fly and will be so bitterly disappointed by its failure that she can't bear to find out one way or the other. Whatever the reason, and she's not sure herself what the reason is, she doesn't touch the plane for two full days.

When she finally does pick it up, in her dark office, she doesn't try it out, doesn't throw it, just hefts it in her hand. Does it bounce a little? Maybe. It's hard to say without the lights on.

After ten minutes or so, she sets the plane on her desk and walks down to the coffee machine, feeds coins into it, and requests light, no sugar. All the while, she looks thoughtful, far away.

When she gets back to her office, she sips at the hot coffee and stares at the folded paper.

Finally, she shrugs, picks up the paper airplane, and tosses it—

And is tugged a few inches up off the floor and toward her door. She smiles.

Imagine that.

The Cube Root of the Universe

Lawrence Buentello

"The distinction between past, present and future is only an illusion, however persistent."
—Albert Einstein

"What is this?"

That was the first question Vince Wolfe asked that night, and perhaps the most pertinent since he'd begun visiting his brother. He'd brought the small cube to the light, as much light as the ineffectual lamp on the table produced, before holding it to his eye. Within the apartment lay any number of exotic artistic inventions, conjured from a mind heavily veiled from the world. His brother was a challenged man, though only a man in years—his body was developed, and his intellect, but he had no practical understanding of the world in which he lived.

Vince asked again, because his brother, brooding over notes written in a tiny script that perhaps only he could interpret, refused to respond. But when he finally raised his head, his still blue eyes peering from a small face framed by unkempt hair, a small smile came to his lips, of satisfaction perhaps, or appreciation.

"It's the universe," Dominick Wolfe replied, gesturing awkwardly with the pencil in his hand before returning to his notes. His head moved slightly, as if nodding to himself, but it was really only a neurological tic left over from one of his many surgeries.

Vince lowered the cube and watched his brother's motion like a man watching an interesting animal, a bird of paradise spreading exotic feathers, or a whale breaching silently near a pier, though his brother's condition was less interesting for its grace than its resemblance to normal human activity. A waste, he thought—

He'd always been fascinated by nature—in his youth he'd wanted to become a biologist, though declared as a business major in college. But his dreams of financial success were as futile as his academic career. The knowledge he retained of either study was fleeting.

As for Dominick's latest creation? Another absurdity. But he was curious, so once again he raised the object to the light.

Now he could actually see something inside the cube, which seemed to be comprised of glass panels held resolutely by a copper latticework. Pale light shone through from the other side; within, suspended in a smoky gel, tiny globules of light glimmered faintly. Its delicate appearance didn't seem to warrant its weight, and he could only wonder what it represented in his brother's oeuvre of meaningless creations.

"The universe?" he said, trying to find the artistic value in it. His mother represented Dominick as a savant, a creative genius, before she died. Now it was Vince's responsibility to look in on him from time to time, just to make certain he didn't injure himself with the tools of his 'genius'. He'd been coming for a couple of months now, but hadn't made any appreciable personal connection, and the intellectual barrier was beginning to wear on him.

He lowered the cube, his arm grown weary from holding it.

"What's it made of?" he asked.

Dominick didn't answer. Equations appeared in the notebook, born of a mind disinterested in human communication.

Vince touched his brother's shoulder. Dominick moved away from the sensation curiously. Vince had always been perplexed by the man's reaction to stimuli, and couldn't help probing its dimensions. It was cruel to provoke such a reaction in a mentally challenged person, but sometimes he couldn't help himself.

"What's it made of, Dominick?"

His brother blinked several times before answering.

"It's made of whatever the universe is made of," he said. "It's the universe. I placed it in a cube. Do you think it's beautiful?"

Vince smiled. "Yes, I do think it's beautiful. The universe, I mean. Is it cast in glass? Is that what it is?"

"No. It's the universe. You're not listening to me. You never listen to me."

Dominick seemed to look past him then, lost in thought. Without saying another word he returned his attention to his notes, writing so quickly it seemed as if he were taking dictation.

Vince grew tired of the game and raised the cube to the light again. Somewhere in the vastness of the cube's interior he thought he saw a faint winking light, but that was probably only the lamplight reflecting off some piece of debris encased in the substance. When he lost interest in the piece, he set it by the lamp and sighed. Though Dominick was now his responsibility, his *personal* responsibility, he considered the matter an immense waste of time. His brother had no personality to speak of, no connection to the world, no social inclination. He was living in the shadow of his own disability, as functional as he was, and it was embarrassing to observe.

But the anger he felt at having to join his life to such a waste of time smothered any empathy he might have otherwise experienced.

After reconnoitering the kitchen to make certain his brother wouldn't starve to death, Vince lingered in the living room, hoping to initiate some other line of conversation. But Dominick sat entranced by his calculations, repeating numbers endlessly in a psychic loop that ultimately meant nothing. Frustrated, Vince held the cube in his hand and tried to understand how his brother had pieced it together.

"Do you mind if I take this with me?" he asked, not expecting an answer.

Dominick raised his head at the question, first glancing at the cube, and then regarding his brother.

"Carry the universe with you as you go," he said, apropos of nothing. Then he nodded and returned to his writing.

God save me, Vince thought, shaking his head. He thought he might use the cube as a paperweight. It was certainly heavy enough.

Marlene was sleeping again.

When Vince returned to their apartment from the store he would usually find her waiting for him, but not lately. An empty wine bottle stood on the table by the sofa. She lay sprawled, one arm hanging wickedly over the side.

Vince closed the door and sat on the chair by the sofa. For a moment he studied the cube again, secretly marveling at his brother's ingenuity, before setting it on the table by the wine bottle. One object contained the universe; the other the fading aspirations of a once-beautiful woman. But perhaps that was unfair. She was still beautiful, her body still carrying the essence of a voluptuous youth—inside she was fading, like an ancient print, the art of her released from its obligations as her potential faded like a poorly kept painting. She used to paint fairly well, dreaming of art shows and notoriety; but the art shows never manifested, nor the notoriety. Together they'd found new ways to insult the dreams of their youth. Alcohol was only one method. Supporting each other's spiritual dissolution was another.

He knew their relationship would die one day, but not today.

He reached out impulsively to stroke her hair, trying to sense some connection to the past.

She stirred at the sensation, groaned, then rolled over on her elbow to face him.

He moved the hair from her eyes, and she smiled, perhaps remembering some pleasant dream, or perhaps it was only the wine's effect.

"How was work?" she said.

"Same as always," he said. "But a paycheck is a paycheck."

"I thought you were stopping by to see your brother?"

"I did."

"And you're back already?"

"What's the use in staying longer? I was only talking to myself."

"You're not trying hard enough."

She didn't seem drunk; this was either a testament to the strength of her constitution, or an indication that she didn't drink nearly as much as he thought she did. In the back of his mind he'd hoped she *would* be drunk—that would have saved him from having to recount his evening in painful detail, something she always seemed determined to have him do no matter how many times he objected to being interrogated.

"I'm not a psychologist."

"Your mother seemed to do just fine with him."

"My mother had a dedication to futility unmatched by mortal man."

"So you keep telling me. But we all have responsibilities in life."

"Responsibilities? That's just a politic way of saying I have no life of my own anymore."

She smiled halfway, a sardonic expression he hated, but which always seemed to follow his displays of self-pity.

"What was your life like before your mother died?"

He said nothing. He had no intention of recounting his mother's virtues, or lack thereof. A beautiful, educated woman abandoned her life to care for a child that couldn't begin to return that kind of love, and used up any love she might have kept for Vince as well. It wasn't fair of Marlene to use her example, but he understood her intent and couldn't really debate the point.

"That's why we're good together," she said, still smiling. "We both talk a good game, but never follow through."

She picked up the empty wine bottle, tilted it, examining it for any liquid still hiding at the bottom, then set it down again. Then she reached past the bottle and picked up the cube. For a moment she held it in both hands, feeling the weight of it, before raising it to her eyes to study it. When it grew too heavy, she held it on her knees and turned to him again.

"What is this?" she said.

He laughed. He couldn't help himself.

"That's exactly what I asked my brother."

"Well?"

Vince, still hurt by her remark, decided to let it go for now. What good would it do to argue?

"He told me it was the universe," he said, leaning closer. "I guess it's one of his weird little projects."

"It's so heavy. What's it made of?"

"The universe."

"I'm serious."

"That's what he told me," he said, leaning back. "And that's when I left. He was writing again in one of his journals and didn't seem interested in talking."

"What's he writing?"

"God knows. Gibberish, most likely."

She nodded. "And he gave it to you?"

"I asked him if I could have it."

"Why did you want it?"

Vince shrugged. "I can use it as a paperweight."

"What papers do you have that need to be weighted down?"

He plucked it from her knees and held in it his hands. He really didn't like being interrogated—it was one of her worst habits. Why did they stay together? He always complained of her need to know every detail of his existence, and she always criticized his negative perceptions of life. What was the equation? The product of two negative numbers is a positive number?

"I just wanted it," he said. "I don't really know why."

"Maybe you *do* want some connection with him."

He laughed again. "Please, no psychoanalysis. Not tonight."

"It's not psychoanalysis, it's just common sense. You want to connect with your brother but you don't know how."

"Do you always have to do the opposite of what I ask you to do?"

"You're afraid, and you know it," she said, rising. She bent and kissed the top of his head perfunctorily. "All you have to do is talk to him. If he's reluctant, just keep trying. You'll get there. Ask him about his writing. Ask him about his work."

"I've tried."

"Really? Have you *really* tried, or just given a half-hearted effort like you always do?"

He bit his lip against his response. She liked to watch him lose his temper; it seemed to be her favorite hobby. But he wouldn't, not tonight. His feelings were too conflicted.

"Maybe you're right," he said.

She stood quietly for a moment, then said, "I'm going to bed now. Coming?"

"In a few minutes," he said, staring down at his hands. He needed those few minutes to regain control of his emotions.

When she left the room he picked up the cube again, then leaned back toward the lamp. Its density not only increased its weight, it also made the material fairly opaque. Still, faint glimpses of light shone through occasionally, quite beautifully. It seemed to contain something he couldn't quite identify, some ordinary material that only appeared exotic in the cube's configuration.

He set the cube on the table again.

Perhaps Marlene was right. Perhaps he did have to apply himself a little more dynamically before his brother would let him into his world.

After a few minutes he rose from the chair and walked toward the bedroom, hoping she was already asleep.

Over the next few days he considered various approaches to the problem of his brother. He'd watched his mother interact with Dominick of course; she was very good at coaxing him from his clinical self-absorption, but he hadn't studied her technique—he'd always been more interested in escaping his mother's devotion than emulating it. One family member trapped by circumstance was all the universe was owed, at least in his estimation.

But Marlene's subtle accusations echoed in his thoughts and angered him even more than the thought of his responsibilities. They argued too often these days, and he wondered if Dominick was really to blame. Perhaps if he could normalize his relationship with his brother she might begin to think of him again as a decent human being. She seemed to be more emotionally distant the last few days and the change in her worried him. It wasn't so long ago that they never used their own human failings as ammunition in an emotional war.

The next time he visited his brother's apartment he immediately attacked his routine duties, picking up laundry and placing the dirty dishes in the dishwasher, closing cabinet doors and checking on the cleanliness of the bathroom, so he would have enough time to implement his plan.

Dominick barely noticed his presence—he sat reading under a lamp, a thick, difficult physics textbook whose pages turned with a disturbing quickness. Vince, standing in the hallway as he dried his hands on a towel, wondered if his brother was actually reading the book. As a boy, he would gloss over the pictures in comic books and beg Vince to read the continuity to him.

Vince had brought the cube with him in his coat pocket and had set it on the table by the sofa before beginning his chores.

Now he lifted it in his hand as he sat near his brother, feigning a close examination of it while surreptitiously watching Dominick.

"I showed your cube to Marlene," Vince said. "You remember Marlene, don't you? She thought it was very pretty."

Dominick continued reading, though he seemed to nod briefly at the mention of her name.

"I told her that you said it was the universe. Do you remember telling me that? But she didn't understand. Dominick, can you explain the cube to me so I can tell Marlene about it when I see her again?"

For a moment he thought his brother would simply continue reading and ignore him completely. But then Dominick cocked his head to one side, never staring directly at Vince, but offering his attention nonetheless.

"It's the universe," Dominick said.

"Yes, I know," Vince said, leaning a little closer. "But what's it made of? It's a model, isn't it?"

"No, it's the universe. The universe is in the cube."

"I know it might seem to you that the universe is in the cube, but it's really not. Otherwise we would be in the cube, too, because we're part of the universe. Don't you see?"

"The universe is an energetic field held within its own properties of existence," Dominick said in a toneless voice. "The energy field exists within a set of co-ordinates reflected in the space-time continuum that holds it, so it also exists within the dimensional representations of itself. But the continuum is timeless, it contains all times, even from the time it was very young. I calculated the co-ordinates for the universal timeframe from when it was very young and translated them into the cube, so the cube holds the dimensional co-ordinates for the early universe within its frame."

Vince sat back a moment, amazed at the complexity of his brother's statement. What in the world was he talking about? Vince wasn't an uneducated man, but he wasn't a scientist, either. He did, however, understand the use of obfuscating language, and so knew jargon when he heard it.

He leaned forward again, rotating the cube in his hands.

"But it's just a block of glass or something," he said. "This cube doesn't hold the universe."

Dominick's mouth moved oddly, as if he were biting the inside of his cheek. Then he spoke again.

"No, it doesn't hold the universe. It holds the dimensional co-ordinates in which the universe of that time exists. The cube is small because the co-ordinates reflect the size of the universe when it expressed itself within those co-ordinates."

"That's nonsense, Dominick. You do know that, don't you? If this cube held the universe it would weigh trillions of tons. It would have an immense mass."

"You're thinking too conventionally," Dominick said. "Gravity was created by the creation of the matter that influenced itself. The universe would have mass only relative to itself in its dimensional timeframe. When the universe was that small it didn't express weight in the same terms because gravity didn't yet exist in the way we know it now. The universe you're holding is different from the one in which we live. In its own dimensional timeframe it has very little weight."

Vince thought about this for a moment, then said, "That's really clever, but if this is really the universe of billions of years ago wouldn't it also express an enormous amount of energy? I only see a few specks of light inside."

"Stars shine because of the nuclear reactions within them," Dominick said. "When the universe was young those reactions hadn't yet occurred. You're still thinking in the wrong terms. You have to imagine the universe at its birth."

"But if it was the universe we know, it would still have incredible mass, wouldn't it?"

"Measured against what? Itself? There's nothing outside of itself to use to measure it."

Vince first smiled, then laughed softly to himself. He was amazed at his brother's ability to create a fantasy of scientific nonsense.

"All right," he said, "let's just say all that's true. How did you capture the universe in a cube?

"I didn't capture the universe, only its co-ordinates."

"Then how did you capture its co-ordinates?"

Dominick said nothing for a moment, then abruptly rose from his chair, letting the textbook clatter to the floor. He stumbled past Vince to his desk where he began sloughing through stacks of papers, pushing them indiscriminately to the floor.

"It's in my notes," he said, slapping the papers, then picking through them, occasionally peering at one like a profoundly near-sighted man.

Vince, startled by the display, stood quickly and waved his hand.

"Never mind, Dominick," he said, watching his brother scatter pages everywhere, "it's not important. You can show me later."

Dominick abruptly ceased his assault on his papers, cast a sideways glance at Vince, then clumsily returned to his chair. He picked up the book and opened it under the lamp. The ensuing silence suggested to Vince that his brother considered the subject now closed. It was a strange, unemotional display that unnerved him.

He sat for a while studying his brother, perhaps too much like someone watching the behavior of an exotic animal in a zoo. But Dominick's behavior was prosaic. Only his conversation was exotic, a finely woven tapestry of illusion. Still, he was functional in his own way. Only his quasi-autistic approach to life illustrated his human tragedy. He was no savant; their mother simply mistook his scientific gibberish for genius.

Vince, suspecting that he'd made absolutely no progress at all with his brother, slipped the cube angrily into his coat pocket and left the apartment.

Later that night, as he sat rotating the cube in his hand waiting to recount his limited success with Dominick, Marlene walked through the door and told him they needed to talk.

He wasn't ready; he knew the subject had been on her mind, he knew she'd been on the verge of saying something but had always turned away from it at the last minute. Now the words found their way into the air, into his heart, and he felt the heaviness sink from his chest to his stomach.

She sat next to him, pulling a hand through her hair nervously, before speaking again.

"We have to talk about the future," she said. "Our future."

He set the cube on the table by the lamp, trying to steal a few seconds to organize his arguments. But they were the same old arguments, and he knew they wouldn't survive close scrutiny.

"You're not happy," he said, more as a statement of fact than anything else.

"No, I'm not happy," she said. She'd been drinking, but she wasn't drunk. Perhaps she'd had one or two drinks to firm her resolve before returning to the apartment. "I haven't been for some time. And I don't think you're happy, either. You haven't been happy with me."

"Yes, I have. I love you, Marlene."

She smiled, a tired, beautiful smile that refused to mock his sincerity.

"I know you love me, Vince. But I don't think you *like* me very much anymore."

"That's not true."

"Yes, it is. I won't make you say it, even though we both know we've been making each other pretty miserable these last few months."

"I'm sorry," he said, taking her hand. "After my mother died things went bad."

"No," she said, "that's not true. They were going bad long before that. It's not your mother's fault, or your brother's fault. This is *our* fault."

He stared at her hand for a long time before raising his head.

"Are you leaving?"

She nodded.

"I talked to Karen about it," she said. "I can stay with her until I find my own place."

He released her hand. There was something final in the act, as if some connection had been abruptly severed.

"I know I haven't been the man you hoped I'd be," he said. "I'm sorry about that. And I'm sorry about getting you involved in caring for my brother."

"It's not that—"

"It's *exactly* that," he said. It was difficult keeping the anger from his voice when he spoke of it. "I'm chained to my brother forever, or until one of us dies. And that'll probably be me. Not that my mother ever gave a damn about what happened to me."

"You have to stop blaming your family for everything in your life, Vince."

"Why shouldn't I? Not only did she make me promise to watch over him, she left all her money in trust for him. Not a dime for me, not even a token gesture of her love. Why shouldn't I feel some negativity?"

"She knew you could make a life for yourself, that's why. She knew you wouldn't have to depend on her like your brother did. What did you expect her to do?"

"I expected her to throw a little love my way," he said. "I expected her share her life with me, too, not just devote herself to my brother. He's emotionally *dead*, damn it, he can't respond to love like a healthy human being. I don't even think he knows what love is. And she expected me to take over where she left off."

"You know, you're really pretty good at feeling sorry for yourself. You should hear yourself talk about it as if you were in prison or something."

"That's pretty much all I have left, isn't it? After you leave? Then what? Do you think a line of women is going to form outside my door for the chance to get involved with a guy who's tethered to some mental defective? Isn't that why *you're* leaving?"

"No, it's not," she said, standing. "I'm leaving because we're not good for each other anymore. Maybe we were never good for each other. I look in the mirror every morning and see the person I've become. I know I drink too much, too. It helps me forget what I see in the mirror. And I haven't painted for a long time now, something I should never have let happen. Vince, I need a chance to be something more than I am. And you do, too. But I don't think either of us will ever have the chance if we keep supporting each other's worst qualities. *That's* why I'm leaving."

She began to cry, though fighting to remain in control of herself.

He didn't rise to comfort her.

"I'm sorry," he said, almost helplessly. It was the only thing he could think of to say that wasn't a lie.

She calmed herself after a moment, then said, before turning toward the bedroom, "I'll start moving my things tomorrow."

He nodded, but said nothing.

When he was alone again he sat turning the cube in his hands, his mind filled with too many thoughts. He loved her, but felt poisoned by her, as much as she felt poisoned by him. He wouldn't argue with her—he knew she was right, and was only vaguely jealous that she'd been the one to find the courage to initiate the process. He'd let his ambitions die long ago, and knew they weren't ever going to return. Caring for his brother had been his most constructive use of time in recent memory, and yet he was decrying its imposition in his life.

If he could turn back time, perhaps he'd turn it back just far enough to recapture his lost ambitions, just far enough to make certain he didn't lose his desire for a better life—

He envied Dominick his ability to live inside abstract concepts of the universe. Having no need for love and comfort left him free to enjoy a mindless existence in scientific delusions.

What do I do now? he thought.

A couple of days later he returned to his brother's apartment through a dense rain, a sudden storm drowning out the grace of the perfectly beautiful stars. He'd stopped in a bar on the way, and knew it was a mistake to visit Dominick afterward, but he was just a little too drunk for self-restraint. He carried the universe in his coat pocket the entire way, having taken it with him when he left his own apartment. He and Marlene had had a loud, sober argument before he left; she'd come to get the last of her things, though he thought it might have been a cheap excuse to lecture him one more time before leaving. Go on, he'd said, leave already, I'm not in the mood for another sermon.

The rain had partially sobered him, though. By the time he got to Dominick's door the pleasant haze of inebriation had softened into a sullen stupor. He was even able to slip his key into the lock on the first attempt.

He sat with a flourish on the sofa, his wet coat staining the cushions.

Dominick didn't even raise his head from his notebook. His writing was fluid, unconcerned.

Vince smiled.

"How're you doing, Einstein?" he said. "Working out the unified field theory for the rest of us?"

His brother failed to respond. Vince felt a subtle anger stirring in his chest.

"Marlene finally left me," he said. "You remember Marlene, don't you? Of course you don't. You don't even remember who *I* am."

He laughed at this, wiping the rainwater from his face. Then he reached into his coat pocket and removed the cube. He stared at it a moment before placing it beneath the lamp.

"It's just as well. We were only feeding on each other, like vampires sucking the blood from one another, only spiritually. Isn't that a pretty picture? Now maybe we can both have normal, productive lives. Achieve great things, find a cure for cancer, who knows? Of course, neither of our accomplishments could ever compare with the product of *your* genius—"

He gestured extravagantly toward his brother, who still sat writing in his journal.

"No, of course not," Vince said, staring at the cube again. "In order for a person to enjoy your level of genius he would have to be an emotionless robot, completely self-centered and dependent only on his own inner world to feel fulfilled. Isn't that true? Isn't that true, you God damned idiot?"

Vince waited for a response. Dominick kept writing.

Vince laughed, then almost choked on a hiccup.

"It must be a beautiful life for you," he said, recovering, "to never be aware of the level of your incapacities, to never be aware of your own profound failure. Well *I'm* aware of my own failure, and let me tell you it's no blissful revelation. So you keep writing, you keep peeling away the layers of creation, so the rest of us can worship at the altar of your genius."

He sighed deeply, then held his face in his hands for a moment, intense memories filling his mind, of growing up, living with his obsessive mother, watching his only brother perform the muted rituals of the tiny world in which he lived; flunking out of college, jumping from one job to the next, finally settling with Marlene into a life that held some promise. Now the promise was gone and he was alone with his brother again, moved back in time to a place he'd never left. He lifted his face from his hands and stared at Dominick.

It wasn't his fault, really. Left to himself he'd continue on until the food was gone, and then he'd slowly starve to death as he furiously wrote equations into a never-ending series of notebooks. His mother was really the only person keeping him alive; and now, it was Vince's turn.

He rose from the sofa and pulled off his coat. The rainwater chilled him, made him shiver. He saw the cube sitting beneath the lamp, gleaming oddly in the light. He picked it up and stumbled toward his brother.

Dominick barely noticed his presence.

"What's the secret of it all?" Vince asked, dropping a hand on his brother's shoulder.

Dominick, startled by the gesture, stared up blankly.

"You know it, don't you?" Vince asked, holding the cube before Dominick's eyes. "What's it all about? What is the meaning of existence? What is the purpose of the universe?"

Dominick's lips trembled, as if he were actually trying to formulate an answer.

"Dominick," Vince said, "*answer* me. What's it all about?"

For a moment only silence existed between them.

And then, after glancing quickly at the cube, his brother said, "The cube root of the universe is zero."

Then Dominick stared down at his notebook again, fingering his pencil.

Vince stared at the moving pencil, almost hypnotized. Then he rose away from his brother and lurched back toward the sofa.

"I guess that's it, then," he said, staring fiercely at the cube. "It all comes down to zero, doesn't it? I'm a zero, you're a zero, Marlene's a zero. Our mother was a *phenomenal* zero, and here we all are in the middle of the universe."

Marlene was right—he sounded painfully self-pitying. Since there was no one else in the room to hear him, he found himself his own audience, and he didn't like the performance. For once in his life he wished he could follow through on something meaningful, something that might benefit or change the world in some small way; something greater than the sum of so many negative numbers.

He held the cube to the light a moment, trying to find them all inside the ethereal gloom, but all he saw was darkness.

Then, suddenly furious at the futility of it, he turned to the wall and raised the cube over his shoulder.

"Maybe I can play God for once," he said. "Let's see what happens when it starts all over again."

He hurled the cube at the wall with all his strength, hoping for some revelation.

But the universe only brought itself back to zero.

The Ring Reclaimed

Jeffrey Greene

On a rainy October evening more than twenty years ago, two hikers traveling in opposite directions on the Appalachian Trail in northern Georgia stopped for the night in one of those doorless log shelters provided by the Park Service at intervals all along the more than two thousand miles of the trail. After their respective meals, the two men sat across from one another in the small, dusty room, a tiny propane lantern hissing softly between them as they talked and sipped strong black tea spiked with a little bourbon provided by the older man. Rain drummed steadily on the log roof and cascaded from the overhang, but it was a mild, if unusually dark, night and there was no need for a fire, which, along with their full stomachs, pleasantly tired muscles and potent tea, made for a mutually expansive mood.

The younger man introduced himself as Alan Schusterman, a recent college graduate from Florida who had been hiking alone since June, having started at the trailhead at Mount Katahdin, Maine. He told the other man, Dr. William Pettit, a retired psychiatrist from Ithaca, New York, that he was only three to four days' hike from Springer Mountain, the southern trailhead and the achievement of his goal to hike the entire Appalachian Trail. He accepted Dr. Pettit's congratulations with thanks, but added that after five months of living outside, he had mixed feelings about returning to the suburbs.

"To be honest," he said, "I'm not sure I want to go back to regular showers, bad traffic, and long lines at the movie theater."

The doctor smiled and nodded, his grey-stubbled face bobbing in and out of the lantern's small zone of light. He was a compact man in his mid-sixties, with sparse grey hair, an angular, deeply-lined face, and a large, oar-shaped nose with a rather distinguished bump on the bridge. His baggy brown eyes were restless and intense, though friendly, and narrowed when he stared directly at Alan, as if he were peering at him through dense fog or smoke.

"I hiked the entire trail myself in 1952," Dr. Pettit said, sipping his tea. "And I'll admit that it only deepened my appreciation of hot showers and warm beds. But yes, I can imagine a person capable of loving this trail so much that he might abandon the indoor world completely, learn to live off the land, using the shelters in rain or snow. In fact, I met someone on Roan Mountain during my hike who may have been a kind of nomad of the trail." He raised his flask inquiringly and Alan nodded, holding out his cup as the doctor poured a generous shot.

"You met someone who lived year-round on the Appalachian Trail?" Alan asked, smiling at the idea.

"I can't say for sure if she actually lived on the trail," the doctor replied.

"She?"

"Yes. At first I thought she was a transient, perhaps mentally ill, who'd probably been hitchhiking where the trail crossed the highway, and followed it to the nearest shelter." He sipped his tea. "The reason I thought she might be crazy, aside from the fact that she was filthy, a bit wild-eyed and in the woods alone was... well, she had in spades that—how shall I put it?—solipsistic self-assurance that is all-too-frequently seen in schizophrenics. On the other hand, she seemed quite lucid; abnormally so, one might say."

"I've met some interesting types myself," Alan said. "And you say this happened at the Roan Mountain shelter?"

Dr. Pettit sipped his tea and nodded. "One of the garden spots of the entire trail, as you know, with its three grassy balds. I'd just been discharged from the Army that spring, and wanted to do something adventurous before the long servitude of medical school. Like you, I started in Maine and headed south. It was late August when I reached the Tennessee-North Carolina border, having slogged through four straight days of heavy rain. I was in good shape by then, but you know how heavy a pack can get after hiking all day in the rain, and by the time I reached the Roan Mountain shelter at dusk, I was exhausted. From a distance it had seemed unoccupied, but as I got closer I noticed a bundle of old clothes in one corner that soon became the figure of a woman, curled on her side and facing the wall, asleep. A mud-smeared army blanket concealed all but a waterlogged pair of boots and a greasy mass of the blackest hair. She didn't move as I changed into dry clothes and hurriedly prepared dinner in the fading light. No other hikers came, and finding that my clumping around didn't disturb her sleep, I went about my business, though all the time wondering who she could be, why she was traveling without a pack, and whether I should risk falling asleep in the same room with someone who definitely wasn't your garden variety hiker, who in fact, to judge by her clothes, could either be a drifter or a nutcase. It occurred to me that she might even be faking sleep, waiting until I was asleep so she could slit my throat and rob me. I considered waking her up, just to know who the hell I was dealing with, but in the end exhaustion overcame paranoia and I fell asleep.

"This may be a damaging admission for a psychiatrist, but I don't usually remember my dreams. For me, they're mostly a ghoulash of the recent and distant past, a senseless jumble of images that fades as soon as I wake up. But that night in the shelter I had a dream that stayed with me. It was very brief and simple, and not at all frightening: I was on a dirt road in an unfamiliar country, a treeless, hilly, desolate place, like the moors of Scotland. Then, without any sense of transition, the way things happen in dreams, there was a woman on the road ahead of me, leading a gigantic horse. It was exaggeratedly tall and thin, with long, spindly legs like a giraffe, and it was clearly ancient, on its last legs. My memory of the woman is more vague. She was fairly tall, though not a giant, and her head was bowed, but I can't recall much about her face except its rather downcast expression. She seemed like a groom or a servant. The horse couldn't have been hers, since she wouldn't have been able to touch the bottom of the stirrup standing on tiptoe, much less mount it, any more than I could have. And yet the horse was saddled. Even in the dream this struck me as significant. It was more picture than plot, and nothing else happened that I can remember.

"I don't know whether it was the dream itself that woke me up, or some sound in the shelter, but I sat right up, as if someone had touched my face. I'd put my pocket knife under the towel I was using for a pillow, and my hand closed on it as I strained to see in the darkness. Then I heard a rustle of clothing, and groping for my flashlight, I shined it where the woman had been sleeping. I got a shock then: she was awake and sitting cross-legged with her back against the wall, staring intently at me, her dark face framed by an almost frightening mass of black hair. It was so unsettling to wake up and find her wide awake in the dark, that I momentarily forgot my manners, and it wasn't until she shielded her eyes with one hand, her long fingernails casting spiky shadows on the wall, that I moved the light from her face.

"'That's better,' she said in a low voice.

"'Sorry,' I said.

"'Could you spare a little food?'

"I first put my pants on, then crossed the short space between us and handed her my canteen and a bag of trail mix. She was dressed in well-worn jeans and a loose khaki shirt, and through her dense hair I glimpsed a wide mouth with full lips, large black eyes and a hawk nose. I noticed that she was wearing a single item of jewelry—a heavy gold ring on her right hand, set with an oval, blood-colored stone.

"'Thanks,' she said. 'We don't need the light, do we?'

"I turned it off and listened in the dark. She ate ravenously, in silence. When she was finished she leaned over and handed back the canteen and the bag, her movements, as well as I could see them in the dimness, conveying a casual grace. 'Thanks.'

"'If you want more, let me know,' I said.

"'I see you're a young man of the better sort,' she said.

"Not sure how to respond to that, I asked where she was heading.

"'Home,' she said.

"'And where's home?' I asked.

"'North.'

"'I'm being nosy because the only hikers I've seen without packs are day hikers,' I said. 'I thought you might be lost.'

"I saw a glimmer of teeth in the dark. 'Well, it's a big universe,' she said.

"'Big woods, too,' I replied. 'But I guess you'd tell me if you were lost.'

"'Why? You want to rescue somebody?'

"'No,' I said, a little hurt. 'I'm just curious. You don't see many women hiking alone.'

"'Did I say I was hiking?' she said.

"'Okay, fine,' I said, beginning to get irritated. 'Just trying to make conversation.'

"'Oh, conversation,' she said. 'Then let's talk about your dream.'"

"This was my second shock of the evening. 'Dream?' I said, though I knew perfectly well what she meant, because the dream had been so simple and vivid that I could almost reach out and touch it.

"She leaned forward, her intense black eyes staring into mine. 'Don't play dumb with me,' she said. 'This little picture around us…' She indicated with a contemptuous gesture the shelter and the dripping forest. 'This is like the newspaper, to be read and forgotten over breakfast. But a dream, a true dream like the one you just had, is a poem from the Gods, written for you alone. So much more real than this paradise of maggots.'

"'How did you know I had a dream?' I asked.

"She laughed, a deep-throated sound that was not in the least infectious. 'I've always preferred poetry to journalism,' she said. I had to smile at that, and she smiled too, as if we were enjoying a joke together. 'Now tell me your dream.'

"I told her, and she listened as if her life depended on reciting it back word for word. There was this quality about her, that I've searched for ever since and never found: her face—or was it just her eyes, her expression?—was like a flame consuming everything inessential. Her unkempt nails, her ragged clothes, her dirty hair, where she came from, where she was going, how she lived from day to day like the rest of us: all these trivial questions that I'd wanted to ask from the moment I saw her, were forgotten. Our positions had reversed very quickly; I was the poor, confused beggar, not her. She was royalty of a different sort.

"She was silent for several minutes. Finally, I asked: 'Do you know what it means?'

"'Not for me to say,' she said. 'But this meeting was no accident. We're here together because the roads running through our dreams intersected. You needed me to remind you of the importance of your dream, and I needed you because in my dream, I was thirsty.'

"'Oh, I thought I was here because it was raining and the trail led this way,' I said sarcastically, put off by her glib mysticism.

"'I think we're somewhat different,' she replied. 'You think truth can be found secondhand, in books or a classroom, that nothing is required of you beyond the ability to assimilate it. For me, there is no truth without blood. I must grab the blade to find it.' She stood up suddenly in one fluid motion, and in the darkness her hair seemed to writhe around her face. 'Think about your dream,' she said. Then she took off her gold ring, and leaning over me, so that her hair brushed my arm, she dropped it in my hand. 'As long as you wear this, you won't forget it,' she said. 'It's the best I can do for you.'

"Not knowing what else to say, I thanked her.

"'It's not a gift,' she said, backing away from me. 'I'll come back for it, and on that day we'll talk again about your dream.' She turned and stepped into the rainy darkness, and was soon swallowed up by it. The skin of my arm tingled where her hair had touched it.

"I examined the ring closely. It appeared to be made of solid gold and was very heavy, with a polished red stone shaped like a tiny egg set in mouth-like clasps on either side. On closer inspection, the clasps proved to be twin serpents with distended mouths trying to devour the egg from each end, their tangled coils forming not only the hollow in which the stone rested, but the ring itself."

"You're describing the ring you're wearing right now," Alan said, pointing to the ring on the doctor's right hand.

"So I am." He held it up to the light. "I put it on soon after she left. It slipped on easily enough, but when I tried to take it off, it wouldn't budge. After I'd tried everything short of cutting it off with a hacksaw, I began to like it. It hasn't been off since that night."

"Well, you've remembered the dream, so I guess it served its purpose," Alan said, smiling. "Do you think she put a spell of memory on it?"

The doctor laughed. "She must have known it wouldn't be necessary, since I had only to look at the ring to recall every detail of the short time I spent with her, including the dream. Anticipating your skepticism, I'll agree that she did nothing supernatural, since her knowing I'd had a dream could just as easily have been a guess, maybe after hearing me talk in my sleep. Aside from a certain fearlessness, an aversion to bathing and trimming her nails, and a fascination with dreams, one could say that she was no different from anyone else. Yet here I am, all these years later, still talking about her. I guess in a way I fell in love with her, or at least with what she represented. I'm not sure what to call it: spiritual audacity, maybe, or having the kind of heart that thrives inside of flames instead of being warmed by them. Now whether she burned with true insight or mere force of personality, I don't know, but for most of my life I've measured myself unfavorably against that fire. Which is not to say I didn't struggle, in my muddling way, with the meaning of the dream; I did, for many years. It's an irony I've never shared with my colleagues, that a single hour in the company of a woman whose name I never learned had more to do with my becoming a psychiatrist than all the years with greybeard attending physicians put together." He drained the last of his tea and poured a dash of straight bourbon into his cup, then offered some more to Alan, who nodded and held out his cup. They drank for a moment in silence.

"Well, after all this, I have to ask what you made of the dream," Alan said. "Or did you decide that sometimes a woman leading a giant, decrepit horse is just a woman leading a giant, decrepit horse?"

The doctor shook his head. "The process of thinking about it wasn't continuous, of course. It came in fits and starts, sometimes coinciding with personal and professional crises, sometimes when I was happy, sad, or bored, or right before falling asleep, even in the middle of listening to one of my patients describing a dream. Then years might pass before it would come back, burrowing up from the depths. I painted pictures of it, papering my study with different views of the same scene, or emphasizing certain aspects over others. I tried Freud on for size, then Jung. If, as Freud believed, all dreams are the expression of unconscious wishes, I asked myself, what was I wishing for on that lonely road in an unknown country? Who was the horse's absent rider and why wasn't he—or she—in the dream? Was he my father, not yet dead at the time, but ill, and if so, was I wishing him dead by making his horse riderless? Perhaps the absent rider was not my father but God the Father, and his huge, enfeebled horse was a symbol of my dying faith. Having already killed God with my science, there remained only the vestiges of childhood religion, the still-running clock of the Church, ticking off its round of rituals and ceremonies long after the clockmaker has died. As you can see, the more I thought about it, the more complex that apparently simple picture became. If true dreams are "poems from the Gods," as the woman had said, which I take to mean that certain rare dreams have the brevity and weight of poetry, using image and incident rather than words, then this opens the door to multiple interpretations. Occurring to me over half a lifetime, they ranged from the grandiose to the absurd. I considered and rejected the notion that the absent rider was one of the Four Horsemen of the Apocalypse, or even my own death, but rather liked the idea that the dying horse represented the moribund Western film genre, which was itself a metaphor for the adventurous yearning for new horizons that fueled the American expansion. As we moderns become ever more urban and sedentary, we grow more nostalgic, perverse and inward in the same proportion. The unhorsed rider might have been my own resurrection of the Lone Cowboy, a role I aspired to as a child. Instead, I grew up, then grew old listening to people describe their obsessions and neuroses. You can't imagine how sick of sick people I became. At some point in mid-career it occurred to me that I was a fraud, pretending to care when all I felt was pity, contempt, weariness, or an uneasy mixture of all three.

"After many years I realized that I was going around in circles, chasing my own tail. There were failed marriages along the way, children who grew up and scattered in all directions, prostate cancer, arthritis, cataract surgery—the usual stuff. But through the years there remained the constant reminder of the ring on my finger, and the woman's promise to reclaim it. I told you I've searched for the fire she came to represent and never found it. At some point I realized that what I really wanted was to see her again, if only to find out how my older self would judge her. I still believe in literary and artistic magic, and in the overwhelming, ungraspable fact of

Existence itself, but the muddy current of everyday life has led me farther and farther away from the more arcane magic that may or may not have taken place in that tiny room in the mountains so long ago." The doctor drained his cup and poured them both another finger of bourbon.

"Is that why you're here now?" Alan asked. "Hoping to meet her again?"

"Partly, yes," Dr. Pettit replied. "And partly to recapture—if it's still possible—some echo of what it felt like to have an adventure."

"May I assume, then," Alan said, adjusting his back against the wall, "that in thirty-five years you came to no definite conclusions about what the dream meant, if in fact it meant anything other than what it was—a picture that appeared in your mind while you were sleeping?"

"If you're asking whether I experienced some Eureka moment of pure clarity, then no, I guess I'd have to say I failed."

"I wouldn't say failed," Alan said. "Remember, the woman asked you to think about the dream, not figure it out. You've certainly done that, more than most people would. And who's to say any dream has just one meaning? Didn't that theory go out of fashion along with Freud?"

"Maybe. But I was hoping for something more definite, the sense of a key turning in a lock, an inner door opening. Unfortunately, I dreamed no sequels: the dream woman never spoke to me, and no ten-foot-tall cowboy mounted the horse and rode into the sunset. I'm still here, as muddled as I ever was."

"I don't know you well enough to agree or disagree with that," Alan said. "But if you don't mind me putting in my two cents...?"

"Not at all."

"Well, this is just an idea, but what if the key character in the dream is the woman, not the horse?"

Dr. Pettit nodded impatiently. "I've thought about her, of course, quite often. But the vagueness of her face, and the fact that she never made eye contact, led me almost from the beginning to discount her as the dream's central image. And the giant horse is so much more memorable, so suggestive of the being capable of riding it, who also evokes potent, invisible mysteries, things so far beyond human comprehension that we can't even see them, much less understand them. The horse was a thing of extremes: extremely large, extremely old, while the woman occupied in every sense—size, age, looks—the great middle way. In a word, mediocrity, a condition that I dreaded as a young man, that I still dread, even though I realized long ago that I'm no different from the rest. Time cuts us all down to size, and youth is the only force strong enough to resist it. For a little while," he added with a sour smile.

Alan laughed. "So what you're saying, doctor, is that the woman leading the horse was beneath your notice because she symbolized everything you fear and despise in yourself. Is that a fair statement?"

"Well, no, not exactly. In a dream with so few characters, nothing is unimportant. I just thought that, since she seemed to be a servant or a groom..."

"Aren't grooms always male?" Alan asked. "Or am I mistaken?"

"Maybe in the real world," Dr. Petit said. "Not in my dream."

"All right, let's follow that thought for a moment," Alan said. "Your dream woman was leading a horse that she obviously couldn't ride, that seemed to be saddled for a giant. Her head was bowed and her eyes downcast, therefore you assumed that she was a groom or a servant. But books and movies had taught you since childhood that grooms are either young men in sackcloth with Prince Valiant haircuts or middle-aged Englishmen with riding caps and a cockney accent, so why would you dream a woman in that role? The stuff of dreams is the stuff of this world, and however bizarre they may seem, isn't there always a thread of internal logic to them? So, if a woman leading a giant's horse is not a groom, what else could she be? The giant's wife? His daughter? Has she stolen the horse, or does it belong to her? Maybe she's a character out of a myth or a fairy tale, a lower-echelon fairy, perhaps, who's been charged by her superiors in Fairyland with keeping this magic horse in a magic stable, feeding and caring for it through the centuries, and sadly watching it grow old as she waits for the hero of the story to come questing, the inevitable handsome prince who must prove himself worthy of riding it. But let's say it's almost too late. By now the horse is ancient, since no one worthy has come in all these centuries, and in the meantime Fairyland itself has retreated to remote and forgotten corners of the world, which might include certain regions of the unconscious mind, accessible only to those willing to undergo the rigorous training necessary for the journey—like psychiatrists, for example. Maybe the horse will die of old age before the prince happens along, and this sense of sadness and futility, mingled with her inbred obedience to the chain of command in Fairyland, is what you see in the woman's face. What you don't see, perhaps, is the hope hidden behind the downcast expression. Here you are standing before her on a lonely road in a dream country where only two people can ever be at any given time: the woman leading the horse and the questing prince, who may or may not be worthy of riding it. She waits for you on the road as she's waited for centuries, expecting nothing but hoping, always hoping. She can't look up at you because the fairy queen has forbidden her to help the seeker in any way. This, as you remember from your Brothers Grimm, is the unbreakable law of the fairy tale: the hero is given magic weapons to defeat evil and win the love of the princess, but he must wield them himself. So this fairy, elf, witch, or whatever she is, keeps her eyes averted, and the horse waits, old and tired, not winged or eternally young like Pegasus, but mortal, as magic is mortal, as the Earth is mortal. A dream giant doesn't need boots as big as wine barrels to convey the idea of stature. There are giants of soul, intellect, talent, bravery, whose horses would throw off anyone they sensed was unfit to ride them."

While listening to the dim figure seated across from him, Dr. Pettit's face had gone pale. He stared hard at the young man, licking dry lips, his eyebrows drawn together, his fingers nervously rubbing the stubble on his cheeks.

"As a young man," Alan went on, "you aspired to greatness, but your trail was not as well-marked as it is for those special few, and after many years you saw yourself meandering, back-tracking, losing precious time. You became 'no different from the rest,' a muddled, groping Everyman, and gradually your youthful aspirations curdled into the regrets of old age. But in the back of your mind, you had stored a picture, a snapshot, of a place beyond the clutter and confusion of this world of sleepwalkers, where a woman who may be a witch always waits for you, with a horse that is more or less than a horse, waiting for its master to remember who he really is. If you don't try to ride him he will never be ridden, because he was bred for you alone and will die when you die. The sky, the hills, the road, the woman, the horse: all of it is part of the William Pettit who is always awake and alive, shouting 'wake up!' to the William Pettit who is always asleep and dying."

"Then why was the horse old, even when I was young?" Dr. Pettit asked, almost whispering.

"Maybe the dream was trying to tell you that it was almost too late for you to become the person you were meant to be. It's always almost too late, from the moment we begin to discount the importance of our dreams. Of course, these are only opinions. Like you, doctor, I lack Freud's gift of certainty. In fact, the only thing I am certain of is that you have something that belongs to me."

Alan held out his hand, and in the uncertain light Dr. Pettit saw it change and darken. He looked up and found the woman of his memories seated in the young man's place. Her hair was still wild and thick, and her clothes were the same, but it was as if she had come through a blizzard, so white was her hair and brows. The only blackness left in her face was her eyes. He stared at her, too shocked to speak, until he understood what she wanted, and held out his right hand. One hand closed hard on his wrist and the scythe-like nails of the other reached for the ring and pulled. He felt no pain, only a sharp, cold sensation, and it was a second before he realized that his finger was gone, the stump bleeding profusely.

"No truth without blood, remember?" she said, gazing at him with something like affection as she slipped the ring on her finger, then casually dropped his severed digit into her shirt pocket. "And we'll shed oceans more before we wake up." She stood up, her movements slower and less fluid than they once were, but no less decisive. "Thanks for the whisky," she said, then, hoisting her pack and shrugging it on, she stepped carefully off the platform and strode into the darkness, whistling a tune he didn't recognize as she picked up the trail heading south.

It seemed to him that he could still hear her gradually fading whistle, long after the bleeding had stopped.

Waiting for the 26

Roderick B. Overaa

Robert Austeridge had been standing at the bus stop a good two minutes before he noticed the guy. Swaddled in the cumbrous layers of his own thoughts, he had stepped immediately to the curb hoping to glimpse his bus through the cottony fog that had drifted in with the eventide. A chill winter fog—the sort which, like heavy snow, mutes sound and hugs the earth so that passing cars seem to slide by like phantoms, ethereal and silent. A prickling sensation over his scalp provided the first hint that he was not alone. The same feeling he'd experienced last summer, when hiking alone in the Cascade Mountains he had suddenly sensed the gaze of some unseen animal (a deer, it turned out). A quick glance confirmed the suspicion—a bulky and bedraggled man occupied the bus stop shelter. Startled more by the fellow's abrupt manifestation than his scruffy appearance, Robert inadvertently splashed a dram of scalding coffee onto the back of his left hand and nearly dropped the bag of donuts he was carrying in his right. Wiping the burning liquid onto his jeans, he silently cursed his inattention.

The stranger sat wedged into the far corner of the shelter, huddled on the slatted bench with his stout forearms girdling his knees. A beard of sooty gray tumbled out over a dingy workman's jacket, beneath which innumerable layers of clothing of varied style and hue were visible. So tucked up into his corner he was that Robert nearly hadn't noticed him at all, and having done so would not have sworn to his existence, even then and there. For he had become aware of the man's presence obliquely; not from the corner of his eye, but rather through inattention, by allowing his vision to glaze over as one does with those "hidden image" autostereograms found in novelty shops. In fact, the more Robert attempted to bring his subject into focus, the more the man went fuzzy at the edges. It was as though he shared some kinship with the surrounding fog; the closer Robert looked, the more quickly the man seemed to dissipate into nothingness.

The uncanny nature of the man's apparition, certainly, did nothing to assuage Robert's sudden alarm at seeing him there, for lately the world—his world, at least, one comprised of interminable hours of study broken only by snatches of sleep—seemed strangely formless and insubstantial. A graduate student at the nearby university, his business of late was reading books. The great books, certainly, but also the books about the great books, which, Robert discovered, were often not bad themselves. Yet the more Robert read about the world around him, the more the objects of that world dissolved into abstraction, like Alka-Seltzer tablets plunked into a tumbler of cold, crystalline water. More precisely, his overworked, juggernaut mind lately had been transposing every new experience into some literary allusion drawn from his reading; disturbingly, this was now the filter through which he made sense of his universe. Thus Robert Austeridge found himself plagued with an overwhelming sense of Lawrencian detachment, all spirit and no sense, a Clarel versed more in his tomes than life. Yet as with that thwarted, embittered whaler of old (he thought, letting his mind once again wax allusive), Robert wanted to feel something in his slippery world that could hold. Having a bearded, bedraggled and apparently homeless man materialize unexpectedly before him was not helping.

Such were the various thoughts, feelings, and perceptions that flared and dwindled in the kiln of Robert's mind in the time it had taken to spill a few drops of coffee. Still unnerved by the advent of the stranger, he thought it might be best to speak, if only to reassure himself with the sound of his own voice.

"Hello," Robert called, breath emerging in thick clouds. "I'm sorry; I didn't see you there."

The man started, then recovered himself, turning a pair of remarkable Nordic eyes upon his interpellator. He uncurled from his deep tuck and straightened what turned out to be an impressive frame, placing a pair of sturdy work boots on the pavement.

"No, it's…quite all right," the man said, the creases at the corners of those impossibly blue eyes betraying his surprise. "I'm pleased that you can see me at all. Really, it happens so infrequently these days…it's a bit of a shock, to be honest."

"People have a knack for not seeing what stands immediately before them," Robert replied.

"Oh, it's absolutely true," the man agreed, nodding with quick, bobbing motions. "I had a short conversation with a little girl the other day—the children, you know, are the most perceptive—and her mother, standing right there with the girl's hand enfolded in her own, never so much as noticed."

Robert nodded politely and sipped his coffee. Resisting the urge to glance at his watch, he turned and looked up the street. The fog had condensed into a roiling mass of gray vapor; it was impossible to see beyond the light pole at the corner. As if to mock his feeble attempt, heavy snowflakes had begun to fall, further obscuring his vision. The man in the shelter remained blurry and indistinct, leaving Robert to wonder if the fellow was merely an illusion, or perhaps even an allusion, of the type that had been recently insinuating themselves, gnat-like, upon his consciousness. Rest, he thought, rest and a break from the books, that's what I need.

"Waiting for the 26?" asked the man.

"Yup."

"It'll be along shortly," he said, with a wink that implied a certainty wholly incongruous with his semi-materialized state. "They run every half hour, like clockwork, and I haven't seen one for some time."

In fact, and quite despite the inchoate stranger's well-intentioned assurances, Robert realized, the very bus he was waiting for was itself a kind of phantom uncertainty. As it happened, his present dwelling lay situated in a kind of metropolitan limbo, for there was no single extant bus route that precisely coincided with his point of origin (the university campus) and his destination (the cozy confines of his apartment). Thus each evening Robert found himself in a sort of mass-transit purgatory, a way station that lay somewhere between where he had been, and where he knew he must, ultimately, end up.

"How long have you been sitting there?" asked Robert, for he dearly wanted to consult his watch, but did not wish to appear rude.

"Hard to say. Too long; not long enough. Depends on the criteria you use to make the judgment, wouldn't you say? The important thing is that I know where I am."

This is what I get for offering a friendly greeting, thought Robert. Of all the homeless nut-jobs in all the bus shelters in all of the greater Seattle area, he had to bump into this one, the Philosopher King of homeless nut-jobs, a latter-day Prospero without even a wretched Caliban over whom he could exercise his will. (Damn, he was doing it again.) It was strain enough having to keep his eyes unfocused enough to discern the fellow; was Robert now expected to listen to his demented ravings?

"Listen," he said, "I've just bought a couple of donuts, which I have absolutely no intention of eating. They're fresh; perhaps you'd like them?"

Robert typically only bought coffee on the way home, but today the glazed donuts, with their ring-like shape and transparent veneer, had suggested to him a *Brahman*-esque perfect unity of form and flavor—a flatulent thought clearly related to the book on Hinduism he'd been digesting in the library that morning.

The stranger eyed him curiously. "You bought some donuts, which you have no intention of eating?" Arched eyebrows like untidy, bristling hedgerows betrayed the man's conviction that it was Robert, rather than he, who was off his proverbial nut.

"It's a long story," Robert replied.

He called it his layover, the eighteen minutes he was forced to wait here each evening in order to transfer from one bus to the next as he made his circuitous way home. Stranded thus by the vagaries of the bus system, it had become his custom to purchase coffee at the donut shop around the corner from the bus stop, as both a fortification against the elements and a quick pick-me-up in preparation for his evening studies. As a result he had developed a potent attraction to the young woman who worked the donut counter—that peculiar and intense sort of attraction that, to a quixotic young scholar of literature such as he was, seems apocalyptic and inexorable in magnitude, something that strikes with all the force and attendant confusion of a *tsunami*, tearing everything in its path asunder.

The name of this enchantress (Robert had just learned, having stolen a glance at the nametag pinned above the perfectly pressed pocket of her uniform blouse), was Miranda, and it was this wonder incarnate that proved the source of his preoccupation that evening. For Miranda—insofar as Robert had constructed her, through both the processes of empirical observation and wild, Romantic extrapolation—embodied the very best of those qualities that he considered distinctly and definitively feminine. In short, she was everything Robert Austeridge had ever imagined or hoped for (which for young men of his particular temperament can amount to quite a lot).

Despite this infatuation (or perhaps because of it), however, Robert had as yet been unable to break through the institutionalized protocols that dictate socially acceptable behavior in the commercial exchange of maple bars. After all, he reasoned, one can hardly blurt out a request for a young woman's phone number when others are waiting in queue. It was *aporia*; dissatisfied with sanctioned modes of discourse (these being perfunctory greetings, the weather, and expressions of appreciation for services rendered), Robert was yet at an impasse as to how, and in what direction, he might proceed. And so, prompted that evening by Miranda's usual "Here, or to go?" her customer, as he was accustomed to do, had given his customary reply, and with his greasy paper sack of glazed donuts in one hand and coffee in the other, had bidden the young woman goodbye, receiving for his trouble a smile so warm and radiant that it might have thawed the winter ice on Thoreau's Massachusetts tarn.

"Look," Robert said to the stranger, who was still regarding him with an impertinent look. "Do you want the donuts, or not?"

The man shook his head vigorously, beard scritching against the fabric of his denim coat. "Never touch the things. You know, you can eat donuts all morning long, and how do you feel at the end of it? Empty, completely vacuous. It's like reading a Thomas Pynchon novel."

It was here, finally, that Robert found some purchase.

"You read books, then?" he inquired.

"Of course I read books," the stranger snapped. "It's the only thing worth doing, isn't it?"

He leaned forward and unzipped his jacket, from which tumbled an assortment of dog-eared paperbacks: Kafka, Melville, Conrad, Hawkes, and Murakami.

"Quite a diverse collection," Robert said.

"Not so much as you might think," the man answered, picking up the books and setting them beside him on the bench. "When all of life has become a hobby, that hobby becomes literature. What else is there, at that sublime juncture, other than ideas? What else remains?"

"Love?" suggested Robert, not then fully apprehending the other man and still preoccupied with tender notions.

"Love? Hah!" The stranger spat an enormous oyster of phlegm onto the snowy pavement. "That's the first thing to go."

He went on to explain that many years before, as a graduate student, he had been walking across campus with his nose stuck in a copy of Baudrillard's *The Ecstasy of Communication*, whereupon, through inattention by both parties, he found himself in direct and decidedly non-ecstatic communication with an impatient cyclist. The resulting concussion left him with a peculiar infirmity that defied the collective efforts of physicians worldwide. He had, in fact (or so he claimed), enjoyed a brief celebrity as a medical curiosity, before the inevitable sands of time had smoothed his case over unto the point of oblivion, at which point his lingering legacy was that of an unexplained footnote in the annals of medicine.

"I can't watch TV," the man explained, clutching his head in so vigorous a manner that Robert was involuntarily reminded of

Kafka's supplicant. "It all looks like gray static to me. Newspapers and magazines are equally incomprehensible. Books are all that's left for me—and even there, I can't parse much of anything written after 1967."

Momentarily bemused, Robert scratched an earlobe, until certain random bits of information passed through his mind like a shower of innumerable neutrinos: in sum, that on or about December 1967, human character had to all intents and purposes imploded.

"What a curious condition," he remarked.

Clearly, Robert mused, he was dealing with a lunatic, albeit an articulate and well-read one. It was equally clear that this ethereal interloper had no intentions of boarding a bus, and was merely utilizing the bus shelter as a bivouac, a temporary refuge from whatever elements most assailed his uncanny sensibilities. In any case, Robert was stuck with him until the bus arrived, for over the course of their bizarre conversation he had established some measure of aptitude in perceiving the fellow. It was an unsettling realization—that the very recognition of the man's existence, however dim his understanding of it, guaranteed both Robert's inability to ignore it and the hopeless inadequacy of a worldview in which the man did not exist. Like it or not, Robert was compelled to address the stranger with whatever powers of faculty remained his to exercise.

"Life," the man replied, leaning forward and grasping Robert by the arms, "is not a condition. The peony branch bends in the wind; the butterfly strains its wings against the same force, unyielding. Life is the fluctuation between these extremes, tempered by our conscious decisions. Ishmael was a branch, and thus floated; Ahab was a butterfly, and perished—but the dichotomy is a false one; in Life these seemingly contrary impulses are wedded for ever, two sides of the same doubloon."

Robert let out a startled yelp. The allusions, though familiar, terrified him. Worse, the stranger's fingernails were digging through his parka and into his biceps. The man's blue eyes had brightened to antifreeze intensity, so desperate did he appear that Robert understand and accept the truths he was revealing. Yet just in that moment, as the young student began to dread his safety, the man released his viselike grip and leaned back on the bench, taking his bewhiskered chin in one hand and throwing an indicative wave with the other.

"Your bus is coming," he said.

Robert staggered backwards to safety and turned. Rows of orange running lights, haloed by the swirling fog, were visible in the distance, although the gathering snows had muted the familiar rumble of the vehicle's engine. Turning back, he discovered that his assailant had disappeared. In his place on the bench sat the stack of books he had earlier produced from his coat. Robert called out, scanning the streets and sidewalks for any sign of the fellow, but he could not discover so much as a single waffle-shaped boot print in the freshly fallen snow.

The bus glided to the curb. The door opened inward, folding itself down the middle with a hiss of hydraulics. A large advertising billboard affixed to the side of the bus bellowed for attention, but perhaps through some fortuitous visual effect created by the inclement weather and his oblique vantage, Robert could not make out the sign's purport; it seemed a turbulent, swirling mass of gray static.

Alarmed, Robert mumbled an excuse to the bemused bus driver and stumbled backwards, the soles of his sneakers slipping in the slush that had accumulated on the muddy strip abutting the sidewalk. Scarcely hearing the engine's groan as the bus pulled away from the curb, he threw a panicked glance at the stack of books the stranger had left behind. He tossed his empty coffee cup into the trash receptacle. Another moment's thought and the bag of donuts followed.

The snow was picking up. Large, feathery flakes stung his cheeks as he trudged back to the donut shop. Miranda looked up as the door chime sounded, her white apron and paper hat dazzling under the fluorescent lights overhead. Her brown eyes narrowed.

"Let me guess," she said, placing a hand on her hip as Robert approached the counter. "Two glazed and a black coffee?"

"Just the coffee this time," Robert replied. Feeling compelled to offer some explanation for his hasty return, he added, "I've been standing out in this snow for a bit, and I could use another cup."

"One coffee, just like God made it," she said, punching the register keys. "Here, or to go, cowboy?"

Robert's lips felt numb, although he couldn't be certain whether this was an effect of the wintry weather or of Miranda's cheeky demeanor. His momentary hesitation, however, enabled him to stifle the reflexive response that lay so ready upon his tongue. She'd probably asked him the same question a couple dozen times by now, he reflected, but for the first time he was determined not to lose himself in musings over just what is was that made Miranda so perfect and so peerless, or what it was that filled him with extraordinary excitement, or whether or no it was possible to be friends with a donut-shop girl; all such allusions proved elusive as he boldly began the intimidating task of originality with a single word:

"Here."

Fiction Contributors

William Alexander forgot to tell you something important. It isn't that he has a website (willalex.net). It isn't that his stories have been published recently in *Interfictions 2* and *Paraspheres 2*. He'll remember what it is eventually.

John Brantingham has been published in hundreds of magazines in England and the United States including on Garrison Keillor's *Writer's Almanac, The Journal,* and *Pearl Magazine*. His chapbooks are published through Finishing Line Press and Pudding House Press, and he teaches composition and creative writing at Mt. San Antonio College just outside of Los Angeles. He lives with his wife and dog who walk three miles every day before dawn.

Daniel Brugioni is a 32-year-old high school teacher living in Hyde Park, Chicago. He's written over one hundred stories and is currently working on his third novel. He's had stories published in *The Timber Creek Review, Spitball, The Sulfur River Literary Review, Words of Wisdom, Struggle,* and *The Skylark.* He and his wife are currently working on visiting all of the fantastic places he's written about so that they might compare his conjured images with those of immutable reality. (They've actually been to Marathon Key, the setting of this story, and in the dead of winter, no less.) Visit Daniel at loner.blogspot.com.

Lawrence Buentello has published more than forty short stories in a variety of genres. He lives in San Antonio, Texas, works in an academic library, and spends his free time, when he's not writing, with his wife, Susan, and dog, Poe (after Edgar Allan). He is also the co-author of the short story collection *Binary Tales* and the novel *Reproduction Rights.*

Jefferson Burson currently spends more time routing internet packets than writing. He would like to correct this imbalance. In the meantime, said routing of packets has allowed him to cool his heels in cities such as Austin, Boston, San Francisco, and Seattle, so it's not all bad (and can even be fun at times). This is his first publication.

Sarah Cornwell is an MFA candidate at the Michener Center for Writers at UT Austin. She is the winner of the 2008 Gulf Coast Fiction Contest and a finalist for the 2009 Keene Prize for Literature. Her stories have appeared or are forthcoming in *Mid-American Review, Gulf Coast, Hunger Mountain,* and *580 Split.* She is currently working on a novel.

Thoraiya Dyer, a NSW-based Australian writer, sends her stories like sparrows into the wilderness. Occasionally someone will shotgun one out of the sky, have a taxidermist carefully reconstruct it, and then slip it into their collection. She hopes you have enjoyed peering through the glass at this particular specimen. http://www.thoraiyadyer.com

Kevin Frazier is an American writer who lives in Helsinki, Finland. His short stories have appeared in *Fiction* and *The South Carolina*

Review, among other places, and he has published a novel and co-written a nonfiction book about Central Asia. A frequent book reviewer and essayist, he has recently written pieces on Hawthorne, Proust, Tolstoy and many contemporary novelists and poets.

Vishwas Gaitonde has lived in the United States, India and Britain. He has been published in all three of those countries, and elsewhere. Examples of publications where his writing has appeared or is due to surface include *Bellevue Literary Review, Mid-American Review, Hawai'i Pacific Review, Fifth Wednesday Journal,* and *The MacGuffin*. He is interested in the intersection between the sciences and the humanities.

Kim Goldberg is an award-winning poet, journalist and author. In 2009 she received Canada's Rannu Fund Poetry Prize for Speculative Literature. Her speculative writing has appeared in *Tesseracts Eleven, On Spec, Chimera, The Dalhousie Review, Istanbul Literature Review* and numerous other magazines and anthologies in North America and abroad. Her latest book, *RED ZONE*, documents homelessness and urban decay through poetry and photography. Her previous poetry collection, *Ride Backwards on Dragon*, was a finalist for Canada's Lampert Memorial Award. She is the publisher of Pig Squash Press on Vancouver Island. Visit: http://www.pigsquashpress.com/

Jeffrey Greene was born in Michigan, grew up in Florida, and now lives in Bethesda, Maryland. He has published short stories in *The North American Review, Oasis, Potomac Review, Reactor Magazine, Tomorrow Speculative Fiction,* and *decomP Magazine*.

Jennifer Griffin Graham might be from Anchorage, Alaska, or she might be from Portland, Oregon, depending on whom you ask. Currently she lives in Austin, Texas, where she's an MFA candidate at the Michener Center at UT. You can contact her at jgriffin.graham@gmail.com.

Trent Hergenrader is currently a Ph.D. student in Creative Writing at the University of Wisconsin-Milwaukee. His fiction has appeared in *The Magazine of Fantasy & Science Fiction, Realms of Fantasy, Weird Tales* and other fine publications. His stories have received honorable mentions in both *The Year's Best Science Fiction* and *The Year's Best Fantasy and Horror*; his story "The Hodag" was reprinted in *The Best Horror of the Year #1.* He lives in Madison with his wife Amy, his dog Athena, and as of May 2009, his son Grey. Visit him online at http://www.trenthergenrader.com.

Andrew Hook is the author of three short story collections, one novel, and most recently a novella: *And God Created Zombies* (NewCon Press). His next publication will be a collection of stories co-written with Allen Ashley titled *Slow Motion Wars* which should appear from Screaming Dreams Press later this year. From November 2002 until November 2008 he also ran the multi-award winning Elastic Press, but that venture has closed so he can concentrate on his own writing. His website can be found at www.andrew-hook.com

Nick Jackson lives in Norwich, U.K., in a rather pleasant and occasionally productive muddle. His stories have appeared in a number of U.K. indie magazines but he is delighted to be appearing for the first time in a U.S. magazine. His 2005 story collection, *Visits to the Flea Circus*, was published by Elastic Press.

M. Lamaga de Sanchez is a writer and photographer living in Baja California, Mexico. She earned an M.F.A. in Creative Writing from Virginia Commonwealth University in 1998. After a ten-year detour into screenwriting she rediscovered her great passion for speculative and mythic fiction. Her stories have previously appeared in *The Tusculum Review* and *Fiction International.* She can be reached at lamagadesanchez@gmail.com

Susannah Mandel's short fiction and poetry have appeared or are coming up in *Shimmer, Strange Horizons, Goblin Fruit, Sybil's Garage, Peter Parasol, Lady Churchill's Rosebud Wristlet,* and the anthologies *Escape Clause* and *Quantum Genre on the Planet of the Arts*, among other venues. She was born in California, grew up near Boston, and has since lived in Philadelphia and the north of France. Her flash fiction appears regularly at the *Daily Cabal* (www.daily-cabal.com). A nonfiction piece confessing to her lifelong passion for apples appeared in the anthology *Evocative Objects: Things We Think With,* published by the MIT Press in 2007.

Roderick B. Overaa holds a MFA in fiction and is currently a Ph.D. candidate and English teacher at the University of Washington. His writing has appeared in such internationally recognized publications as *Kyoto Journal* and *Hiragana Times.* He taught English in Japan for three years, where he served as editor of *AJET Across Japan,* a magazine for participants of the JET Program. His dissertation explores the impact of Eastern religion and philosophy on 19th and 20th century Western literature.

Originally from Brooklyn NY, **Joseph R. Quinlan** lives and works in Asheville NC. He holds a BA in literature from the University of North Carolina at Asheville. His work has appeared in *Zahir, Space and Time,* and *The Leading Edge*. Also, look for his work in an upcoming *Main Street Rag Short Fiction Anthology,* scheduled for release in 2010.

Natalie Segal worked as a technical writer, copy editor, and proofreader before teaching technical writing in an engineering, technology, and architecture school in central Connecticut where she also blogs for the college. In her spare time, she enjoys ballroom dancing—currently she's learning Argentine tango. Aside from academic publications, her haiku has appeared in *Bottle Rockets*, and short stories have been published in the now defunct *Connecticut Writer*.

Alexander Weinstein is the director of The Martha's Vineyard Institute of Creative Writing. He leads fiction workshops in the United States and Europe and currently teaches creative writing at Indiana University. His work has appeared in *Hawaii-Pacific Review, Acapella Zoo,* and *Infinity's Kitchen.*

Richard Wolkomir is a long-time contributor of articles and essays to magazines, ranging from *Reader's Digest, Smithsonian*, and *Woman's Day* to *Geo* (in Europe), *Playboy*, and *National Geographic*. Now he is turning to an original interest in speculative fiction, with fantasy and science-fiction stories either currently published or archived in a variety of on-line literary magazines. His writing has received a variety of awards, such as the American Association for the Advancement of Science Award for Distinguished Science Writing in Magazines, the American Society of Journalists and Authors

June Roth Memorial Award, and the Clarion Award. Currently, besides writing short stories, he is finishing a fantasy novel.

Dallas Woodburn is the author of two collections of short stories and a forthcoming novel. Her short fiction has been nominated for a Pushcart Prize and has appeared in *Monkeybicycle, Arcadia Journal, The Newport Review,* and *flashquake*, among others. She studied creative writing at the University of Southern California and the University of East Anglia in Norwich, England. Dallas is the founder of Write On!, a nonprofit literacy foundation and youth publishing company; learn more at www.writeonbooks.org.

John Zackel lives and teaches creative writing in Portland, Oregon. His fiction is forthcoming in *Third Coast* and *Monkeybicycle*. He'd like to get a dog named Norma Jean. He can be contacted at jzackel@gmail.com.

Art Contributors

Adam Yeater was born in the swamps of Ft myers, Florida. After traveling the U.S he has settled in the arid desert of Tucson, Arizona, where he spends his free time with his wife, son and daughter. *"I primarily paint city scenes with acrylic on canvas or on masonite board. I have been concentrating on the cityscape for about seven years now. I am entranced by the modern day city. The buildings, people and all of its movement are all very majestic to me."* www.myspace.com/adamyeater

Yael Degany, a native Israeli, has lived in the United States since 1999. She holds 2 B.A.s from Columbia University, one in Visual Arts and one in Mathematics. Her works on paper, the majority of which are abstract, are created using pastels, ink, watercolor, graphite, and food color. She makes many of the works by directly responding to music. You can see more of her work at www.yaeldegany.com.

Dan Ruhrmanty is a mixed media artist whose work explores the dependency of the tangible upon the intangible and visa versa. Ruhrmanty's goal is to create something that resembles the very essence of our ever changing world. Notable publications featuring Ruhrmanty's work include *Barefoot Muse, Exquisite Corpse* and *Ars Medica.*

Alyson Lamanes resides in Hamilton, Ontario Canada, and is currently studying English and Multimedia at McMaster University. Other than photography her interests involve writing, music, and growing local arts culture in her home city.

www.ingramcontent.com/pod-product-compliance
Lightning Source LLC
LaVergne TN
LVHW091029080826
845145LV00002B/411

9780983109006